O9-AID-255

CLEAR AND PRESENT DANGER

The killing of three U.S. officials in Colombia ignites the American government's explosive, and top secret, response . . .

"A CRACKLING GOOD YARN."

—*The Washington Post*

THE SUM OF ALL FEARS

The disappearance of an Israeli nuclear weapon threatens the balance of power in the Middle East— and around the world . . .

"CLANCY AT HIS BEST . . . NOT TO BE MISSED."

—*The Dallas Morning News*

WITHOUT REMORSE

The Clancy epic fans have been waiting for. His code name is Mr. Clark. And his work for the CIA is brilliant, cold-blooded, and efficient . . . but who is he really?

"HIGHLY ENTERTAINING."

—*The Wall Street Journal*

continued . . .

Tom Clancy's
NET FORCE®
BREAKING POINT

**Created by
Tom Clancy and Steve Pieczenik**

Written by Steve Perry

B

BERKLEY BOOKS, NEW YORK

This is a work of fiction. Names, characters, places, and incidents are
either the product of the author's imagination or are used fictitiously,
and any resemblance to actual persons, living or dead, business
establishments, events, or locales is entirely coincidental.

TOM CLANCY'S NET FORCE®: BREAKING POINT

A Berkley Book / published by arrangement with
Netco Partners

PRINTING HISTORY
Berkley edition / October 2000

The Penguin Putnam Inc. World Wide Web site address is
http://www.penguinputnam.com

ISBN: 0-425-17693-2

BERKLEY®
Berkley Books are published by The Berkley Publishing Group,
a division of Penguin Putnam Inc.,
375 Hudson Street, New York, New York 10014.
BERKLEY and the "B" design
are trademarks belonging to Penguin Putnam Inc.

PRINTED IN THE UNITED STATES OF AMERICA

10 9 8 7 6 5 4 3 2 1

ACKNOWLEDGMENTS

We'd like to acknowledge the assistance of Martin H. Greenberg, Larry Segriff, Denise Little, John Helfers, Robert Youdelman, Esq., and Tom Mallon, Esq.; Mitchell Rubenstein and Laurie Silvers at Hollywood.com, Inc.; the wonderful people at Penguin Putnam Inc., including Phyllis Grann, David Shanks, and Tom Colgan. As always, we would like to thank Robert Gottlieb of the William Morris Agency, our agent and friend, without whom this book would never have been conceived, as well as Jerry Katzman, Vice Chairman of the William Morris Agency, and his television colleagues. But most important, it is for you, our readers, to determine how successful our collective endeavor has been.

"And who wrote the tune, you dare to ask?
You know who wrote it—
it's the Devil's own music, hot and sweet, and surely
damned will be the man who turns his ear toward it."

—SEAN PATRICK O'MAHONEY

PART ONE

All Politics Are Local

PROLOGUE

Wednesday, June 1st, 2011
Daru, China

The sun rose from the gray sea and cast a fitful light upon the wrinkled features of Old Zang where he sat on the weathered bench outside the house, leaning forward slightly on his cane. He was often up with the sun these days to enjoy the dawn, knowing he would not have so many more he could afford to waste them. But instead of making him sad, the thought made him angry.

This day seemed somehow sharper than normal. His clouded sight was clearer, his hearing keener, and even the wan rays upon his skin felt somehow more intense than usual.

Old Zang had but recently moved to the village of Daru. A mere dozen years or so ago, a blink of an eye for a man his age, he had been forced to leave his real home, which was flooded by the monstrous dam project that forever altered the face of China's rivers. At ninety-four, he had outlived his wife, several of his children, and even a few of his grandchildren, and he did not like it here, staying with one of the grandchildren he had not outlived. Oh, his room was comfortable enough, the bed soft—not an inconsequential thing when one's bones were as old as his—but the village was a mud hole of a place and not where one wished to depart from the Earth to join one's ancestors.

On the mainland across the stormy Formosa Strait from Taiwan, on the coast just north of Quanzhou, Daru was peopled with many elderly residents, some victims of the cursed dam, such as himself, some who had actually lived and grown old here. Save for a few younger souls, fishermen mostly, it was a place of old men and women waiting to die.

Thinking about his forced relocation brought Zang to anger again, and this time, the rage seemed to fill him with a hot glow, from his feet to his face, staining red even his thoughts. How *dare* they do such a thing? The foolish communists who saw everything in terms of their immoral philosophy had ruined the country in but half a lifetime. He had hoped to live long enough to see the children of Mao plowed under, but he was beginning to realize it was not to be. And this angered him even more. He was old, old! He had worked hard all his long life, and what was his reward? To be shunted to a half-wit grandson's home in a mud hole village unfit for pigs? It was not right.

Zang gripped the heavy cane tightly, and the veins in his hands stood out to join the tendons and gnarled arthritic joints under paper-thin and brown-spotted skin. His rage enveloped him like a silkworm's cocoon, warming his chilly flesh. No, it was *not* right!

His sow of a granddaughter, only thirty-four and already so fat she could hardly waddle, lumbered up the graveled path to stand in front of him, her doughy hands on her massive hips, blocking the sun. She said, "Why are you out here again, Grandfather Zang? You will catch pneumonia! I would be happy if you did and died, but Ming-Yang would be distressed, and I will not have it! Get up and come inside, right now!"

The sow seemed fairly angry herself, which was unlike her. Usually she was merely torpid. Dense as a post and twice as stupid, Zang reflected, and the best his idiot grandson Ming could do for himself. A shame.

"You are blocking the sun," Zang said. "Stand aside."

"Are you grown deaf as well as stupid, you ancient fart-maker? I said, 'Get up!' " And with that, she reached out, as if to grab him and physically drag him into the house.

This was a mistake. With a speed and strength that surprised him, Zang snapped the cane up and jabbed it into the sow's belly.

"Oof!" she said, as she leaned forward, grabbing at her stomach.

Zang stood, pulled the cane back as if it were an axe, and delivered a mighty blow to the side of her head. The bone made a wet, but satisfying *crack!* and the sow went down in a heap.

Ha-ha!

Zang leaned over and smashed the cane into the sow's body with all the strength he possessed. Ah, this was good. He hit her again. Better. And again. Better still!

He was not the man he had been, but there were still a few moves left in him, and the sense of rage he felt continued to burn as he beat upon the prostrate and unresponsive sow. Block his sun, would she? He would show her!

He grew tired after a while, and decided to rest before resuming his chore. As he stood there contemplating the sow, he chanced to look up, and thus saw his idiot grandson charging toward him, a three-tined pitchfork in hand.

Amazing, since his grandson was the meekest of men, who would step around a beetle to avoid crushing it, who let others prepare his chum for him because he could not stand to hurt the bait fish, and who had never in Zang's memory uttered even a harsh word in anger at another human being.

"Old fool! I will kill you!" Ming-Yang screamed.

Old Zang smiled wolfishly. "Yes? Come and try, wiper of asses!" He raised his cane to meet the charge.

Zang was paying attention to how he planned to dance around the fork's tines to strike Ming, but even so, with his heightened senses, he was aware of his great-grandson Cheng, aged thirteen, rushing up behind his father, a gleaming fish gaff lifted over his head.

Now, who was Cheng planning to skewer?

Well. It did not matter, did it? Zang would deal with him in due course, just as he would deal with every other person in this mud hole of a village.

He would kill them all.

Finally, a happy thought. He laughed aloud.

1

Alex Michaels pedaled his recumbent trike along the wide
bike path between Net Force HQ and the Chinese restaurant where he sometimes had lunch, pumping hard. The
day was hot and muggy, despite a cloudy overcast, and
sweat had already drenched his T-shirt and spandex
shorts. He shifted up another gear as he zipped past a trio
of Marine officers from the base, jogging along at a pretty
good clip themselves. Ordinarily, he enjoyed riding the
trike, feeling the burn in his legs and lungs, knowing he
was working his muscles and cooking off that half carton
of Häagen-Dazs he'd eaten the night before. Ordinarily,
the commander of Net Force enjoyed a lot of things, but
like his feet toe-clipped into the pedals, a lot of what he
had been doing lately had been no more than going
through the motions.

Work was pretty good. Aside from the ten thousand usual small fish Net Force had to school and round up, there weren't any major problems in the world of computer crime just at the moment. Nothing like the mad Russian who'd wanted to take over the planet, or the senator's aide who wanted to buy up the world bit by bit, or even the dotty English lord who'd wanted to bring back the glory days of the Empire. Congress hadn't cut him off at the knees lately, and his boss, the new FBI director, was sometimes hardheaded, but basically not too bad, and she mostly left him alone.

Work was fine. It was his personal life that was an absolute wreck.

He guided the trike to the right, to make sure the two bicyclers coming from the other direction side-by-side had plenty of room to get by. The couple, an older man and woman, waved as he went by. He gave them a quick lift of his hand in return.

His ex-wife, Megan, had gotten engaged, and was petitioning the courts in Idaho for sole custody of their daughter, Susie. Her new love wanted to adopt the girl. Susie liked her mom's new friend, which was more than Michaels could say. That he had decked the man at a family Christmas gathering had not helped the situation any—even though it had felt pretty good at the time.

Michaels could fight it. His lawyer said he had a pretty good chance of winning in court, and Michaels's knee-jerk reaction at first had been to do just that, fight it until his last breath, if need be. But he loved his daughter, and she was at a tender age, still years away from being a teenager. What would a nasty court battle do to her? The last thing he wanted to do was traumatize his only child.

Would it be better for her to have a mother and father—

even a stepfather—there with her all the time? Washington, D.C., was a long way from Boise, and Michaels didn't see his daughter as much as he wished. Had shuffling out to see him in the summers done some kind of irreparable harm to Susie? Would it make her life worse in the long run?

The big banked curve on the bike trail was just ahead, and rather than slow down, Michaels decided he was going to power his way through it. He upshifted and pumped even harder. But as he started into the curve, he saw a group of walkers ahead, residents of a local nursing home. They were spread almost all the way across the path. He didn't have a warning horn on the trike, and he had a sudden fear that if he yelled for them to get out of the way, one of the old folks might well keel over from a heart attack.

He stopped pedaling and squeezed the handbrakes. The heavy-duty disk brakes on all three wheels squeaked from the sudden pressure, and there came the smell of burning circuit boards as the trike slowed dramatically. On a two-wheeler, he'd probably be going sideways now, but the trike just wobbled the rear end back and forth a little as it came almost to a stop.

None of the geriatric crowd, most of whom looked to be in their eighties, even noticed him until he crept around them at walking speed.

That would have been all he needed, to plow into Grandma and Granddaddy on his trike at full tilt. One more brick on the load.

And, of course, there was the big problem in his life: Toni.

She was still in England, practicing *pentjak silat,* the Indonesian martial art in which she was an adept, studying with that Carl somebody. There hadn't been anything personal between Carl and Toni when Michaels had left the U.K., but—who knew about now? It had been more than a month. A lot could happen in a month.

Toni Fiorella was smart, beautiful, and could kill you with her hands if she felt so inclined. She'd been his deputy commander until she'd quit. And she'd been his lover—until she'd found out about his indiscretion with the blond MI-6 agent Angela Cooper.

Near indiscretion, Alex, his little voice said. *We didn't actually* do *anything, remember?*

Yeah, we did. It never should have gotten to the point where I even thought *about it.*

We were tired, half-drunk, and Cooper was working at it—the massage and all—

No excuse.

It was an argument he'd had with himself a thousand times in the last six weeks. With a thousand variations. If only Toni hadn't gone under the channel to France. If only he hadn't agreed to a beer and fish and chips with Angela. If only he hadn't agreed to go to her place to let her massage his back. If, if, if.

It was all pointless speculation now. And he couldn't lie to himself about it, no matter how much he wished it.

He thought about bringing the trike back up to speed, but it suddenly didn't seem worth the effort. The Chinese place was not that far away. It wasn't as if he was in any kind of hurry now, was it? Or was hungry. Or gave a rat's ass about getting back to work on time.

Even the thought of getting a new project car hadn't given him any great joy. He'd done a Plymouth Prowler and a Mazda MX-5, a Miata, but the garage at his condo sat empty now. The Miata had been the car in which he'd first kissed Toni. He couldn't keep it after she'd quit on him and stayed in England.

He blew out a sigh.

You sure are a sorry, self-pitying bastard, aren't you? Snap out of it! Suck it up! Be a man!

"Fuck you," he told his inner voice. But that part of him was right. He wasn't a sensitive New Age kinda guy who got all weepy in sad movies. In his world, men took care of business and soldiered on. That was the way his father had taught him, and that was how he'd lived his life. Wailing and wringing your hands was not what a man did. You screwed up, then you took the heat, and you got on with your life, period, end of story. What was that old saying: You can't do the time, don't do the crime? That was pretty much it.

In theory, anyway.

Thursday
Sperryville, Virginia

"Ow," Jay Gridley said. He slapped at his bare arm, and when he pulled his hand away, there was a splotch of liquid red surrounding the crushed body of a mosquito. At least he thought it was a mosquito—it was hard to tell.

"Murderer," Soji said. She smiled.

"Self-defense," he said. "If I'd known I was gonna be attacked by all these itty-bitty vampires, I'd have thought twice about going for a walk in the woods with you. Or maybe brought a bunch of matches I could carve into wooden stakes. This would be so much more pleasant in VR."

"My father used to say that God made two mistakes," she said. "Mosquitoes and politicians. Of course, he was an alderman, so he could say that. But he was wrong—both mosquitoes and politicians have their places."

Jay shook his head. "Sounds like more Buddhistic smoke and mirrors to me. You got to go some to justify mosquitoes."

"Really? Tell that to the bats who eat them."

"They could eat something else. Plenty of bugs that don't bite people. They could double up on gnats or something."

"Come on, Jay. If you take away everything that causes you discomfort, there's no way to measure your pleasure."

They were on a narrow dirt trail that wound through a section of mostly hardwood forest. There was enough shade so the day's heat didn't lay too heavy a hand on them, and the air was rich in oxygen, the smells of warm summer vegetation, and decades of damp humus. The backpack was a lot heavier than anything Jay was used to carrying, but since Soji's was every bit as heavy, he could hardly complain. He had the tent, but she had the cooking gear.

He shook his head. He couldn't successfully argue philosophy or religion with Sojan Rinpoche. She could talk circles around him. Though only in her twenties, she was much more educated in such things than he was. They had met after the on-line injury he'd got stalking the creator of a quantum computer that had caused Net Force all kinds of problems. Since they had come together initially in VR—virtual reality—via the internet, they had been in persona, and hers had been that of an aged Tibetan monk. She was a lot better looking as a young woman than she had been as an old man. And she had been instrumental in helping him recover from a brain injury that theoretically wasn't even possible.

"See, that's the problem with you, Jay. You spend too much time on-line. You need to get out more."

"I could put mosquitoes in a scenario if I wanted."

"You could. But have you ever?"

"Well, no."

"And without experiencing real bugs sucking your blood and going splat when you slap them, you wouldn't be able to do it accurately. And even then, it would only be an imitation, and not the real thing."

"But isn't this all just an illusion?" He waved one hand to encompass the wooded hillside.

"Wrong religion, white boy. Try the Hindus or the existentialists. Buddhists aren't into denying reality. We like to get down and roll around in it."

"What about that old man persona of yours on the net?"

"A tool, that's all. Got me past a lot of preconceptions, and made my patients relax. Besides, an illusion is by definition not real, so altering it one way or the other doesn't make it any more or less real, now does it?"

He chuckled. Boy, he liked being with her.

"So how much farther is it to this secret place of yours?"

"Not far. Couple more miles."

He gave out a theatrical groan. "You didn't tell me I was going to have to hike halfway around the planet carrying a house on my back. This better be worth the walk."

"Oh, it will be. Guaranteed satisfaction or your money back."

Well, that sounded promising. He slapped at another mosquito, and was inclined to agree with Soji's father on at least one point, despite what she'd said.

2

Quantico, Virginia

When John Howard walked into the range, he heard, "Tens-*hut*! General in the house! Morning, Brigadier."

Howard fought the grin, but lost. Amid the familiar tang of burned gunpowder, Sergeant Julio Fernandez stood at ramrod attention, a perfect salute in place. Any crisper and he would have crinkled.

"No such thing as a brigadier anymore, you know that."

"It has a nice ring, *sir*!"

"At ease, Lieutenant," Howard said. He returned the salute.

"Not funny, John."

"Hey, I can do it, you know. Me being a general now instead of a colonel. What do you think, Gunny?"

Behind Julio, the rangemaster grinned. "Oh, yes, sir, I believe Sergeant Fernandez is excellent officer material, sir. Never *has* earned his money."

"I get promoted, first thing I'll do is fire your sorry ass," Fernandez said. "You'll be out whitewashing rocks on the parade ground eighteen hours a day."

Gunny laughed. "Long arms or sidearms today, sir?"

Howard said, "I believe the sergeant needs a lesson in how to shoot his pistol."

Gunny nodded and set two plastic boxes of ammo on the counter. The blue box contained .357 cartridges, the orange box 9mm. Howard grabbed the blue box, Fernandez the orange.

"Lanes eight and nine," the rangemaster said.

Howard put his earplugs in as he headed for the entrance to the gallery, Fernandez hurrying to beat him to the door so he could hold it open. "Let me, General. I wouldn't want you complaining you hurt your hand or anything after I shoot the pants off of you. I never got to beat a general before."

"And not likely you'll start today, Sergeant."

In their respective lanes, the two Net Force military men set their ammo down and started up the holoprojectors. They used identical scenarios when they went for scores against each other, so there would be no doubt who had outshot whom.

Howard slipped the Fist paddle holster with his Smith & Wesson .357 Model 66 revolver nestled in it into his waistband and adjusted things. The S&W was an antique, stainless steel and not nearly as efficient as the polymer tactical pistols Net Force issued. The H&Ks and the Walthers carried almost three times as much ammo, and had all kinds of bells and whistles—lasers, suppressors, flashlights, all very modular. Until recently, the Smith had been pretty much stock, unmodified. Howard had allowed Gunny to talk him into trying a red dot scope, a tiny one

that mounted where the iron sights were, which had im-
proved his shooting immediately. Even so, it felt like sac-
rilege—the old wheel gun was as much talisman as
anything, his good luck piece, and in the same category
as the tommy gun he had gotten from his grandfather. It
worked, but it couldn't really run with the newer hardware
out there, even with the Tasco scope.

Julio was still smiling every time he saw the scope, too.

"You ready, John?"

"Crank it up."

Fernandez was using his blued Beretta Model 92, not
as ancient as the Smith, but certainly not in the same class
as the tactical pistols, either. Two old and grizzled types
they were, set in their ways. If they weren't careful, the
future was going to blow right past them.

The mugger, armed with a crowbar, materialized thirty
feet away and ran toward Howard. He snatched his piece
out of the holster, brought it up, and did a fast double tap,
aiming at the chest. The mugger stopped and fell down.
The holographics on the range were pretty good, and the
computer registered the hits and kept track of everything.

"Got me by a quarter second," Fernandez said from the
other side of the bullet-resistant barrier. "General's luck."

"Right," Howard said. "Rack 'em up and I'll show you
how lucky I really am."

The second mugger had a long knife, and Howard's
first round caught him a hair high, just at the base of the
throat. Good enough, since the second round didn't go
off. Instead, there was a metallic *pop!* and the cylinder
jammed.

"Got a mechanical malfunction here!" Howard yelled.
He kept the weapon pointed downrange, waiting.

Julio came around the barrier, an eyebrow raised in question.

"Something broke. Cylinder won't turn."

"I'll get Gunny out here to take a look. So much for your six-for-sure theory."

The rangemaster said, "Sorry, sir, but sooner or later, everything wears out. You probably put thirty or forty thousand rounds through this thing over the years, you got to expect it to metal fatigue and start nickel-and-diming you to death. I can fix it, but it's gonna take a few days to get the parts and get 'em installed."

"General will need a loaner," Julio said. "Can't have him walking around naked. Why don't you show him the Medusa?"

Gunny smiled and went to the gun safe. He came back with a Styrofoam box. On top of it was a little pamphlet. It said "Phillips & Rodgers, Inc.," over a little logo with a reversed "P" and an "R" separated by a big "I." The words "Owners Manual" were under that. Gunny handed Howard the pamphlet. Howard flipped it open to the first page and saw "Firearms Are Dangerous Weapons" in bold print at the top of the page.

He shook his head. That's what came of too many lawyers without enough to do. A maker had to warn you that a gun was dangerous. What was the duh-factor there?

Gunny opened the box. Inside was a flat-black revolver with what looked like ivory grips. It had an unfluted cylinder, and seemed like a K-frame S&W with a funny-looking squared-off and grooved barrel.

Fernandez took the revolver from the rangemaster. "General, this here is a P&R Model 47, aka Medusa. Three-inch, match-grade, one-in-nine twist barrel, 8620 steel, heat-treated to 28 Rockwell, with a vanadium cylinder at 36 Rockwell. Got a neat little red fiber-optic front sight, and fully adjustable rear sight. Coated with black Teflon, so it won't rust."

He handed the piece to Howard. It felt good, familiar, if it looked a little squarish for his tastes. "You getting a commission from these people, Julio? And why would I like this more than my Smith?"

Fernandez grinned widely. "Well, sir, if we can't get you to use a semiauto, at least we can get you *closer* to the current century. These first came out in 1996, I believe, and they have a big advantage over your antique Smith. They will chamber and fire everything from an anemic .380 ACP to the hottest .357 Magnum rounds, and a whole bunch of stuff in between. You can load it up with any variation of 9mm you can think of—Kurz, Largo, Long, Luger, Mauser, Parabellum, Steyr, whatever, as well as .38 ACP, .38 auto, .38 Super, or .38 Special. Bunch of other calibers will work, too, but the manufacturer doesn't recommend 'em."

"And how many cylinder changes do I have to carry to accomplish this miracle? Three? Five?"

"No, sir, not a one. Pop the cylinder and push back on the extractor rod."

Howard did so. The extractor looked very odd.

"Those are springs, those little things in the chambers. Anything that'll fit, they'll hold in place, and it'll cook 'em off just fine."

"Really?"

"Yes, sir. You happen to find yourself on a battlefield somewhere and you run out of .357, you can always find 9mm somewhere, it still being the most popular military caliber worldwide. It'll shoot the stuff we use in our subguns."

Howard looked at the gun. "What's the catch?"

"Well, sir, there are three. It doesn't much like speed-loaders, because of the springs. You can make them work, but there's a little trick to it. Speed strips would be better, and they are easier to carry anyhow. Second, if you are going to mix calibers, you should shoot the longer stuff first, so as not to gunk up the chambers. And third, if you are mixing calibers, the sights won't be dead-on for the different ones, so you have to adjust the rear sights. But that's the same with mixing bullet weights, and most of the time, you'll be shooting the same ammo. Still, you can put a different caliber in every chamber and fire them off just fine. At close range, you don't need to worry about the sights, anyhow."

Howard hefted the revolver. "Interesting."

Gunny said, "Only thing I got in .357, General. I have a snubnose Smith M60 in .38 Special if you want to try that, but even with plus-P, it ain't much gun, and it only holds five."

Julio nodded at the Medusa. "Why don't you put a few through it, long as we are here? Unless you want to, uh, forfeit the match?"

"You wish."

Gunny said, "Lemme see your ring, sir."

Howard nodded and slipped the Net Force signet ring from his right third finger. It looked ordinary enough, but inside the mounting was a tiny computer chip powered by a capacitor whose stored electricity came from a small kinetic generator, basically a little weight that shifted back and forth. As of a month ago, all Net Force who carry and field-issue sidearms, subguns, and rifles were equipped with smart technology. The guns had an internal chip that kept the actions from operating unless they received a coded signal. The rings sent the signal, and had a range of a few centimeters, no more. The Net Force guns were all tuned to the same signal, so if needed, they could shoot each other's weapons, but if anybody not wearing the transmitting signet ring tried to fire a Net Force small arm, it would simply refuse to go off.

Howard was not happy with the things, but he had been made to understand that there was no choice in accepting them. *All* federal agencies would eventually be using smart guns, and the FBI was taking the lead.

So far, the new guns had operated at 100 percent, no failures. So far.

Gunny put the ring into a slot on the coder and checked the program, then did the same for the new gun. "All set, sir." He passed the ring and revolver back to Howard.

Howard looked at the gun as he slipped the ring back on. The theory was fine. If your kid found your weapon and hadn't been taught properly, at least he wouldn't shoot himself or one of the neighbors. It wasn't fool-proof—somebody could snatch one of the rings and use it—but it was supposed to keep Net Force people from being shot if they lost a gun in the heat of battle. And once a month, you were to run your ring through a coder that reset the command signal, so any lost rings would no longer work after thirty days. He didn't like it, but that was how it was going to be. End of story.

Back at the lane, Howard loaded the revolver using his .357 ammo. The shells were a little harder to put into the chambers than they were in the Smith, but not that much harder.

He set a stationary bull's-eye at fifteen meters, lined the

sights up. The front sight had a red dot on it, easy to see under the overhead lane lights. He squeezed off a round. He was surprised. Even though it fired the same cartridge, the recoil seemed considerably less than the Smith. Probably because it was a heavier piece, plus the barrel was a half-inch longer. He looked at the counter. A centimeter below dead center. Probably zeroed at twenty-five meters.

He cooked off the rest of the cylinder, and managed a grouping that went maybe four or five centimeters, all in the X ring. Damn. This was great for a gun he'd never fired before. Hell, it was great for a gun he'd been shooting for *years*. Pointed fine, too; it felt very ergonomic in his grip.

"Not bad for an old guy," Julio said. "Want to get back to it?" He waved at the target.

"You and the Beretta you *sleep* with against a gun I've just picked up? Right."

"Tell you what, to make it fair, I'll go and borrow that snub .38 Special Gunny has. Ten bucks says I can beat you with that."

"If you are determined to give up your money, Sergeant, I *will* take it."

Fernandez grinned. "Be right back."

London, England

Toni Fiorella deflected Carl Stewart's right punch to her throat with her own strike at his face—

Because he had his punch backed up with his left hand, the wipe was there, and he took it, and fired a backup elbow at her temple—

Because her strike was also covered with her off hand, she had the parry for his elbow and she rolled it aside—

Carl switched tactics, twisted, went with her move, looped his parried hand across her chest and stepped in for a throw behind her leg, the *kenjit*—

Toni dropped her weight, knees bent deeply, leaned forward, and reversed the move, snapped her own foot back, caught his leg for a *beset* takedown—

Carl leaned in, put his head on her shoulder, stole her base, and switched feet—fast!—and did the inside sweep, *sapu dalam*—

She wasn't quick enough with the counter, and she went down, dived and tried to make it into a roll, but he was there, tapping her on the floating ribs with the heel of his wrestling shoe, just hard enough to let her know he had the shot.

Toni grinned, took his offered hand, and got back to her feet.

The entire sequence had taken maybe three seconds.

"Good series," he said.

"Yes."

They were alone in the school where he taught his classes, a version of the Indonesian martial art of *pentjak silat* that was similar to her own system. Toni had been training since the age of thirteen; she knew the eight *djurus* of the entry-level style called *Bukti Negara*, plus the eighteen *djurus* of the more complex parent art, *Serak*, and until she had met Carl Stewart, had never sparred with anybody who could beat her. Well, except for her teacher, Guru DeBeers. Guru was in her eighties now, still shaped like a brick and dangerous to anybody who might be stupid enough to think she was a helpless old lady, but if push came to shove, Toni knew she could best her teacher in a fight. Barely.

That was the thing about *silat;* it didn't depend on strength or speed, but more on principles. In theory, a player always expected to go up against bigger, stronger, and multiple opponents, who were probably armed, and at least as well trained. Being able to survive and even prevail under such circumstances meant your technique had to be very good, and your system absolutely scientific. There were no perfect arts that would handle every possible attack—when Toni talked to martial artists who claimed their ancient systems were complete, she'd always ask them which form taught them how to defend against a twelve-gauge shotgun at thirty feet—but some arts were more effective than others. In her opinion, *silat* was better than most. Of course, she would think that, given her years of training in it.

Carl glanced at the wall clock. "Got an hour before the beginning class gets here. You want to get a cup of tea? Or coffee?"

Toni hesitated a second, then said, "Sure."

There was no reason not to. Alex was back in Washington, and she was still not happy with him. She had programmed her com to bounce his calls, though he still tried to get through at least once every day. They were officially broken up, and she didn't work for Net Force anymore. She had enough money to stay in London through the summer, if she felt like it, then she was going to have to find a job, and that would have to be back in the U.S. Meanwhile, she was learning a lot from Carl, who was easily the best *silat* player she had ever seen in person. He was a good twenty years older than she was, but there was an attraction that went beyond martial arts. He was in good shape, good-looking, and, she had found out by accident, rich. He hadn't pushed it, but Carl knew she and Alex had split, and he was interested in her as a woman.

So far, she hadn't pursued a relationship beyond exchanging ways to beat attackers to various kinds of pulp. So far. It was tempting—Alex had done so with Angela Cooper, the MI-6 operative they had worked with on the Goswell operation, and Toni was still very much pissed off at him for that. Yeah, sure, she had stumbled with Rusty that one time, but that was before she and Alex had become lovers. That didn't really count.

The thing was, as angry as she was at Alex, as much as she wanted to break things and yell herself hoarse at him, she still loved him.

It was kind of hard to get around that, loving him.

Still, Carl was here, he wanted to get to know her better, and there were no strings on her. She had an idea that Carl would probably be a caring and considerate lover, and she and Alex hadn't spent much time making love the last few weeks they had been together, and that had been more than a month ago. It was a thought.

Carl was halfway to the door before Toni realized she was lost in her thoughts.

She hurried to catch up with him.

"I've been thinking, there's a place you might like to see," he said. "You busy Saturday morning?"

"Not at all," she said.

"Fine. I'll pick you up at your flat. Around eight A.M.?"

"Great."

Quantico, Virginia

Howard had to admit that the P&R had some advantages over the Smith. He recovered the sight picture for his second shot quicker, and the slightly longer sight radius made him more accurate. He was doing better than he usually did with the Smith, and for a new gun, that was fairly amazing. The trigger was crisp, maybe four pounds single-action, ten or so double-action. These people did good work on their hardware. Made in Plano, Texas, according to the information stamped into the black steel. Who would have guessed that? Texas.

Even so, Julio was *beating* him, just barely. And using a snub-nose Chief's Special he had never shot before, *that* ought to be impossible.

After the last go-round, Howard put the Medusa down. He liked it. He could use it for a few days until the Smith was repaired.

"Sergeant Fernandez, bring that little revolver here, I want to take a look at it."

"God hates a sore loser, John."

"Let me see it."

Fernandez came around the barrier, holding the .38 Special snubbie on his palm, cylinder latch up.

Howard looked at the weapon. Stainless steel, two-inch barrel, plain ramp-and-notch sight, nonadjustable. The grips were black plastic, boot-style, cut small so as not to reveal a concealed weapon under a thin jacket. The Chief was basically a smaller version of his revolver, a J-frame to his K-frame, a five-shooter instead of a six-honker. In the hands of an expert, this gun could certainly put the bullets on target, but the short barrel and minimal sights made such a thing difficult on a good day without a lot of practice. Julio shouldn't be able to do it right out of the box.

"Satisfied?" He started to pull his hand away.

Howard grabbed the revolver and turned it over. When he did, he noticed the little bulge at the top of the other grip panel. At the same time, he felt the small button on the inside of the grip, under his middle finger. "And just what is this?" He pointed the gun downrange and squeezed the grips.

A hundred meters away, a bright red spot appeared all the way out on the back wall.

There was a laser built into the grips.

"You cheating bastard. You set me up."

Julio laughed. "Gunny showed it to me before you got here. It's from somebody called Crimson Trace—cool, ain't it? You adjust it with a tiny little Allen wrench, right there, and up there, and it fits inside a regular holster. Doesn't add any appreciable mass or weight, and unlike a dot scope, you don't even have to bring the weapon up to eye level, you can hip-shoot. Gets a couple thousand rounds per set of batteries, and you can carry a spare set in the other grip panel. They make 'em for K-frames, too, so you could get them for the Medusa or the Smith."

"You work for *these* people, too, Julio?"

Julio laughed again and pointed at the dancing dot. "Old guys like us, we need some advantages. You can see that sucker a couple hundred meters away in the dark and, according to Gunny, it shows up okay at handgun combat range even in daylight. Wherever the red spot is, that's where the bullet hits. If it's foggy or you're worried about giving away your position, you can use the regular sights, 'cause the laser don't get in the way. Gunny says they make these for a whole bunch of guns, including my

Beretta. I'm gonna get one before Joanna has our kid and we have to start putting away every penny for his college education."

"God hates a cheater more than he does a sore loser."

"No second-place winner in a gunfight, John. You know that. What do you think about the Medusa?"

It wouldn't do to admit to Julio how much he liked it, so he said, "I can force myself to use it until Gunny gets the Smith back on-line."

Julio gave him a knowing grin. "Ah. I see."

They'd been serving together too long for Howard to get much past his old friend. He grinned. "Okay, so it's a great piece, you happy?"

"You *working* for these people, John? Getting a *commission* on sales?"

It was Howard's turn to laugh, and he did.

3

Sitting in his Dodge Caravan, Patrick Morrison rode the ferry from Seattle toward Bainbridge Island. This was the first leg of a journey that would involve driving north after the boat ride, another ferry, then another short stint in the car, to finally arrive back at Port Townsend. The picturesque little town on the little peninsula where the Straits of Juan de Fuca turned south into Puget Sound was only about forty miles away from downtown Seattle as the crow flew, but a two-hour trip by car and boat, if you were lucky enough to make the ferry connections just right.

Morrison owned a house on the hill in Port Townsend, where Shannon, his bride of four months, was doubtless still in bed asleep at this hour. She was twenty-five, gorgeous, a trophy wife half his age. Shannon was his second marriage, the first one having gone bad after almost twenty years. Marian had also been beautiful when he'd met her, and brilliant, which he'd always thought was the bigger attraction. But she'd let herself go, had gotten fat and lazy, and, it turned out, had been too smart—especially with her mouth. He liked intelligent women, but he found that he liked them at a distance. Too close, and they were like fire, you got burned by their brilliance. Marian had turned that heat onto him too many times, and she knew all the spots where it would hurt him the most.

Shannon, on the other hand, was not the sharpest knife in the drawer. She wasn't really stupid, probably about average intelligence; she thought *he* was a genius, being a scientist and all. Actually, he just missed the cut for genius by an IQ point or two, but he was pretty sure she would never throw that in his face. Nor would she stab him with the pointed question that, if he was so smart, why hadn't he won a Nobel?

Besides, Shannon knew tricks with her hands and her body that Morrison had never dreamed of doing in nineteen years of marriage to Marian. Her mouth was smart— but in an entirely different way . . .

He shifted a bit, suddenly excited by the idea of being home and in bed with Shannon. *Easy, big fella,* he told himself. *It's a ways yet.*

The big ferry blasted its warning horn at a sailboat that ventured too near. Sail craft generally had the right of way over powerboats, all things being equal, but a ferry hauling scores of cars and hundreds of passengers was more equal than a thirty-foot sailboat foolish enough to tack in front of it. A sailor and a retired airline pilot that Morrison knew liked to say, "If you fly your plane into a mountain, you don't get to blame the mountain." Nobody had any sympathy for a day sailor who cut in front of a ferry—or plowed into one, which also happened from time to time.

Morrison opened the Dodge's door and stepped out. The van was six years old, but a Dodge, so it was good for years if he took care of it. Not that he intended to keep it that long. Pretty soon, he'd be able to buy a new car. A fleet of new cars, if he wanted, with a ship upon which to transport the fleet, and a navy to escort it, if he so wished.

He smiled at the thought.

The air had that salty, seaweed tang to it, and even though it was early and there was the passage wind blowing, the day was already warm, and promised to be hot before it was done.

He worked his way across the hard rubber gratings toward the railing—he was parked forward and on the deck under the sky, outside of the superstructure enclosure where all the foot passengers rode.

Gulls flew past. It was a great morning.

Of course it was a great morning. The test had gone so well he couldn't believe it. The Chinese had clamped down on it fast, squelching the incident into official silence deeper than that in a tomb, so there hadn't been any reports in the media, even in China. Maybe especially in China.

Morrison had his sources, though, and he found out quickly enough. The test had replicated the experiments with animals even better than anticipated. Well within the cutoff that separated "chronic" from "acute." It might not work on a battlefield with shifting troops, but the device would definitely work on a permanent settlement.

He'd known that it would. Well, to be absolutely honest, he had been *almost* certain. There was always the worry about field testing versus the lab. One never got over that. It took only a few failures to keep that anxiety alive forever, rather like Frankenstein's monster, shambling around in the dark looking for a friend.

Failure, unfortunately, had no friends. Which was how Dr. Patrick Reilly Morrison, with his Ph.D. in physics from MIT, had come to be involved with the project in the first place. He'd had a spectacular failure in his extremely low frequency experiments involving chimpanzees, and he'd lost his grant and funding big-time and damned fast. It was as if he had developed a sudden case of pneumonic plague—the first sneeze, and every professional contact he knew scattered as if they were parts of a bomb—*ka-blamm!*—leaving him stinking of smoke and failure and very much alone. No rat leaving a sinking ship had ever moved as fast as his grad students and research assistants had bailed on him, bastards and bitches, each and every one of them . . .

He smiled at his own bitterness. Well, it really *was* an ill wind that blew no good, wasn't it? If the ELF simian protocols hadn't gone south on him, he'd never have gotten the job in Alaska, would he? And look where *that* had taken him. He could hardly *be* positioned better, could he?

Well, yes, he supposed, *academically* he could be. And certainly in pure scientific circles, with major universities begging him to come and present papers? Well, he was not at the top of that list. Ah, but if somebody just up and gave you five or six hundred million dollars, maybe more, to fund whatever research your heart desired, no strings, no oversight? Well, that would go a long, long way to assuage one's wounded ego, wouldn't it? People would *kill* for that kind of funding, and rightly so.

Money would get you through times of no Nobel better than a Nobel would get you through times of no money, that was the cold truth.

With half a billion in his pocket, he could thumb his nose at the journals, take his time to do whatever he damned well pleased, and when he was ready, *then* they'd come begging, by God! Because his theories did work after all, didn't they?

True, he didn't want to take the credit for it just now, given the mode and manner in which he had finally proved himself correct, but someday it would be his to claim. Perhaps he would hire the Goodyear blimp and have it fly back and forth across the country with lights flashing and blazing it out for all to see:

"I *told* you so!"

He looked at his watch. He would go home, spend the day with Shannon, then catch a plane back to SeaTac for the flight to Washington, D.C. After the second and third tests, the events would surely be public, and it was of primary importance that he be prepared for that. He *was* one of the sharper knives in the drawer, and he knew that it was not enough to be smart, you had to be clever as well.

Smart, clever, a beautiful young wife who thought the sun rose and set in his shadow, and rich—he had it all but the last, and that was coming, a mere matter of a few weeks or months. When you got right down to it, how important *was* academic recognition compared to those? He could *fund* research if he wanted! Be a foundation unto himself!

Hah!

Life was good—and it was about to get better.

Washington, D.C.

"We're going to Oregon," Tyrone Howard said. He grinned.

Nadine Harris, who at thirteen was the same age as Tyrone, returned his smile in a larger, white-against-chocolate version. "Exemplary, Tyrone. Congratulations!"

They were at the soccer field at their school, where they had gone to practice throwing boomerangs.

"No," he said, "*we* are going to Oregon. My dad, my mom, me, and *you*."

She blinked at him. "What?"

"I asked if you could go. My parents said it was okay. We can both enter the tourney. I might even let you win."

She laughed. "*Let* me win? In your dreams, funny boy. Last I looked, my best hang time was seventeen seconds better than your best. Your 'rang comes down, you're packed up and halfway home before mine even apexes."

"That was *then*, honey chile, this is *now*." He waved his backpack.

"It came?" She knew right away what he was talking about. That was one of the things he liked about her. She wasn't the most beautiful girl in the world, but she was athletic, and she was very quick.

He nodded. "Yep. In this morning's mail."

"Lemme see, lemme see!" She reached for his backpack, and he quickly jerked it back.

"Hey, easy! I don't want you to damage it."

"I'll damage your head if you don't give it up right now!"

He laughed. From inside the backpack, he produced the object in question—a new boomerang.

And not just *any* boomerang, but a Larry Takahashi

KinuHa—a Silk Leaf—a paxolin MTA L-Hook identical to the one that Jerry Prince had used to win maximum time aloft at the Internationals last year. It had cost him sixty-five dollars, plus insured shipping, and it came pre-tuned and ready to throw. Prince had spiraled his up at the Internationals in Sydney last summer and hung it for five minutes and sixteen seconds—with a thirty-klick-per-hour wind blowing. On a calm day, word was he could keep it in the air a whole lot longer, in practice anyway.

The boomerang was lightweight, thin, and flexible, made from layers of linen and glue, and colored a psychedelic electric blue with a black leaf stenciled on the long arm. The blue made it easier to spot if you missed a catch and it augered into the grass.

"Wow," Nadine said.

"So, are you going to come with us?"

She looked up from the 'rang. "I dunno. My mom planned to have me doing yard work this summer. Mowing the lawn, helping the old lady across the street with her garden, like that."

"It's not the whole summer, it's only three weeks. My mom said she'd talk to yours. C'mon, Nadine, how often are you going to get a chance to enter the Junior Nationals, if they aren't here in town?"

"Oh, I'll ask, 'cause I'd love to go. Oregon." She pronounced it "Ory-gone."

"My dad is borrowing an RV from somebody he knows," he said. "It'll be cheaper than staying in motels and eating out. It'll sleep like eight, and there's only four of us. Dad says we'll take five or six days to drive out, spend a week there, then a leisurely drive home. We'll get there like two days before the JN, have time to practice."

"It sounds great. Doesn't it rain all the time out there, though?"

"Nope. My dad goes out there in the winter sometimes for survival training. It's desert and snow and all on the eastern side of the state in the winter, but pretty green and sunny in Portland in the summer."

"They still have Indians out there, don't they?"

"Yeah, they own *casinos*. And the cowboys herd cattle in helicopters or riding on ATVs. It's the northwest, dummy, not Bali."

"You talk too much. Show me what you got." She waved at the new 'rang.

"No, you get to throw it first," he said.

"Really? No, I couldn't."

"Yeah, you can. Then I can beat you and make you feel bad."

"Hah. Gimme it."

He smiled as she took the new boomerang and headed out to where they had chalked a throwing circle. He sure did like her. She wasn't gorgeous like Belladonna Wright, and Nadine didn't make his heart race as Bella had done with a touch or a look, but he enjoyed being around her. She was somebody he could hang with, not exactly like a sister, but not somebody who stirred up his hormones too much, either. Outside of his pal Jimmy-Joe Hatfield, he didn't have any other close friends. And boy, she could *throw*.

He watched her limber up her arm and shoulder, drop some pixie dust to check the wind direction, then set herself for the throw.

The new boomerang whirled from her hand and soared, climbed steeply, twirling into the morning sunshine. *Man. Look at it go.*

4

As he usually did when things got dicey in his personal life, Alex Michaels buried himself in work. Which was why he was at the office at nine P.M. on a Friday night, keeping busy. He scanned computer files, logged into reports annotated by his staff, and tried not to think about anything else.

Somebody was scamming old people by selling phantom retirement property from a website that appeared to be located in some kind of moving vehicle in south Florida.

Another third world country had joined the net, peddling drugs you couldn't buy without a prescription in the U.S., and for a third the cost.

Some hacker had broken into the Sears mainframe and

was threatening to wipe all the memory clean if they didn't pay him half a million dollars.

It was the usual kind of thing that Net Force handled, and there seemed to be more and more of it coming their way every day.

It had been a long day. He noticed he was getting very stiff in his chair, hunched over the keyboard. He could operate his computer with his voice, of course, and voxax was as fast as he could do it manually—faster, even—but he'd never quite gotten used to dictating reports. He'd speak, the words would appear on the screen, and he could do it leaning back and comfortable, but it somehow didn't feel the same. Maybe they used different parts of the brain, keyboarding and speaking.

Or maybe he was just getting old and the future was passing him by . . .

He thought about going down the hall to the gym and doing his *djurus*. Toni had been teaching him *pentjak silat* for six months, since after he'd almost been assassinated, and he officially knew four of the short forms. She'd started him with the simple ones from *Bukti,* but after he'd gotten two of those, she decided to skip over the rest and go right into the more complex *Serak* system. *Bukti* was pretty much a filter, she'd said, a perfectly good system of self-defense, but used to strain out casual students from the really serious ones. After you learned the eight *Bukti Negara* forms, then you were allowed to proceed—if you were lucky—into the parent art, *Serak.* Toni had decided he was serious enough, apparently. So he had already learned the first two from the mother art and had bagged practicing the others. This was pretty quick, she'd told him. Some teachers only showed students two or three *djurus* a year, and he had twice that in six months.

And Michaels already knew the third one, pretty much. He'd watched Toni enough to pick up the moves, though he didn't tell her that. So he was way ahead of the learning curve here.

Probably helped if you were working out every day. Not to mention sleeping with the teacher, Michaels thought.

Though *that* wasn't happening anymore.

Shit. Let's not even go down this road again, okay? Either work out or get back to the computer, but don't sit here whining!

Yeah. I hear that.

The computer. He could practice his *silat* later.

He looked around. Most of his regular crew was gone, only the night shift was on. Gridley and Howard were on vacation, and Toni was in England.

Very quiet around here.

Saturday, June 4th
London

"Why all the secrecy?" Toni asked.

Carl smiled. "Come on, everybody likes pleasant surprises, don't they?"

"Well, not really. I know some people who wouldn't answer the door if somebody showed up on their porch with a check for a million dollars—not unless they had called first."

They were in a section of London that Toni didn't recognize, a fairly well-to-do neighborhood. They had passed Elephant's Castle, and she thought they were heading north and west, but she had gotten turned around during Carl's tour of interesting places.

He laughed as he downshifted the Morgan's manual transmission. He'd told her that the car, a classic from the fifties, spent most of its time in the shop, but that when it was running properly, he much enjoyed driving it. The problem with old British cars was that they only worked if they liked you. If you accidentally insulted one, it would pout, he said, and simply refuse to go until you had suffered enough.

They passed a big building off to the left. "Imperial War Museum," Carl said. "We're not far now."

She had to admit, she had been enjoying her time with the *silat* instructor. Enough so that she considered getting to know him better than just as a teacher and friend. But despite having quit her job, and the breakup with Alex, she wasn't ready to get into another relationship just yet. The wounds were still too raw.

"Here we go, then."

He pulled the two-seater to the curb.

"This is a no-parking zone," she said.

"Right. And the meter maid who usually works this stretch is one of my students. Orinda? Short, built like a fireplug? Be hell to pay in class if she had my motorcar towed." He smiled.

The building they parked in front of was another of those sixteenth- or seventeenth-century things with columns and dormered windows and all, not particularly large or imposing, but stately enough.

They walked up to the front. A uniformed, but unarmed, guard saw them, tipped his hat, and said, "Morning, Mr. Stewart."

"Hello, Bryce. Lovely day."

Toni looked at him. "Come here a lot, do you?"

"Now and then."

There was a brass plate on the wall next to a pair of tall wooden doors, and Toni saw that they were about to enter the London Museum of Indonesian Art.

Ah.

She happened to notice a list of the board of directors for the museum posted just inside the door, and prominent on the list was the name "Carl Stewart."

She looked at her companion. "You're on the board of directors here?"

He shrugged. "My family contributes to various foundations and such. Give enough money, they put your name up somewhere. It's nothing, really."

"Place seems to be empty except for us," she said.

"Well, that is one of the perks of having your name on the wall. They'll open a bit early for you."

When she'd first met Stewart, just after going to his *silat* school in a bad section of town, she'd used her access to the local computer nets to check him out. His family was more than well-off, a thing he had not mentioned. The rich were different, and not just because they had more money.

"This way."

She followed him down a corridor with shadow puppets mounted on the walls, and into a room at the end.

"Wow," she said.

All around here, in freestanding glass cases, or in clear-fronted cabinets against the walls, were scores—hundreds—of *krises*. Some were in wooden sheathes, some out, revealing a multitude of shapes and patterns of whorled steel in the blades.

"Wow," she said again.

"Impressive, isn't it? The largest collection of such daggers outside of Indonesia."

Toni nodded absently, looking at a seven-waved black steel blade with inlaid lines of gold outlining the body of a dragon whose tail undulated all the way up to the weapon's point. The dragon's head was at the base of the blade, opposite the longer side of the asymmetrical hilt.

"*Raja naga,*" Carl said. "Royal dragon. It was made for a Javanese sultan around 1700. Both of those sheathes there belong to it—that one is the formal *ladrang,* the one shaped like a ship, the other one, with the rounded ends, that's the *gayaman,* for informal wear."

The sheathes were made of carved wood, with embossed metal sleeves over the long shaft in which the dagger rode.

"What's the *pamor*?" Toni asked.

He looked away from the exquisite blade to her. "You *know* about these things?"

"Not really," she said. "My guru presented me with one a few months back. I know just enough to ask questions."

"Ah. Well, the *pamor* on this one is *bulu ayam,* cock feather. I don't know enough about them to be sure about the *dapur.*"

Toni nodded. *Pamor* was an Indonesian word that described the pattern found in the steel. Genuine *krises*—sometimes spelled *k-e-r-i-s*—were generally made of hammered, welded steel mixed with nickel. When the final grinding and staining was done to finish the weapon, the iron in it would turn black, but the nickel would tend to stay shiny, thus creating designs in the metal. According to her guru, the staining process usually involved soaking the metal in a mixture of lime juice and arsenic, which probably accounted for the *kris*'s reputation as a poisoned blade.

Dapur was the overall shape, the proportions and esthetics of the blade combined with the handle and guard. *Krises* could be straight or curved, the latter ranging from a few undulations to more than thirty, but always, she had been told, an odd number of waves.

For hundreds of years, especially on the larger islands, no Indonesian boy could officially become a man until an elder, usually his father or uncle, presented him with a *kris*. More than a few were given to young women, too. They were not only weapons, but imbued with magic as part of their construction. The size, shape, pattern, time it was made, and desires of the potential owner were all taken into account by the smith, called an *empu,* who forged the weapon. Some *krises* were reputed to draw fire away from a house, protect the owner against black magic, or to rattle in the sheath to warn of approaching danger.

Toni's heirloom, a gift from her *silat* teacher, was in a safety-deposit box back in New York City. Her guru had given it to her so that its magic might help her get Alex. It had apparently worked.

Too bad it hadn't worked to *keep* him.

Carl led her around, pointing out the various configurations of the daggers. They were beautiful, if you could take the time to look at them properly.

"This is my favorite, right here," he said. He opened the glass case, which was not locked. The British were a lot more trusting about such things, Toni had noticed. In some of the Royal museums, you could literally touch priceless works of art with your nose, if you were that stupid. They just hung unprotected on the walls.

Carl took the *kris* and its sheath out. He gave it a quick nod, a kind of military bow, then held it up so she could see the designs in the steel. "This is a five-wave *dwi warna*—a two-colored, or double-*pamor*—blade. By the guard, it's *beras wutah*, rice grains. From here to the point, it's *buntel mayit*—the twisted pattern called death shroud. A very powerful *pamor,* this latter, particularly suitable for a warrior.

"It's a Balinese blade, they are generally longer and heavier than the Javanese make, though it has been stained and dressed in the Javanese style. Solo seven-plane *ukiran* handle, of *kemuning* wood. Look how intricate the carved *cecekan* is on the inside, here and here."

He pointed at the tiny stylized faces, said to represent *kala,* or protective spirits.

"According to the history, this probably belonged to a mercenary who moved to the area of Solo, Java, from Bali, sometime in the mid-1800s. As a mercenary, he would likely have been employed by the local ruler."

He handed her the blade, and she took it and touched it to her forehead, a gesture of respect her guru had taught her. She noticed him nod in approval at her gesture.

The sheath was an informal one, the corners rounded, the wood a light color with a couple of darker splotches, and the shaft was covered with a plain tube of reddish copper.

"This is your favorite? Out of all these? Why?"

He nodded, as if expecting the question. "Because it's a working weapon. It was never worn in the sash of a *maharaja,* but belonged to a professional warrior. It probably saw duty on the field of battle, and as such, it is full of fighting spirit. Might just be my imagination, but I can feel its power every time I touch it."

"Too bad it's in the museum's collection," she said.

He glanced away from her. "Actually, it's on *loan* to them." He grinned.

She shook her head and returned his smile. Of course.

It did have the feel of a fighting instrument in her hand. *Krises* were stabbing weapons, with a pistol-shaped grip, this one angled slightly inward, pointed where a thrust, if it hit a torso, would drive it into the body's center, where it would likely find a major organ. The waves would gouge a wider cut as it went in, and allow more blood to flow when it came back out. They were ceremonial weapons and cultural artifacts these days, but you could skewer an enemy just as well with one now as you could two hundred years ago, human anatomy not having changed much in the past couple million years.

Her own weapon had been used at least once that way that she knew of—she had seen John Howard take down a gunman who would have killed him, had she not thrown him the *kris* in time.

Remembering John reminded her of her days at Net Force, though, and she did not want to travel that path right now.

"I have trained with knives, but not the *kris* proper," she said.

"I know some of the methods," he said. "I'll show you, if you want."

"Yes. I'd like that."

"Over here, look at these, a matched pair . . ."

She went along to see. She was enjoying herself here, despite all that had happened. Yes, sooner or later, she was going to have to go home. But, like Scarlett O'Hara, she could worry about that *another* day . . .

5

Luther Ventura sat in the Koffee Me! store in the mall near the new entrance to Underground Seattle, holding a triple espresso. The textured cardboard sleeve around the paper cup allowed just enough heat to warm his hands slightly as he inhaled the fragrant vapor wafting up from the fluid. The brew smelled bitter, and it was as dark as a pedophile's sins.

He inhaled the scent, connecting to it as a wine expert might enjoy the aroma of a great vintage.

When he was ready, Ventura sipped the espresso, let the hot liquid swirl around his mouth a bit, then swallowed it.

Ah.

When he drank or ate, that was what he did. He didn't read the paper, he didn't watch television, he didn't split his attention—well, save for the basic Condition Orange he always maintained in public, but he had been doing that for so long it was almost a reflex. After twenty-five years of practice, you didn't have to think about that consciously. You automatically sat with your back to the wall. You checked the entrances and exits of any building into which you went. You knew what kind of construction the building was, which walls you could smash through, which ones would likely stop a bullet. You were always aware of what was going on around you, tuned into the currents of who came and who left, alert for any small sign that danger might be casting a glare in your direction. You expanded your consciousness, relied on all your senses, including your hunches, tuned out nothing, but allowed yourself enough quiet that you could experience the total reality of the place where you were. *Zanshin,* the swordplayers called it. The Zen of being in the moment, no matter where you were and what you were doing, of being and not merely doing. To Ventura's mind, this was all unthinking and basic, absolutely necessary to a man who wanted to stay alive in the business he'd been in.

Once upon a time, Luther Ventura had been an assassin. And, once upon a time, he had been the best in the business. He had worked for governments, he had worked for corporations, and he had worked freelance. Twenty-three years he had done it. Seventy-six major assignments, ninety-one people taken down in the doing of them, and he had never failed to complete a job.

Not any longer. He hadn't assassinated anybody in a while, and if you didn't sharpen your edge regularly, you got dull. Oh, he could still run with *most* of the elite; his skills had been considerable and they had not deserted him completely—but his time had passed. Somewhere out there was a man for whom hunting and taking human prey was a total focus. A man who was faster, stronger, younger, whose entire being was wrapped around what he did, and that made him better than Ventura. His ego didn't want to hear that, but he wasn't going to lie to himself. Experience could balance many things, but no fighter stayed champion forever. Those who tried to hang on too long always lost. Always.

He could still do twenty chins, he could run five miles in half an hour, and he could hit any target his weapon was capable of hitting, but he was pushing fifty, and his reflexes weren't what they had once been. He wore glasses to read and, these days, he missed some of the high notes he knew were there when he listened to a Mozart concerto or a Bach fugue.

He could have tried to fool himself into thinking he still had all the moves, but that was the road to hell, sure enough.

Three years ago, he had taken out a Brazilian drug dealer protected by a hundred troops and a dozen skilled bodyguards. The tap had been extremely difficult and it had been perfect in every way.

Perfect.

Even if your talents never wavered, you couldn't improve on perfection. The best you could ever do was match it, and there was no joy in that. It was not worth the risk. He was on the downhill slope, and the lean and hungry days were long gone. There weren't any old assassins, not at the level he'd played on. So he'd folded his cards and walked away from the game a winner.

Sure, he had *killed* people recently, but those didn't count, those had been defensive, more or less. Once, he had gone forth and stalked. Now he made his money *pro-*

tecting people from other assassins. It was, in many ways, more difficult. There were still challenges to be met. That was his focus, and while it did not have the same level of excitement, it had some advantages. It was legal. It was less risky. And although he didn't need the money, it was lucrative.

He put the espresso down, finished. All he needed was the first sip. He didn't need the caffeine, didn't want the artificial mind-set that came with it. One sip was enough. It was the essence of the experience, no more was necessary.

Finished with the coffee, he looked at his watch. It was one minute past eight A.M. He had a new client, though he was not to start officially working for the man for several days. But as soon as Ventura took on a job, it occupied his attention, and he did what it took to get into the proper mind-set.

Although he was out of town for a few days, at around seven-thirty A.M. on Saturdays his client usually arrived in Seattle via ferry and came to this coffee shop, where he had a cup of triple espresso. For the next several days, Ventura would walk in his client's shoes, go where he went and do what he did, as much as possible. He would get to know the man's routine, just as he had gotten to know the routines of those he had sought out and killed. And when he knew what he needed to know, then he would notice anything that did not belong.

He pulled a small phone from the pocket of his gray silk sport coat. He pressed a button on it, waited for a moment, then said, "All right. Let's move."

The rest of his primary team—two men and two women—were in the coffee shop or covering the street outside. He watched the man and woman pretending to be a married couple stand and walk arm in arm toward the door. Both kept their gun hands clear—the woman was dexter, the man a sinister, so the man walked on the left, the woman the right.

Ventura tucked the phone away and surreptitiously adjusted the hidden pistol on his hip as he stood. The leather was a custom pancake holster from Ted Blocker, the gun a Coonan Cadet, a stainless .357 Magnum. The pistol had been attended to by Ventura himself, the feed ramp throated and polished, the action slicked, custom springs installed, with the magazines hand-tuned so there would be no failures to feed. .357s and .40s had the best record of one-shot stops in street shootings. A one-shot stop meant that one round to the body put a man out of the play. The Coonan held seven cartridges, six in the magazine and one in the chamber, and he carried it in condition one—cocked and locked. All he had to do was draw, wipe the safety, and fire. Using handloads he built himself, Ventura's one-shot stops should be right at 97 percent. Practically speaking, you couldn't get any better than that with a handgun. A subgun was better, a shotgun more so, and a good rifle best of all, but such things were hard to carry around in public settings, so one made do with what was available.

He had three other pistols identical to it. If he had to shoot somebody, the gun had to go away, and since he liked the design and action, he had bought several, through a dummy dealer. Three years ago, he'd had eight of the pistols. They were good hardware.

Of course, the mark of a good bodyguard was not having to *use* the hardware. He allowed himself a small smile as he headed for the exit. Like a perfect crime, the best bodyguard was one you never knew about.

He might not be the best yet, but there was still time for improvement.

Quantico, Virginia

"Sir? Somebody to see you. A Dr. Morrison, from Washington State?"

Michaels looked up from his computer, blinking away the reading trance he'd been in. Morrison, Morrison . . . ? Ah, yes, he remembered. Morrison had called yesterday, said he was in town, and needed to speak to somebody at Net Force about a problem with something called HAARP. Michaels had done a fast scan of the archives to find out that this was short for High Altitude Auroral Research Project, a joint endeavor that involved the Air Force, Navy, and several universities. Something to do with microwaves or some such. Sounded like a snorer to him.

"Show him in."

The man who followed Michaels's secretary into the office was tall, thin, nearly bald, and looked to be about fifty. He wore a plain black business suit and a dark tie, and carried a battered aluminum briefcase. He could have passed for a professor just about anywhere.

"Dr. Morrison. I'm Alex Michaels."

"Commander. I didn't expect to be meeting with the head of the organization."

Michaels considered telling him that his assistant had quit and that his best computer guy was tromping around in the woods somewhere with his new girlfriend, but decided it wasn't any of the man's business, and he probably wouldn't care anyhow.

He smiled. "Have a seat. What can I do for you, sir?"

Morrison sat, awkward in his movement. Not a jock, this one.

"As you may recall, I am one of the project managers on the HAARP project."

"You're a long way from Gakona, Alaska," Michaels said.

Morrison raised an eyebrow. "You know about the project?"

"Only where it is located, and that it has to do with the ionosphere."

Morrison seemed to relax a little. He opened his brief-case and produced a mini-DVD disc. "Here is a rundown on HAARP—I know you have a higher security clearance than do I, but this is all pretty much public background material."

Michaels took the disc.

"HAARP went on-line in the early nineties, has been operating on and off since. We are in summer hiatus just now, for repairs to equipment. Essentially, HAARP is the world's most powerful shortwave transmitter. It was designed to beam high-energy radio waves into the ionosphere, and thereby to perform various experiments to learn about space weather—for our purposes, that's basically the flow of particles from the sun and other sources into the Earth's atmosphere. These things affect communications, satellites, like that."

Michaels nodded. Yep. A snorer. He tried to look interested.

"The array, called the FIRI, consists of one hundred eighty antenna towers on a grid of fifteen columns and twelve rows, on a gravel pad of some thirty-three acres. Each tower consists of a pair of dipole antennas that run either in the 2.8-to-7 MHz, or the 7-to-10 MHz range. Each transmitter can generate some ten thousand watts of radio-frequency power, and the combined raw output of the three hundred and sixty transmitters is thus three point six million watts. When focused on a single spot in the sky, this is effectively multiplied a thousandfold, to three point six *billion* watts."

"Better than the old pirate Mexican radio stations," Michaels said, smiling.

"By a factor of about seventy thousand," Morrison said, returning the smile.

"So it's a very powerful system. And . . . ?"

"And there are several things we've learned along the way. Research has been primarily in four areas: communications, such as with extremely low frequency waves, or ELF, for such things as contacting submarines in the depths; tomography—the ability to see great distances underground—and even the possibility of some rudimentary weather control. There have also been some experiments with pulse generation, EMP, to knock out enemy missile guidance systems, that sort of thing."

"Interesting."

"Yes, it is. And as a by-product of the ELF research, the possibility of affecting and altering biorhythms of plant and animal life has been . . . explored."

Michaels frowned. "You want to clarify that last part for me?"

"We've known for a long time that long-term radio-wave exposure can affect people. Increased rates of cancer under power lines and the like. Civilized people live in a virtual *bath* of non-ionizing low-frequency waves—

everything electrical produces them. At HAARP, certain areas of research involving the 0.5-to-40Hz frequencies, the same ones that the human brain uses, have been experimented with."

"Meaning?"

"Meaning that the Navy and Air Force are very interested in the possibility that HAARP could give them a nondestructive weapon technology."

Michaels leaned back in his chair. "What, are we talking about *mind* control?"

"It is a possibility, though not yet feasible."

This really *was* interesting. "It's been a while since my last physics class, Dr. Morrison, but the difference between hertz radio waves and megahertz is considerable, isn't it? How is it that a transmitter that produces frequencies in the—what was it? 2.8-to-10 MHz range—will do anything in the 0.5-to-40 Hz range?"

Morrison gave him a smile as might a professor discovering a bright student who has picked up something the rest of the class missed. "Ah, very good, Commander. You are correct. A hertz is *one* cycle per second, a megahertz is a *million* cycles per second. So in order for such high-frequency broadcast energy to be, ah, stepped down by this magnitude requires a considerable change in the length of the broadcasting antenna. Generally speaking, an antenna must be as long as the wavelength it transmits. So 30 MHz waves would require a ten-meter antenna, and 30 Hz waves would need about a thousand-kilometer antenna."

"I wouldn't think there are a lot of thousand-kilometer antennas lying around," Michaels said. He kept his voice dry.

"You'd be surprised. An antenna needn't be made of

steel girders—you can make one out of coils of wire, or transmitters linked electronically, or several other ways. For our purposes, we use the sky itself.

"The Earth is essentially a giant magnet, surrounded by incoming cosmic and solar radiation. A certain number of these solar winds spiral in and down at the magnetic poles, in what is known as the electrojet. This is what causes the aurora—the northern and southern lights. With HAARP, we can, in effect, turn the length of the electrojet into a kind of antenna, and by certain electronic manipulations, make it as long as we want, within limits, of course."

"I see. And this means you can generate frequencies that might affect human mental processes with a lot of broadcast power behind them, over a long distance."

"It does."

"Are you here as a whistle-blower, Dr. Morrison? I'm the wrong guy, you want to be talking to the DOD—"

"No, no, nothing like that. There's nothing wrong with the military seeking out new weaponry; that's part of their job, isn't it? The Russians have been playing with this stuff for years, and it would be foolish for our government to ignore the potential. It would be much better to be able to tell an enemy to lay down his weapon and have him do it than have to shoot him, wouldn't it?

"No, I'm here because I am certain somebody has been sneaking into our computers and *stealing* the information about our experiments."

"Ah."

"Yes. And because I don't know who might be doing it, I came to you rather than my superiors."

Michaels nodded. Now it made sense. "And how is it

you came to believe somebody has been stealing information?"

Morrison smiled and took another DVD disc from his briefcase. "They left footprints."

6

Vermillion River, Lafayette, Louisiana

Michaels sat in the stern of a twelve-foot aluminum bateau, his hand on the control arm of the little electric trolling motor. The sluggish waters of the bayou flowed past, the motor just strong enough to hold the boat's backward movement to a slow drift. The boat had been dark green once, but was rain- and sun-faded to a chalky, lighter shade. It was hot here, probably in the low nineties, even on the water, and the humidity of the air wasn't much drier than the bayou itself. On the shores to either side, huge live oaks loomed, gray Spanish moss hanging down like ragged, organic curtains. A three-foot-long alligator gar broke the surface half a body length, fell back, and splashed the murky water next to a bobbing incandescent lightbulb somebody had thrown in somewhere upstream.

Michaels pulled on the rubber handle of the Mercury outboard motor's starter. The starter rope was nylon, and

had once been white, but was now soaked with enough
two-cycle oil and grease so it was nearly black. The
fifteen-horsepower motor caught, burbled, and rumbled.
He shut off the electric, geared the Mercury, and twisted
the throttle. The smell of gasoline and lubricant enveloped
him.

The bateau surged against the slow flow. He angled
toward the east bank to avoid a half-submerged log floating toward him. Or was that a gator?

On the shore, a big snapping turtle sunned itself on a
rock. The approaching boat made it nervous, and the turtle
slid from the rock and vanished into the dark water.

Michaels smiled. Jay had done a terrific job on this
scenario. It felt so real.

Ahead, the virtual reality construct that represented the
HAARP facility's computer system stood on the east bank
of the bayou, the image of a backwoods bar, a juke joint.
The building was wooden, painted white with a slanting,
corrugated metal roof, and the exterior walls were hung
with metal beer and soft-drink signs whose paint was flak-
ing and peeling: Falstaff, Jax, Royal Crown Cola, Dr Pepper. A small mountain of rusting steel cans avalanched
toward the riverbank to the side of the ramshackle building. Michaels was close enough to see that the empty cans
had pairs of triangular-shaped holes punched into the
tops—opened with what his father used to call a church
key, long before pull- or pop-tops were invented.

He guided the boat toward the shore.

Virtual reality hadn't turned out quite the way the early
computer geeks had imagined. With the power and input
devices available, virtual reality could be, well, virtually
*any*thing—it was up to the person who designed the scenario. The constructs were analogies, of course, but con-

figured so that people could relate to them intuitively. Normal people didn't want to push buttons or click on icons, no matter how cute these things were. What they really wanted was to be surrounded by a setting in which they could behave like people. Instead of tapping at a keyboard, they could hike a mountain trail, ride a horse through the Old West, or—like Michaels—take a small boat down a dark and slow-flowing bayou. There were no limits to what you could do in VR, save those of imagination. You could buy off-the-shelf software, have it custom designed by somebody who knew about such things, or do it yourself. Michaels was the head of Net Force, so he had to at least have a passing familiarity with doing it himself, and he did, but it was much easier to let Jay Gridley or one of the other hotshot ops build them. These guys were detail oriented, and they really got into it.

You could go places, interact with other people, get into computer systems, and what you saw and did might have no relationship to what other people in the same location saw or did. It was personal, unless you opted for the default scenario, or agreed to a consensus reality. A lot of people did that, picked one setting, in order to have a common experience, but Michaels liked his or Jay's imagery better. If you could do it, then why not?

The bateau bumped against the pilings of the little dock, and Michaels killed the outboard and hopped up onto the creosoted wooden planks. He tied the boat up and started for the bar. From this angle, he could see the name of the place: The Dewdrop Inn.

Oh, boy.

In reality, he was sitting in his office more than fifty years away from this place, wearing ear and eye bands, hands in skeletal sensory gloves, seeing and feeling the computer's imagery, and he was aware of that on some level, though he had learned to tune the "real" reality out, as had most people who spent any time in VR.

Normally, he would have had Jay or one of the other serious players investigating this. But the truth was, he needed the diversion; otherwise, he'd have to pack up and go home, and while work wasn't always a cure for what ailed you, sometimes it was better than nothing.

He ambled toward the juke joint. A swarthy, bearded man wearing overalls, no shirt, and no shoes leaned against the wall next to the entrance. The man spat a stream of chewing tobacco juice at a little chameleon perched on a stump nearby, missed. The man smiled, showing gaps in his mostly rotten teeth.

In VR, fire walls came in all kinds of configurations.

Well, yeehaw, Michaels thought. *Welcome to the shallow end of the gene pool, boy.*

"Ain't open," Overalls said.

Michaels nodded. "Uh huh. Guess I'll have to come back later."

"Reckon so."

Michaels smiled and walked away. He retreated to the small dock, got into his boat, cast off, and cranked the motor. Around the next bend in the bayou, maybe three hundred yards farther upstream, he put back into shore, tied the bateau to a low-hanging willow tree branch, and hiked back toward the Dewdrop Inn. He circled around behind it, being careful not to let Overalls see him.

The back door was of unpainted wooden planks, crude, but solid. He fished around his pocket and pulled out a skeleton key. In reality, the key was a password provided by Dr. Morrison, but one couldn't expect to have a coded keypad lock in this kind of scenario; it wouldn't be appropriate.

The spring lock clicked open. Michaels quickly stepped inside and closed the door behind him.

The inside of the place was pretty much a match for the outside, a 1950s backwoods bar. There were scarred wooden tables, beat-up cane-bottomed bent back chairs, and a row of stools in front of a bar that had seen decades of spilled beers and misplaced cigarettes. Two big rectangular coolers marked with beer logos were behind the bar, and a single shelf under a long, cracked mirror held bottles of bourbon, gin, sloe gin, scotch, and vodka.

It took only a minute or so for Michaels to find the built-in lockbox under the bar, a steel plate with a huge Master Lock padlock on a finger-thick brass hasp.

Michaels had a key to the padlock, but since he didn't know what was normally in the lockbox, it wouldn't much matter what he'd find in it if he bothered to look. If something was missing, he wouldn't be able to tell by looking.

It was dim behind the bar, light shining through two grimy windows on the sides of the building, hardly enough to see by. He pulled a small flashlight from his back pocket and shined it at the lock.

Sure enough, there were fresh scratches on the lock and on the hasp. Somebody had been at it, trying to pry or pick it open. No way to tell if they had managed it, but it confirmed Morrison's story, at least in part.

Michaels stood, brushed off his hands, and started for the back door. Morrison could have done it, of course. Somebody yelled "Fire!" a big part of the time he was the guy with the match. Then again, why bring it up? Nobody would have noticed without Morrison's report, at least nobody in Net Force. And Morrison had access to the lockbox—which was, of course, nothing more than a protected set of files inside the HAARP computer system. He could open it whenever he wanted, there was no need for him to break into it.

Well. At least it gave Michaels something to go on. He'd have to call Morrison back, get some more specific information. It didn't seem particularly vital, whatever was in the box, no reason to break a leg hurrying to get to it. There were people he could pass it off to, or he could wait until Jay got back from his vacation; he was only going to be gone for a week.

It had been a nice little exercise, maybe helped keep his VR muscles from atrophying completely, but nothing earthshaking.

He could drop out of VR now and unplug, but what the hell, might as well finish the bateau ride, enjoy the sights a little more, hey?

Monday, June 6th
Mammoth Cave, Kentucky

John Howard smiled as the guide turned the lights off and the inside of the cave went black, a darkness deeper than most people had ever seen. The only things visible were phosphorescent or tritium watch dials, and they seemed really bright against the inky jet so tangible you felt it hang on you like a damp coat.

In the gloom, the guide said, "No sunlight ever gets down here, and yet people explored this cave much farther along than we are now using only candles and burning torches. Before the electric lights were wired in, everybody carried a lot of spare batteries and bulbs for their flashlights, believe it."

The tourists, unseen in the dark, chuckled nervously. Somebody punched a digital phone's keypad and a green light went on; somebody else tapped a control on his or her wristwatch and lit the face up.

The guide switched the lights back on, and there was a collective sigh of relief to be able to see again. She said, "We guides have a standing bet that anybody leading a tour group that *doesn't* light a phone or watch or even a cigarette lighter or key ring flash during the thirty seconds of darkness here gets treated to lunches for a week. No-body has won the pool in six months."

Again, the small crowd laughed, a little less nervously this time.

Howard looked at his wife and son, saw Tyrone smile at his girlfriend, Nadine—who just happened to have the same name as Howard's wife. Howard resisted the urge to smile at how cute they looked. Besides, early teens were dangerous, they were either a million miles—or a single step—away from adulthood at any given moment. Right now, Ty and his friend were boomerang-throwing buddies. A month from now they could be either indif-ferent or trying some entirely new game that Howard knew they were much too young to be trying. Not that it had stopped him from trying at their age.

Nadine—his Nadine—slipped her hand under his arm. "Where'd you go? You just developed the long stare."

He did smile at his wife. "Just watching the kids."

"Feeling old?"

"Oh, yeah. But that's only half of it. Feeling helpless is the hard part. I have all this accumulated wisdom—"

"You wish."

"—okay, *experience,* then, and Tyrone doesn't want to take advantage of it."

"You still talk. He still listens."

"Mostly on autopilot. I don't think he's paying much attention to the actual content."

"Of course not. Did *you* pay much attention to what your parents had to say at his age? Every generation has to reinvent the wheel, hon."

"It seems like such a waste."

"But that's how it is. Rain's gonna come down no matter what you want, you can't stop it. You can stay inside, go out and get wet, or take an umbrella, the rain doesn't care."

"I knew there was a reason I married you," he said. "Your mind."

"That's not what you used to say."

"Well, I suppose you had a couple other attractions."

"You mean you used to think so before I got fat and ugly?"

He turned and looked around behind him.

"What are you looking for?"

"For whoever you must be talking to. You sure ain't talking to me. You better lookin' than the day we met. Going senile and losing your mind, maybe, but fat and ugly? Sheeit, woman, gimme a break."

She smiled. He liked making her do that. Even after more than fifteen years, it still made him feel good.

"It's good for us to get away for a while," she said. "I'm having a good time."

"Me, too," he said. And he was. He hadn't thought about Net Force for the better part of an hour, easy.

Seattle, Washington

Morrison pushed an electronic card across the table to Ventura. "Here is the retainer. A hundred thousand." He'd had to drain his savings and take out a second mortgage on his house to get the money. Ventura's services weren't cheap—thirty thousand a month for the basic plan, and it went up from there—but he was supposedly the best there was, and Morrison knew he needed the best. He'd be broke by the end of July if the deal didn't happen, but there wasn't any real doubt that it would, only with whom and for how much. He needed to stay alive until then, of course.

Ventura took the card with its embedded credit chip, turned it in his fingers, then tucked it into the inside pocket of his sport coat. "Beginning when?"

"Immediately," Morrison said.

Ventura took a small phone from his pocket, touched a button, and said, "We're on," then put the phone away.

Morrison couldn't help but look around. The restaurant was not all that crowded, but he couldn't see anybody who looked like a bodyguard lurking about.

Ventura smiled. "You won't see them."

"Them?"

"There are two ops in here with us, two more outside. Now, I need some information if I am going to protect you properly. Let's start with the level of threat and the reason. Who might be wanting to kidnap or kill you, and why?"

Morrison nodded. Here's where it got tricky. He could offer a good story and probably have the man buy it. Or he could tell the truth. Since his life was going to be on the line, he did not want to make a misstep here.

"I'm not certain of the 'who' yet. Probably the Chinese, but it could be the Russians or maybe the Israelis. The 'why' is because I am in possession of certain, ah, highly useful information they would like to get their hands on."

"From HAARP?"

Morrison blinked, taken aback for a moment. Well. Of course, the man would have checked him out. And it really wasn't all that much of a leap to that assumption. Still, his estimate of Ventura's abilities did go up a notch.

Morrison considered his response, and while he was doing it, Ventura said, "Doctor, I don't much care what it is you are doing, but if I am going to keep you alive, I want to know what I am apt to be dealing with. It makes a big difference in how we proceed, you understand? If you boinked somebody's wife and he wants to beat you to a pulp, that's one thing. If we are going to be dealing with the secret police of a major foreign country, that's something else. I'll take the job either way, but I need to know *everything*. We're talking about your life, and the lives of my crew."

Morrison nodded. Yes. He understood. He took a deep breath. "All right." And for the next fifteen minutes, he laid it out, answering questions as he did so. Ventura did not take notes. He also did not seem disturbed to hear what Morrison had to say.

When he was done, Ventura said, "All right. I'll need your itinerary. Anywhere you go, I will make the travel arrangements. In matters of security, I am God. If I think a situation is too risky, I will tell you, and you will follow my recommendations without question—is this a problem?"

"No, no problem."

"Fine. The situation probably isn't hot yet, but we have to assume that somebody might be able to figure out who you are, so from this point on, we're on alert. What are your immediate plans?"

"I have to go up to the project. We're on hiatus, officially, but I am running some, ah, 'calibrations.' Over the next couple of weeks, I need to do at least two more of these. Possibly three."

"What is the situation with security at the facility? Can I bring my people in?"

"No. I can get you in as an observer from one of the universities—we can fabricate enough background to pass the Navy and Air Force checks—but that's it. There are armed guards patrolling the perimeter of the project, gates, guards at the door, and so forth. It's not exactly a worry that somebody is going to drop by and steal the antennas or the generators."

Ventura nodded.

"There is one complicating factor you should know about. The facility and its computers are being investigated by Net Force."

"Net Force. The FBI suspects what you've done?"

"No. They are being guided down a path I've provided for them."

"Ah, I see. Smart. But they will suspect the messenger, you know, they always do. That's standard procedure."

"I expected they would. I'm covered."

Ventura shrugged. "I hope so. I might be able to keep you from being shot by the Chinese, but I can't keep you out of jail if you have the feds after you—unless you are willing to go completely underground—and leaving the country would be better."

"I understand." Morrison felt a cold hand clutching his bowels. He had started down a dangerous road. He wasn't some absentminded professor who thought about the universe only in abstract theory; he knew that the world was not always a nice place. He had taken this into account, had made the assumption that the people with whom he would be dealing would be treacherous, as trustworthy as foxes guarding a henhouse. Even at this point, he could scrap the whole deal and walk away without being caught, he was certain of it. But no risk, no gain—and the gain here was enormous. People would buy a lottery ticket when the odds were millions to one against them winning. How many people would buy the ticket if they could get their hands on the winning numbers before the drawing?

No, he was committed. He was going to step very carefully, and when he left, it wouldn't be walking, it would be in a solid gold limousine with diamonds for headlights.

There was a price to be paid in human life, of course, but he was willing to pay it—well . . . as long as it wasn't his.

7

A light rain pattered tiny wet fingers on the tent, but the
rip-stop Gortex was up to it—water beaded and ran down
the roof sides in meandering rivulets.

It was just after dawn. Jay Gridley lay on his back
watching the drops. He was inside the two zipped-together
sleeping bags next to Soji, his head propped on his rolled-
up jacket. She'd been right—he hadn't been the least bit
disappointed in this camping trip, no sir, no way. This
was the best vacation he had ever had, no two ways about
it. He wasn't a fan of the great outdoors, he was much
more comfortable creating a VR version of it and plug-
ging into that, but no matter how good a programmer you
were, you couldn't begin to approach the reality of sex.

Nope, nossir, no way, no how.

Jay glanced over at Soji, who was still asleep. He resisted the urge to reach over and stroke her dark hair. God, she was beautiful. Smart, wise, everything he could possibly want in a woman. The only question was, how could he make it permanent? Would she, he wondered, laugh at him if he asked her to marry him?

Soji opened her eyes and smiled at him. "Thinking about asking for your money back, white boy?"

"I'll have you know I'm half Thai," he said, "and *that* for your white boy." He gave her a slapped biceps and raised fist. "And no, I wasn't thinking about asking for my money back, thank you."

"Scenery was worth the trip?"

"All the scenery I need is here in the tent."

She laughed. "Uh-oh, a flatterer trying to reattach me to my ego."

"Yes, ma'am, I'm a Buddhist's worst nightmare. Listen to me, you will fall right off the edge of the eightfold path."

"Never happen," she said. "We Buddhists are middle-of-the-roaders, remember?"

Now he did reach out and softly run his hand through her hair.

She caught his hand, brought it to her mouth, kissed the palm. "Hold that thought," she said. "I'll be right back."

"Going to go and meditate in the rain?"

"No, I'm going to go pee behind the tent."

"You're ruining my image of your holy nature."

"Sorry. You'll just have to get used to me being a lowly human."

"Like the rest of us."

She unzipped the sleeping bag and rolled out, gloriously nude. "Well, not as lowly as *some* of you."

He watched her crawl out of the low-roofed tent, smiling at her tight backside as it vanished past the mosquito netting. They were in the middle of nowhere, hadn't seen another soul for four days, not since they'd left the main trail. They could run around naked in the sunshine—as long as they slathered themselves in sunblock and bug dope, of course—and nobody would see them. If it stopped raining and there was any sunshine—and as far as he was concerned, he didn't care if they ever left this tent except to go pee.

Jay laughed. Boy, had *he* come a long way from being a dedicated computer op. Going back to work had no appeal whatsoever. *This* was what life was all about.

Yes, *sir*.

London

Toni had rented a small place when Alex had gone back to the U.S.—she had some money in the bank, but hotel prices in London would eat that up in a big hurry, now that she wasn't on an expense account. Carl had introduced her to one of his students who had a granny flat, and the cost was more than reasonable. In fact, Toni wondered if maybe Carl was somehow subsidizing it on the sly. So far, she hadn't worked up enough nerve to ask him—if he wasn't, he might be insulted by the thought. And if he was, then she'd have to move out, and that would be a pain in the butt.

Either way, her money would be depleted by the time her visa ran out, and she'd have to leave the country by the end of the summer.

She was sitting at the small table in the kitchen—a kitchenette, really—when the doorbell chimed. Who could that be? Save for Carl and her landlord, nobody knew she lived here. A salesman? Somebody come to the wrong address?

When she opened the door, the last person she expected to see stood there:

MI-6 agent Angela Cooper.

Toni was stunned. The bitch! How *dare* she come here?

Toni clamped a lid on the rush of anger that threatened to boil forth. Polite might be too much to ask for, but she kept her voice even: "What do you want?"

Cooper flashed a weak smile. She was a beautiful woman, no doubt of that. Toni could see the attraction. "I need to speak to you. May I come inside?"

"Why? We don't have anything to talk about."

"I think we do. Please."

Toni offered as bored a shrug as she could. "Sure. Come in."

Once inside, Cooper looked nervous. *She sure as hell should be,* Toni thought. She might be a trained secret agent, but Toni's martial abilities were a lot sharper than what the Royal secret service would be passing on to its operatives. If push came to shove, she could take Cooper—even if she had James Fucking *Bond* backing her up. And she would enjoy whacking Cooper. A lot.

"What?"

"I won't be here but a moment or two. Listen, I've wrestled with this and I can't come up with any clever way to say it, so here it is, flat out: I didn't sleep with Alex Michaels."

"No, I expect you *didn't* get much *sleeping* done."

Cooper shook her head. "You have it wrong. We did

not have sex—is that clearer? Not in any way, shape, or form, not even by Clinton definition. I wanted to, but he turned me down."

It caught Toni flat-footed. "What?"

"Yes, I know I made it seem as if we had, but—it didn't happen. I wanted to, believe it, and I tried my best, but he wouldn't go for it."

Toni waved at the table. This was astounding. "You want to sit down?" As it always did when she got flustered, her Bronx accent came back: *Ya wanna siddown?*

Was she telling the truth? Had Alex put her up to this?

Cooper read her mind: "In case you are wondering, no, Alex didn't tell me to talk to you; I haven't spoken to him since he left the country. I heard what happened between you two. I was going to let it pass. When he wouldn't do me, I was, well, a bit put out, so I decided to sting you a little by letting on that he had. I suppose I wanted you to take him to task, make him squirm a bit. But despite his rejection, I did like Alex, and it isn't really fair to make him suffer because he was doing right by you."

"Alex didn't deny it when I brought it up," Toni said.

"I don't understand why not. It had been a long day. We had supper in a pub. He had one beer too many, and I offered to give him a massage. But that was as far as it got. He was half-asleep facedown on the massage table when I stripped and tried to get him to have it off with me. I was ready—and it was obvious *he* was ready, too— but instead of his willie, he waved *you* in my face."

She paused, took a deep breath, and went on. "I was furious. And I resented you for having him, so that's why I did what I did. I'm sorry. That's it."

She turned and started for the door.

Toni had trouble finding her voice, barely made it before the woman got the door open. "Angela?"

"Yes?"

"Thank you for telling me. It couldn't have been easy."

Cooper smiled, more genuine this time. "I'd rather be having a bloody root canal. You're lucky to have a man like that interested in you. Maybe you can patch things up."

When she was gone, Toni sat at the table, staring at the wall. Why hadn't he just *told* her? He *knew* she thought he'd slept with Cooper; all he had to do was *deny* it, she would have believed him. At least she thought she would have believed him. Why hadn't he spoken up?

She replayed their last meeting, trying to remember exactly how it had gone. Had he ever actually *said* he'd been with Cooper?

No . . .

Well, *shit!* What the hell was wrong with him! Why had he let her think he'd done it!

Abruptly, Toni felt the emotions well, and tears spill. *Dammit, Alex!*

She was angry all over again, but this time for an entirely different reason. *What on Earth could he have been thinking?*

8

"Is that where we're going?" Ventura had to raise his voice for Morrison to hear him. Normally, a plane like the Cessna Stationair was not that noisy while cruising, but this one had a slightly warped door edge on the passenger side that added a loud almost-whistle.

"That's the place," Morrison said.

Ventura looked down from what he guessed was about eight thousand feet. Most of what he saw looked like virgin evergreen forest. In the distance was a snowcapped mountain range with a few very tall peaks. The HAARP site itself was cut out of the forest—it was as if somebody had cleared a large area in woods in the rough shape of a skeleton key. Several buildings and a parking lot in a ragged circular area were connected by a straight road to the array itself—which looked as if somebody had planted seeds that grew up to be giant 1950s-style television antennas. Beyond that was a second rectangular array, as large as the first. Behind the control buildings and just coming into view was a long, straight paved strip a couple of thousand feet long.

The pilot banked the plane slightly, then throttled back as he straightened the Cessna out.

"We've got our own landing strip now," Morrison said. "Better security. It wasn't a problem when they built the place—anybody could just walk up to the front gate, they even had open house every now and then—but there was some ugly vandalism by eco-terrorists, so now there's a big chainlink fence and armed military guards. The nearest town, such that it is, Gakona, is over that way. There's a post office, a gas station, a motel and a couple of bed-and-breakfast places, a restaurant, a bar, like that. They get a lot of tourists, hunters, and fishermen up here. If you want, you can get a dogsled custom-made for you here, too, but if you are looking for nightlife, this isn't the place. Forty-nine permanent residents."

Ventura nodded. He had been in backcountry towns so small and isolated that a big topic of conversation on a Sunday morning was the size of a particularly large icicle hanging from a bar awning. "Gets a little chilly for street dancing," Ventura said.

It was not a question, though Morrison treated it as such. "Yes, it drops to forty or fifty below in the dark of winter, and usually there are a couple feet of white fluffy powder on the flats, piled higher against the buildings. Sometimes the wind blows hard enough to scour the ground clean in places, though. Plays hell with the runners on your snow machine when you hit one of those."

Ventura smiled politely. He had done some background

research before they'd flown into Anchorage. He probably knew more about the terrain and local country than Morrison did, but he didn't let on. In almost every situation, knowledge was power, and because you worked for a man didn't mean that you trusted him.

From what he had learned, the HAARP site was a hundred and some odd miles northeast of Anchorage, almost to the Wrangell Mountains, the high range that divided Alaska from the Canadian Yukon.

He already knew that the nearest town was Gakona, and that it was about fifteen miles north and west of the town of Glennallen, which wasn't exactly a major metropolis itself. Up here, people gave directions differently than in a city—the Sourdough Motel, for instance, was at Milepost 147.5—you didn't need to say which road, there weren't so many you'd get confused. Gakona was on the Glenn Highway, though the locals called it the Tok Cut-Off, a couple of miles from the Richardson Highway intersection. The town, what there was of it, was near the confluence of the Copper and Gakona rivers. The original inhabitants were Ahtna Indians, though few of them lived here now. Few of anybody lived here now. During the busy season, there were more people working at the HAARP site than lived in town. People who chose to be up here enjoyed the great outdoors, and they were either hardy or they didn't stay.

The landing strip at the site was new, and according to his research, there wasn't a commercial airport closer than Gulkana, a few miles south of Gakona. No railroad, and the roads called highways were more like state roads.

A hundred years ago, somebody had built a roadhouse, the Gakona Lodge, and it was still there, now a restaurant.

If you didn't work for HAARP—or against it, and there were some who did that, work against it—you came up here to hunt, fish, hike, canoe, kayak, ski, or snowboard. There were a couple of paramedics with the volunteer fire department, but no hospitals, clinics, or doctors around, so if you chainsawed your foot off, you were shit out of luck.

The pilot, who was a grizzled man of maybe fifty, lined up on the narrow runway and dropped his airspeed. A lot of these bush pilots were experts, and this one was better than most at flying this little bird, because after he'd left the Navy, where he'd flown jets off and onto an aircraft carrier, he had flown crop dusters for a living down in central California. Ventura had checked him out, too. When you took on a client, you didn't take any chances— you examined everybody who got within rifle range of your charge if you could pull it off. It was easier up here in the middle of nowhere, at least insofar as the numbers went. And it wasn't that hard to do, much easier than a lot of people realized.

Ventura subscribed to a computer investigative service. You logged onto the site, gave them your password and the name of whoever or whatever you wanted to know about, and within a few minutes, usually, they came back with as extensive a report as was available. The service had access, however legally, to social security, state motor vehicle departments, credit bureaus, police computer nets, and a bunch of others they wouldn't talk about. It was an expensive service, but they were pretty good. Not perfect—all they had on Ventura himself was what he allowed anybody to have on him—but as good as you were going to find outside of a serious spook shop. Good enough to track and define most honest people. Spotting the others was his job—if it took one to know one, he certainly ought to know a shooter.

The pilot brought the plane in smoothly, didn't even hop once when he touched down, and taxied toward a wind sock on a steel post next to a corrugated metal shed with a very steeply angled roof.

Once they were out with their bags, the pilot headed from the apron back to the runway, never even killing his engine.

It was warm—high seventies or low eighties, Ventura figured.

Morrison said, "Didn't think it would be so warm, eh?"

"Actually, I was wondering where the mosquitoes were. They're usually pretty bad this time of year in the lake valleys."

Morrison blinked, apparently surprised that Ventura wasn't surprised by the temperature. "Um. Well, the DOD has a guy who comes out and fogs the site every now and then. The mosquitoes are worse away from here. So, you've been to Alaska before? Why didn't you say so?"

"It never came up," Ventura said. He smiled.

"Um. Come on, I'll show you the setup. There's a fuel-cell cart in the shed; it's a mile or so to the front gate from here. We'll ride."

Ventura nodded. He adjusted the pistol in his belt holster. It had been there since they'd left Seattle. There were half a dozen ways he knew of to avoid having to pack your weapon in your luggage. People who thought you couldn't carry a gun onto a commercial jet were only fooling themselves.

Fooling himself was not Ventura's game.

I-80, just northwest of Laramie, Wyoming

"Wow, look how *big* they are!"

Tyrone glanced away from the small herd of buffalo penned next to the truck stop, and at Nadine. "Yeah. I've seen vids, but you don't get the reality of it. They stink, too." In the heat of the early afternoon, the dry air carried the musky, dusty odor of the animals. It was kind of hard to say exactly what it smelled like, but it wasn't something you smelled on a street in Washington, D.C. This was a fairly level spot, but they were into the northern Rocky Mountains now, and it was a lot slower going in the big RV than it had been on the flatlands of Kansas.

He and Nadine stood next to the tall wooden rail fence bounded by a single wire plastered with warnings that it was electrified, and not to touch it, not more than twenty or thirty feet away from the nearest buffalo as it chewed on hay or something. As they watched, the creature let loose a big dump, clumps of brown and yellowish stuff plopping onto the ground under its tail. It never even lifted its head from its grazing. Poot and eat at the same time. Yuk.

"Puu*wee!*" Nadine said.

Before it had smelled kind of rank, but now it *really* stunk.

"Yeah, well, I'm impressed. No wonder they wiped them out. Come on, let's get upwind," he said.

Behind them, the thirty-foot-long RV Tyrone's dad had borrowed from an admiral he knew was parked at the gas pumps, sucking up fuel. The thing would hold like fifty or sixty gallons in the tank, and it needed it, because it got only eight or ten miles to the gallon. On a round trip that was probably going to run almost six thousand miles, the RV was going to drink a *lot* of gasoline. Even with the new clean-burn technology and the solar-assist panels, the RV was a big old tank, big as a bus, and it lumbered along like a dinosaur. Of course, it was huge on the inside. There was a bedroom in the back with a queen-sized bed, where his mom and dad slept. A bathroom with a shower and toilet and sink, lots of closet space, and even a tiny bedroom up front that pulled out from one side of the main body like a drawer when they were stopped. Nadine slept in that little room behind one of those plastic accordion doors. Plus there was a dining area with a table, a kitchen with a stove, fridge, sink, microwave oven, and a pretty good-sized TV set and computer, with an automatic track-and-lock sat dish on the roof that caught narrowcast audio-vid, and telecom signals. You could sit there and eat a bowl of Häagen-Dazs pineapple-coconut ice cream and watch entcom stuff, or log onto the net, all while your dad was driving down the interstate at sixty. Pretty amazing. A lot more fun than being cooped up in the back of the family Dodge. Although being cooped up hip-to-hip with Nadine wouldn't be so bad. She wasn't gorgeous, but she was smart, athletic, and definitely female.

There was a couch behind the passenger seat that pulled out into a bed, and that was where Tyrone slept. He'd gotten used to it after the days on the road, and it was almost as comfortable as his bed at home. His dad had said it ought to be, since the RV had cost the admiral as much as they'd paid for their *house*.

He saw his mom and dad coming back from the direction of the truck stop. They had a couple of big paper bags and a cardboard carrier of soft drinks. This was a treat, since Mom usually cooked in the RV.

"There's a place to park around the side of the buffalo pen," his dad said. "We can eat and watch the buffalo roam." He rattled the bags.

"Flawless," Tyrone said. "As long as it's not downwind."

The fries were good, the onion rings really good, and the burgers had a kind of smoky, odd flavor. Not bad, but different. Tyrone swallowed a bite of the burger and said, "They cook burgers kinda differently out here."

His father smiled. "It's not how they cook them, it's what they *make* them out of."

Tyrone looked at him. "Huh?"

His father pointed out the window over the table and grinned real big.

Tyrone looked at the buffalo. He looked at his burger. Ah . . .

Both Nadines laughed.

All of a sudden Tyrone wasn't that hungry. Then again, he *was* going to eat this burger, and he would do it if it *killed* him. No way was he going to let his dad get this one, no . . . *way.*

He smiled, took a big bite, and smiled again, mouth full. "Good. I love it."

9

Michaels felt as if he were a thousand years old and mostly turned to dust as he held the phone's receiver in a death grip that threatened to break his hand or the instrument. He kept his voice as light as he could.

". . . really great, Dadster, and all the kids in my class love him."

His daughter was talking about Byron Baumgardner, a teacher at her school in Boise—and his ex-wife Megan's boyfriend.

No, not boyfriend—*fiancé*. They were getting married at the end of the month. And they wanted to have Byron the bearded wonder adopt *his* daughter, move in and take over as her father, and deny Michaels visitation—if he allowed it.

Needless to say, Michaels had not been invited to the wedding.

His initial inclination had been to fight it to the death—preferably Megan and Byron's death. He didn't like either of them right now, and at their first meeting had put the bearded wonder on his ass when the man had grabbed him. Megan had been doing her usual slash-and-burn number on him, and when he'd said something back in an angry retort, dear young Byron had taken it upon himself to defend her honor. Without thinking about it, Michaels had decked the man, thus proving that the *silat* he'd been learning actually worked.

In retrospect, that had been a mistake, but boy, it sure felt good at the time.

Well, Byron the bearded wonder would find out about how much *honor* his new love had the first time he crossed her—Megan fought dirty, always had. Michaels had overlooked that for a long time, blaming himself for a lot of their troubles, but eventually he realized it wasn't *all* his fault. Yeah, he had spent too much time at the office, and yeah, he could withdraw into his own head and not engage even when he was home, but he had been a good father, and when Megan started throwing the lousy-dad crap in his face, it was hard to smile and shrug it off.

But would taking his ex and her new love to the legal mat and trying to choke them out benefit Susie? How would an ugly custody battle affect her? Sure, kids were resilient, they could bounce back after really nasty trauma—mental, physical, whatever—but did he want to be the one who *caused* that trauma?

No. Even if it was mostly Megan's doing, she was going to be the person who got Susie out of bed every day, the person Susie would come crying to when she fell and skinned her knee, the person who could, with a few well-chosen words, plant a lot of lies about dear old dad that would slowly and surely turn his daughter against him. And he wouldn't put it past Megan, not after what he'd learned about her after they had split up. She had a mean streak, and it was a lot wider and deeper than he'd ever imagined it could be.

Getting into a tussle with her mother over Susie's affections would be a losing proposition, no question. At least until she became a teenager and rebelled . . .

Susie, now eight, continued to talk about what a swell guy Byron was, and as much as he didn't want to agree with *that*, Michaels didn't say so. Poisoning a well was never a good idea in his mind, you never knew if somebody you loved might drink from it—or if you might have to drink from it yourself someday. Susie was going to be living with the man, and what good would it do her to be in the middle of a pissing match between her real father and the new stepdad?

What harm might it do her?

Truth was, Byron probably *was* a nice guy. If he'd met him away from Megan, he suspected he wouldn't have had any problems with him. Yeah, he'd been out of line when he got between a divorced couple in a long-running fight he didn't understand, but he would have done the same thing in Byron's place. Michaels had been ragging on Megan—justifiably so, in his mind—but what kind of man were you if you didn't step up to protect your woman? Even if she was in the wrong?

Or even if she was somebody like Toni, who could protect herself better than you could?

Michaels shook his head. *Toni isn't your woman anymore. Don't go there.*

"So when are you coming to see me, Dadster?"

"Pretty soon, Li'l Bit. Next month."

Yeah, next month. Friday, July 1. The day of the first round of the custody hearings. His lawyer, Phil Buchanan, was confident they could win, or at least stall things for a long time, or so he said. But the question was: Did he really want to do that?

"Spiffy! Did Momster tell you that Scout caught a rat?"

"A rat?" Scout was a toy poodle Michaels had come by when an assassin, a woman disguising herself as an old lady walking her dog, had used the little beast as part of her subterfuge. Fortunately for him, the dog had barked at just the right time, saving his life. He'd thought about keeping the pooch, but figured he needed more attention than he could give a pet, so now Scout was his daughter's companion.

"Oh, yeah, we heard them fighting under the porch last night and then Scout came out dragging it by the neck! It was a big rat, all brown and bloody, and it was dead, but he bit Scout on the leg, so we had to take Scout to the vet to get a shot so he wouldn't get rat disease. He's okay, though."

The idea of the toy poodle tangling with a wood rat and coming out the winner was amusing. When he'd lived there, Michaels had used D-Con or traps to keep the rat and mice population down. *That* was a long time ago, in a galaxy far away . . .

"I gotta go, Daddy. Daddy-B is coming over to take us to the new IMAX 3-D. I love you."

"I love you, too, honey. Bye."

Michaels stared at the phone. *Daddy-B.*

Well, okay, sure, what was she going to call him? An eight-year-old using his first name somehow wasn't right, but "Daddy-B"?

Michaels sure as hell didn't need to hear that, regardless of what was best for his child. That wasn't right, either.

So, what was he going to do about all this? He had only a few weeks to decide, and the decision would affect him and his daughter for the rest of their lives.

Wasn't *that* just one more straw his camel didn't need. His life had become a damned soap opera.

London

"Are you sure?" Carl asked.

Toni nodded and sighed. "Yes. I have to go."

They were in Carl's *silat* school, which occupied the second floor of a four-story building between a tandoori restaurant and a boarded-up charity shop in a less-than-posh section of town called Clapham. The school was bare-bones, old wooden floors and a few mats, run-down, but kept spotlessly clean by students offering *hormat* and *adat*—basically honor and respect—to their instructor. The first evening class would be starting in about an hour, and the students who volunteered to sweep and mop the floors would be there soon.

Carl nodded in return. "I understand."

Impulsively, Toni put her hand on his chest. Under the thin white T-shirt, the muscle was tight and warm. "Thank you. I appreciate all you've taught me."

He caught her hand with his, pressed it against his pectoral a bit harder. "It has been mutual. Listen, if things don't go well with your Mr. Michaels, let me know soonest, would you?"

"I will."

"I have occasion to visit the States now and then. I'd be pleased to see you there whether this works out with Alex or not."

"I'd like that," she said.

"Are you going to stay for class?"

"No, I need to get packed. My flight leaves early in the morning."

He nodded again. "I'll miss you."

"I'll keep in touch, I promise."

He bent and kissed her gently on the lips, leaned back, and smiled. "Travel safely," he said.

Toni nodded and smiled. Carl was a path not taken, at least not fully, and she had a feeling she would always wonder how it would have been to travel that way.

Back at her flat, Toni looked through the things she had gathered during her weeks in the country. Some of it would fit into her bag. Some of it she could have shipped if she wanted. Most of it would stay here. A coffeemaker, a blender, a small microwave oven—they would be useful for the next tenant. What she would mostly take would be her memories, and now they were jumbled in a way she had to reconsider. Alex hadn't slept with Cooper, whatever his reasons for allowing her to think otherwise. It made a difference to her, and she had to resolve it.

She could have had her com receive his daily call. Could make the connection herself and ask him about it from thousands of miles away. No risks to that. But no long-distance voice, even complete with a video image, was enough for such a conversation. She needed to be able to see into his eyes, watch him closely, pick up the little movements of his body language, to touch, smell, maybe even taste him. She didn't kid herself that she could always tell if somebody was lying to her, but she thought she could tell if Alex was lying, if he was standing right in front of her and if she was looking for it. So if what Cooper had said was true, if he *hadn't* cheated on her, then what would that mean? She had left him, quit her job, and if she had done it because she had made a mistake—it was a very *big* fucking mistake. If she had been that *wrong,* then what did *that* say about her?

She had to know. One way or another. And if she had to swim across an ocean and then walk the rest of the way when she got to dry land, then that was what she was going to do.

The doorbell chimed.

A deliveryman dressed in blue shorts and a matching shirt and cap stood there, holding a small package. She signed for it, then went back inside. What could this be?

Inside the box, enveloped in fat green plastic bubble-wrap, was an eight-inch-tall, dark blue glass bottle, about as big around as a cardboard toilet tissue tube.There was a small sheet of print rubber-banded to the cylinder, and a note in the box. The note said, "Toni—I thought you might be able to use this. It won't do anything for your ego or your soul, but it might help with external aches and pains. Cheers, Carl."

The sheet of print turned out to be instructions for using what was inside the blue bottle: *Balur Silat,* also called *Tjimande Silat,* or if you liked the newer spelling, *Cimande,* where the "C" was pronounced the same way as the "Tj."

Toni grinned. *Balur Silat* was a training aid, coupled

with conditioning devices like padded punching and kicking targets. Toni didn't use it much anymore, but she still had a striking ball that Guru had made for her years ago. It was an old athletic sock with about three pounds of copper-coated steel BBs in it, the kind used by air guns. The BBs were tied off in the toe of the sock, which was then clipped to make a globe about the size of a baseball. This was then wrapped tightly with layers of duct tape. What you did with this was to punch it, or hold it in one hand to bang it against your forearms or elbows or shins, to help get them used to being hit.

Balur Silat was a blend of coconut oil and different roots and herbs, a concoction that took about a month to make. You ground the herbs up, cooked and mixed them together, put the resulting goop into a dark glass bottle, and stored it in a dark cool place for months, or even years, to age.

After a bruising session of bone-to-bone contact during a workout, battered shins and forearms were common. Like the Chinese herbal remedy *Dit da jow,* or "iron hit wine," the classic Indonesian preparation was said to be a great help. Literally, *balur* means "to crystallize" or "to harden." The stuff was solid at room temperature and had to be heated slightly to liquefy. The liniment thus created was used to help speed healing of bruises, and to help to condition and toughen the skin. There were practitioners of some fighting arts who had shins so hard and impervious to impact they could break baseball bats over them without apparent harm or pain. Toni had seen a picture of an old *Serak* stylist who could do that once, and she had no desire to have her shins scar and knot and wind up looking like his; still, a certain amount of conditioning was a good idea, and *Balur Silat* was a help, though finding the authentic stuff wasn't easy—every other guru out there had his or her own recipe, and some were better than others. She was pretty sure that Carl Stewart's stuff would be decent.

She hefted the bottle. If it *would* work on bruised egos, the maker could name his price and retire rich in a few days. She smiled again, and went back to her packing.

10

Morrison had given Ventura the tour of the facility, but the man hadn't seemed too awed or even interested by anything, other than the main power generators. Those were fairly impressive. The power building, more than twenty thousand square feet of it, was constructed originally to house a huge coal-fired steam generator that was to run an Air Force Over the Horizon Backscatter Radar installation originally sited here. At the termination of the OTH-B program and the shift to HAARP, the steam generation gear was hauled off, and the backup diesel generators were used instead. They had plenty of power to operate the transmitter and the ISR. Originally, HAARP had been tapped into the local power grid for lights and heating and like that, but interruptions during really bad weather were sometimes a problem—nobody much enjoyed sitting in the cold and dark even if the transmitter still worked, so the local grid was eventually switched over to their own generators. Power-wise, they were self-sufficient—as long as the monster fuel tank was kept filled.

Morrison could understand why Ventura wasn't all that impressed—a lot of the older buildings that were supposed to have been temporary were still there, and they weren't anything to write home about. These were no more than trailers with cheap wood paneling and external conduits for switches and electrical plugs, beat-up old computers and monitors, steel desks and press-board filing cabinets. Not what you thought of as cutting edge.

Still, impressing Ventura was not the point. Running the next test was.

Which was what he was about to do. He had another target, and the conditions were as good as they were going to get this time of year, so he was ready to begin.

Ventura stood behind him, wearing a disguise that ought to fool anybody here into thinking he belonged—black polyester slacks over brown loafers, a white shirt with a pen protector in the pocket, an ugly vest, uglier tie, and dark plastic rimmed glasses. A perfect geek.

There was a gun tucked under the vest, Morrison was certain, but even though he knew it was there, he couldn't see it.

The controls in the auxiliary trailer worked as well as the main ones, but they were less likely to have unexpected visitors here, and unexpected they would be if any showed up.

Morrison said, "With our computers up, and if the sunspot activity isn't too bad, we can hit the mark ninety-eight times out of a hundred." He adjusted a control, and a liquid crystal display of numbers flashed new digits.

He and Ventura were alone in the HAARP auxiliary control room. The ACR was where Morrison usually conducted his calibrations and, in this case, an unauthorized use of the equipment. The thing was, you couldn't tell by looking where the energy generated by the array was going. Since the project was shut down for the summer, except for maintenance and calibrations, no real scientists would be looking over his shoulder—and the guards wouldn't have a clue what he was really doing.

In his guise as a geek scientist, Ventura chuckled.

Morrison frowned. "Something funny about that?"

Ventura said, "In some circles, ninety-eight percent accuracy is considered failure."

Morrison adjusted another dial, then turned to look at Ventura, the question apparent in his raised eyebrows.

"In the late 1800s, there was a trick shooter named Adolph 'Ad' Topperwein. In December of 1906, he decided to try for a record. He had a sawmill in San Antonio, Texas, make up a bunch of wooden cubes, two-and-a-quarter-inches square."

"A bunch? *There's* a scientific term."

"Give me a minute, I'll get there."

Ventura held his thumb and forefinger apart, about the thickness of a modestly fat reference book. "Blocks were about so, a little bigger than a golf ball."

Morrison glanced at his control board, tapped a key. The computer screen scrolled more numbers. "Fine. So?"

"So, Ad went to the San Antonio Fair Grounds with a couple of relays of throwers, some official witnesses, three Winchester M-03 self-loading .22 rifles, and a—here's that word again—*bunch* of ammunition. He had his assistants stand about twenty-five feet in front of him. They tossed a block high into the air, and he snapped off a shot, only one, per block.

"He shot more than fourteen hundred of the little blocks before he had a miss. After that, he went more than *fourteen thousand* straight, hit every one."

"Jesus. That's a bunch, all right."

"Not yet it isn't. He did this for a week, seven hours a day. At the end of that time, he had fired at *fifty thousand blocks*. Of fifty thousand tries, he missed exactly . . . four."

"Good Lord," Morrison said. "With a *rifle*? Not a shotgun?" Morrison had done some target shooting as a boy with his father's .22 rifle. The idea of hitting fifty thousand blocks sitting on a *table* at twenty-five feet and only missing four was amazing. To hit them flying through the air? That was *astounding*.

Ventura smiled. "It gets better. He was averaging more than a thousand blocks an hour, one every three and a half seconds or so, and so he finished ahead of schedule—he had allowed himself ten days. He had the record and could have quit, but he didn't. Instead, he had his assistants salvage some of the least-damaged blocks, got more ammo, and started shooting again. He was getting a bit tired after a week of constant shooting, so his tally fell off a little, but he shot for three more days.

"All totaled, he fired at seventy-two thousand, five hundred blocks. His final score was seventy-two thousand, four hundred and ninety-one. He missed nine.

"Sixty-eight and a half hours of point-and-shoot. Although there have been shooters who have actually potted *more* blocks since, none of them have done it under the same conditions, so the record still stands. I have a picture of Topperwein, in a black suit—with a tie—boots, and a campaign hat, sitting atop a mountain of shot-up blocks, his rifle cradled in his arm."

Morrison shook his head. "I can't even imagine waggling my finger seventy thousand times, much less maintaining enough concentration to shoot accurately that many times."

"Frankly, neither can I. Topperwein was the best exhibition shooter who ever lived. But he was also a relatively uneducated man from a little town in Texas, using bare-bones .22 rifles, no laser sights, no shooting glasses, no electronic hearing protection, nothing. Not exactly what you'd call high tech, and *his* accuracy percentage was .99988. More than a hundred years later, with all of this"—he waved one hand to take in the computer gear— "at your command, you'd think you could improve on target shooting."

Morrison considered that. Yes, you'd think so. Then again, with a tap of a single finger, he could drive seventy thousand people mad in a few hours. No man with a rifle could begin to match that.

Morrison powered up the system for his "test." Warning buzzers started to sound, a red light flashed on and off on the control board. He reached for the control, a covered button. The buzzers continued their howl, the lights their strobe, as he raised the cover, then pressed the button.

I got your blocks of wood right here, *pal . . .*

Multnomah Falls, Oregon

John Howard stood by the stone restaurant watching his family look at the thin ribbon of water cascading down from a great height to splash into a cold pool at the base of the cliff. They were about twenty-five or so miles outside of Portland, in the Columbia River Gorge, looking at one of the highest waterfalls in the country, more than a six-hundred-foot drop in the second stage here. It was beautiful, though more impressive in the spring as the snowmelt fed the tributary a lot more water.

Everything was damp here, lots of moss and mold, fed by the constant spray off the falls.

Howard reached for the virgil—the virtual global interface link—hooked to his belt. This was a great toy, not much bigger than a standard pager or small cell phone, and it not only had a com, it was a working GPS, clock, radio, TV, modem, credit card, camera, scanner, and even a tiny fax that produced weavewire hardcopy. There were civilian models, but the military units were better—at least for now. Sharper Image was gaining, or so he had heard.

Sergeant Julio Fernandez appeared on the virgil's tiny screen, smiling.

"Congratulations, General. I didn't think you'd make it this long. I guess one of the others will win the pool."

"I am merely calling to check in, Sergeant."

"The country is getting along fine without you, sir. No wars, no terrorists taking over at Quantico—well, if you don't count the new feeb recruits—and the Republic endures."

"I just wanted to let you know where I was."

"John, your GPS sends us a homing signal as long as it's got power, remember? We *know* where you are. You want me to give you your longitude and latitude?"

"Nobody likes a smart-ass NCO, Julio."

"C'mon, you're on vacation. Relax. Enjoy yourself. I'll

call if the Swiss or the French decide to invade the country, I promise."

Howard made a suggestion that was anatomically impossible and unlikely for a heterosexual even if it had been possible.

Fernandez laughed. "That's a discom, General. Adios."

Howard smiled as he rehooked the virgil to his belt. Well, yes, he did sometimes think things would go to hell if he left town. So he was a worrier, what could he say?

Nadine and the children were hot to climb up to the little bridge closer to the falls, and Howard went along. It was all part of the ambience, to get wet, wasn't it?

As they hiked up the damp macadam path, he recalled the first time he'd ever been to this part of the country. Back in '99 or '00, in the late fall or early winter. A friend of his from the army, Willie Kohler, had scored some two hundred buck tickets to a boxing match out on the coast. Not the best seats, but pretty good, only about fifty or sixty feet from the ring. It was in one of those Indian casinos that the local tribes had put up. Chinook something? Chinook Winds, that was it. In Lincoln City.

He remembered the event better now that he thought about it. They had given it some silly name, like the Rumble in the Jungle or the Thrill in Mantilla, it was . . . ah, yes, Commotion at the Ocean. He and Willie had gotten some funny mileage out of that one.

He wasn't the world's biggest boxing fan, but he'd done a little in the service when he'd been younger, fighting camp matches as a light-heavyweight and giving about as good as he got. No future there for him, getting bashed in the face, but he didn't mind watching somebody with real skill demonstrate it. As he remembered, there had been six or eight matches at the casino, all fairly low weight classes, and a couple of them were championship bouts. The most interesting fights had been on the under card. Some black kid from Washington, D.C., with sweet moves had put his man down in the second round. And there had been a couple of female fighters, one a little girl in red, a featherweight, all of a hundred and twenty-two or -three pounds, who had great hands—and great legs, too. Only her third pro fight, but she had real boxing skills. Of course, this was back when boxing wasn't considered a brutal crime against humanity, and women were just getting into it. And when it still wasn't too politically incorrect to admire a woman's legs . . .

What he remembered most of all was that they played bad rap music—if that wasn't redundant—between each fight, and it was way, way too loud. Earmuffs should have been mandatory; it was noisier than a shooting range, and probably less musical. After the second or third fight, he and Willie were ready to go and kick out the damned speakers to kill the noise. But like at gun shows, you needed to be polite at a big boxing match—you never knew but that guy you just sloshed your beer on might have been the number one contender for the cruiserweight title a few years back, and no matter what self-defense system you knew, a good pro boxer was going to get at least a couple of shots in if he smiled—and then threw the first punch.

Howard smiled as they climbed into the waterfall mist. There was a lot of green on the hillside now—moss, ferns, all kinds of water-loving plants.

Julio was right, he needed to relax and enjoy his vacation. His son was growing up, and pretty soon he'd be a lot more interested in girls and cars than boomerangs and family trips. Might as well enjoy it while he could. He was out in the Wild West, nothing of any major military importance was apt to happen here, certainly nothing he needed to worry about.

Nadine looked back at him and smiled. "Isn't this fun?"

"Yep," he said, "it is."

11

Jay Gridley wasn't exactly thrilled about having to go back to work. Yeah, sure, it was what he did, and yeah, sure, he loved it, but rolling around with Soji, even in a drafty tent in the rainy woods? Well, that had work beat all *hollow*.

He never thought he'd hear himself think that, but there it was.

Truth was, even though he was dropping by the Net Force compound late Thursday afternoon, he didn't really have to be back until Monday. But Soji had clients she had to counsel, and she refused to take a laptop or net-phone with her into the woods, so they had packed up the camping gear and came back to civilization. In her net persona of the old Tibetan priest Sojan Rinpoche, Soji taught basic Buddhism and also offered a kind of psychospiritual first aid to people who had suffered various forms of brain damage, usually secondary to drugs or stroke. That was how they'd met, on-line, when Jay had been zapped while chasing the guy with the quantum computer.

Soji had an apartment in Los Angeles, but she was going to be working out of Jay's place, at least for now. And he hoped he could convince her to make it permanent, though he hadn't yet worked up the nerve to ask her to move in, much less to marry him. But he was gonna. Eventually.

Commander Michaels was in his office when Jay got there. He waved at the receptionist. "He busy?"

"No, go ahead in."

Jay tapped at the door, then opened it. "Hey, Boss."

"Jay? What you doing here? You're not supposed to be back until Monday. How did it go?"

"The mosquitoes got so bad we had to come back for a transfusion. Other than that, it went great. How's business?"

"Slow. Nothing major. Usual net scams, viruses, illegal porno stuff. Nobody trying to topple the world that we've noticed, thank God."

Jay wanted to ask if Michaels had heard from Toni Fiorella—her quitting had hit the Net Force group hard—but he didn't bring it up. Toni had called Jay from London and he had heard that she'd called a couple of other people in Net Force, too, but he still didn't know what exactly had gone down between her and the boss. It must have been bad, though. Michaels had been pretty miserable about it, even if he tried to pretend otherwise.

"Nothing interesting at all?"

"Nope. Well, one little thing. You know about something called HAARP?"

"Sure, the atmosphere burner up in Alaska. The guys in aluminum-foil hats *love* that one. What happen, it melt down?"

"According to one of the scientists working on the thing, somebody sneaked in and stole something from their computer."

"Who would bother? The technology is moldy, goes back to Tesla, more than a hundred years ago."

Michaels shrugged. "Got me. I did a little web walking in VR, and it does look as if somebody got into their computer."

"Kid hacker, maybe," Jay said.

"Could be. You want to check it out, be my guest."

"Soji is gonna be busy for the next couple days. I'll take a look at it, get a jump on work."

"Background and what I saw is in the work file under 'HAARP.' "

"Copy, Boss. See you Monday morning."

"My best to Soji," he said.

Jay went to his office and looked around, but there wasn't much new to see. Some hardcopy reports was all. He had checked his e-mail and phone messages using a virgil he'd checked out and taken with him, so he was pretty much up to date.

Just for grins, he lit his computer and read over the information on HAARP the boss had given him, including the hiddencam vid of the interview with the scientist, Morrison.

Very interesting stuff. Mind control? That would be worth stealing, but that also didn't seem likely. People had been playing with low-frequency stuff for a long time without much in the way of results. Still, it was intriguing.

Jay logged off his computer. He'd been here for a couple of hours. Time to head home. Soji didn't have to be on-line *all* the time . . .

But as he started for the door to leave, his com chirped, and the sexy, throaty female vox he'd programmed into his computer said, "Jay! Priority One com, Jay! Heads up! Answer the phone, you hunk of burning love!"

Friday, June 10th
Longhua, China

When he had been a member of the Chinese Army twenty years before, Jing Lu Han had apparently at some point collected a Russian Makarov pistol, and kept it hidden away for two decades afterward. No one had ever seen him with it—at least no one alive who could testify to that. There seemed no other way he could have come by such a thing, there not having been any Russians in or about Longhua in anybody's memory, and Jing having lived there all his life, save for his time in the army.

However he came by it, it was with this pistol that Jing proceeded to shoot seventeen members of his home village in the wee hours of Friday morning. He walked calmly through the town, plinking at anybody who came out to see what the noise was about, and he did not discriminate as to sex, age, or familial relationships. By dawn, he had shot men, women, children, friends, and relatives. He had two dozen rounds of ammunition remaining for the pistol after he shot number seventeen— his butt-ugly and ignorant cousin Low Tang—but it was moot as to how many more he might have wounded or killed, given that he was overwhelmed at that point by half a dozen villagers and hacked to pieces by their sickles and scythes. The bloody tatters remaining of Jing were pounded into the hard ground under their sandals—before the six took their weapons to each other.

The only apparent survivor of this melee had a short-lived triumph, as he was murdered shortly thereafter by a middle-aged schoolteacher wielding a pair of hedge-trimming shears, with which she deftly snipped his left carotid artery. He bled out in less than a minute, judging from the blood trail.

The teacher then used the shears on herself, plunging them into her belly more than ten times before shock and loss of blood overcame her.

A block away, four women were killed by a fifth when she drove a forty-eight-year-old Ford tractor into, and then back and forth over, the four until the tractor ran out of gasoline an hour later. She fell asleep sitting there.

In the town's only decent food market, nineteen people who had fled there to avoid the carnage were trapped inside when a teenaged girl set the place on fire. They were all cooked. The girl in turn was killed by an elderly woman who sneaked up behind her and smashed her skull with a shovel, and *she* in turn was slain by a very large naked man who grabbed and fell on her, suffocating her under his bulk as he lay there giggling.

In a period of six hours, ninety-seven residents were killed, twenty-one others were wounded seriously enough so that they would later die from their injuries, and a hundred more were injured badly enough that they needed hospitalization. Nobody knew about this immediately, because the landline communication wires out of town had been cut and then burned by a man who used part of the wire to hang himself.

The town of Longhua had seen better days.

Thursday
Quantico, Virginia

Michaels looked up from his laptop and the hardcopy reports, photographs, and vids, at Jay. "How did we get this? It's so detailed."

Jay said, "Some of the pictures and vids are retro-spysat and computer augs, some came from the Chinese investigating team, some from a bashed up and bloody camera found on the scene. The reports we got from my friend in the CIA, who got it like the CIA usually gets such things—they bought it from one of their Chinese computer spies set up to find such things. It's all fresh stuff, really fresh."

Michaels looked back at the hardcopy picture of the women who had been murdered by tractor. They were mostly mush, and hardly recognizable as humans.

"What do we know? And why do *we* at Net Force need to know it?"

Jay said, "Longhua, China, a mountain town, a hundred and fifty kilometers or so north and east of Beijing, approaching old Mongolia. Nothing much happens in Longhua—or at least it didn't use to.

"According to my CIA mole, there's another village, called, ah"—he looked at the laptop on the table in front of him—"Daru, which is a couple thousand kilometers south of Longhua, on the coast across from Formosa. Same thing happened there a few days ago. The Chinese, of course, are sweating buckets trying to keep the lid on, but our sources say it was another verse of this song. Group insanity coupled with murderous violence. Survivors in both towns tell the same tale. All of a sudden, everybody went bugfuck and started attacking everybody else, no reason. This includes those who lived to be in-terviewed. They were minding their own business and *blap!* they were enveloped in a killing rage that over-whelmed them. None of them can explain it. It just sud-denly seemed like a good idea to fold, spindle, or mutilate their family and neighbors to death."

"What do the Chinese investigators think?"

"They don't have a clue. They've checked for drugs, poison, psychedelics in the water, diseases, the weather, earthquake activity, even bad *feng shui*, and they haven't found anything. Whatever caused it came and went, and it didn't leave any traces."

"And what does the CIA think?"

"The CIA doesn't think, Boss, it just collects data and passes it along. I have a standing order with my pal for anything weird, it comes in as a Priority One Call, which is why we got it."

"I'm sure your friend would be happy to hear you have such a high opinion of him. What do *you* think?"

"Well, what this looks like to me is some kind of de-liberate test."

Michaels stared into space. "And you think it is the Chinese doing it to their own people?"

"Can't say for sure, but why not? Take out a few, who's gonna miss 'em? They got more than a billion more where those came from."

"Jay—"

"Sorry, bad taste, I apologize."

"But the Chinese investigators seem surprised from these reports. Wouldn't they know?"

"Left hand not telling the right what it's doing? Hap-pens all the time, all over. State doesn't tell the CIA. The spooks don't tell the Army. We're *part* of the FBI, and the feebs don't tell *us* a whole lot of things. Why would things be any better in China? That's assuming the investigators aren't part of the cover-up."

"And why it is our problem, Jay? How does this end up floating in our punch bowl?"

"When you asked me to poke around in that HAARP thing, this came in almost immediately. It rang a bell. You remember the guy you told me about who came by while I was camping. The scientist from HAARP?"

"Morrison, right."

"Uh-huh. Well, he mentioned something about mind control and low-frequency radio waves."

"He said it wasn't feasible."

"Maybe not. Or maybe it is. Maybe the Chinese were the ones poking around in the HAARP computers and maybe they swiped it. It just seemed awfully coincidental, given that this was *exactly* the kind of thing somebody would want to do if they could do it."

"The Chinese?"

"Possible. They have some people who are pretty good hackers. Maybe the HAARP guys found some piece of the puzzle and the Chinese knew where to use it. Nothing for certain, and it's kind of a stretch, but I'd check it out."

Michaels nodded. "I hope you are wrong. I hope nobody else makes the connection and thinks it is our problem to solve. All right. Find out what you can. If this thing in China is connected to it, I don't want us to be caught flatfooted. At the very least, we need to be able to say we're investigating it if somebody should ask."

"Gotcha, Boss. I'm on the case."

After Jay left, Michaels took several deep breaths. *Let it be some virus they couldn't find and not something they swiped from a U.S. computer. Please. I really don't need this right now. Or ever ...*

12

It was well after dark when Toni's plane landed at Dulles. She'd had to switch from the jumbo jet to a smaller craft in New York, and she knew she'd catch hell if her mother found out she had been at JFK and hadn't called the Bronx to at least say hello, but she couldn't deal with that yet. Her mother would want to know all about it, what had happened with Alex, and even Guru would need more details than Toni was ready to provide. She'd thought the story was over, but maybe it wasn't, and until she had a better sense of things, she didn't want to start downloading it into sympathetic ears. She needed a girlfriend for that, anyhow, somebody who could listen to the gory details—not her mother or her elderly teacher. Mama Fiorella had raised a houseful of children, mostly sons, and with six kids, she certainly knew about sex, but knowing it and *talking* about it were two different things. Toni remembered a discussion she'd had with one of her older brothers when she'd been about nineteen. He'd been asking about women, when their mother had wandered into the room. Mama heard the words "female orgasm" and disappeared faster than Houdini stoked on methamphetamines.

No, the conversation about Alex and sex and love would have to wait until she could pay a visit to one of her college buds, Dirisha Mae, or Mary Louise, women she'd kept in touch with since school. Women who had been there and done it themselves, and had come back to cry on her shoulder about it. The Man War, they had dubbed it in the dorm when they'd lived there. Some battles you won, some you lost, but the war itself never ended.

The cab ride through the sticky summer night to Alex's was incredibly fast, as of course it would be, since she was suddenly not in a real hurry to get there. Back in London, thousands of miles away, this had seemed urgent and absolutely necessary. The closer she got, the less brilliant the idea seemed. Just showing up on Alex's doorstep, no call, no warning? What if he wasn't home? What if he didn't want to talk to her?

What if he wasn't *alone*?

That had just come to her for the first time. What if he had a woman in his bed and they were giggling and playing games under the sheets?

The grinning, green-eyed monster popped up like magic in her mind and chortled its nasty laugh. This jealousy crap was really hard to take. It wasn't like somebody coming straight at her she could elbow or throw, it was this sneaky, insidious beast that popped up unexpectedly, stabbed her with a long trident when she wasn't expecting it, then ran like hell before she could gather herself to react. She hated the feeling, and she *really* hated not being able to prevent it. Toni wasn't altogether dense about this kind of thing. You don't spend more than half your life learning a martial art that would allow you to kick serious butt without recognizing that you have some . . . control issues. She didn't really think Alex would have found somebody else, given his track record—he hadn't dated anybody to speak of for years after he and his ex-wife split—but you never knew. Having jumped back into the pool finally, maybe he would have found a new partner for synchronized swimming. And certainly that would screw things up, wouldn't it?

Toni shook her head at her thought. Okay, fine. Whatever. She wasn't going there for some kind of tearful movie reconciliation, she was going there for some answers. Answers that Alex, by God, *owed* her.

And thinking of there, all of a sudden, here they were.

Alex's condo was on a fairly quiet street in a solid upper-middle-class neighborhood filled with condos and houses much like his. Rich people wouldn't stoop to live here, poor couldn't afford to, but the residences were comfortable and in keeping with the kind of job Alex had. Nice place, nice neighborhood, and until that horrible moment in London, nice guy.

She had to know what had happened to change that. It didn't make any sense.

Toni paid the cabbie, towed her single suitcase on its built-in wheels to the front door, and stood there.

And stood there. And stood there some more.

There were lights on inside, and it wasn't that late. All she had to do was push the doorbell.

She realized that she was breathing too fast, and that
her hands were damp. It was a warm, humid night, but
that wasn't what was causing her to sweat. She was, she
realized, afraid. And coming from a solid base of being
able to protect herself, that was really scary.

She took a deep breath, let half of it out, and gathered
her resolve. She pushed the doorbell. She heard it ring.
There was a space of time, how long she couldn't say,
but subjectively, about ten or fifteen thousand years.

"Yes?"

His voice over the intercom was the first time she'd
heard him speak since he'd left London seven weeks ago.
It was a sound she hadn't realized how much she had
missed until she heard it, and the simple question stunned
her, so that all she could say was "Hi."

"Toni!? Don't move, I'll be right there!"

And despite whatever she had felt, it warmed her to
hear the joy in his voice.

Gakona, Alaska

Ventura made the rounds of his surveillance stations. He
was running a basic six-person team, not counting himself, and that was not really enough, considering what his
client was into, but as much as he was likely to get away
with up here in the middle of nowhere. Disguised as a
birdwatching club out looking for owls, it gave his people
a reason to be out with binoculars and starlight scopes
and cameras, but it was still something of a stretch to have
them wandering around in the woods. The locals would
surely notice his people, and while they had all the proper

gear and had done enough quick research to fake it, they wouldn't fool any real birders they might run into.

Fortunately, there wasn't much in the way of law enforcement up here, so even if somebody thought the birders were a bit odd, they weren't likely to call the cops, and even if they did, it probably wouldn't be the top priority for an overextended Alaskan police force. *Weird-looking birdwatchers? Isn't that redundant? What are they doing? Walking around in the woods looking through their binoculars? Oh, wow. How sinister! What, you think they've come to steal the trees? Smuggle Kodiak bears down into the lower forty-eight? C'mon!*

Ventura had installed them at the Two Moose Lodge, a relatively new fifteen-unit motel a few miles from the HAARP site, a place that looked like a bunch of log cabin condominiums. Aside from five ops tromping around outside where they could watch the comings and goings around the last room on the west end of the building where Ventura had put the client, there was an op in the room, a young woman. Armed with a short-barreled shotgun, a snub-nosed revolver, and a couple of knives, Missey White would surely be a big surprise for an unsuspecting assassin who assumed from her bubble butt and perky breasts, all of which were barely hidden under a miniskirt and halter top, that she was a piece of fluff and harmless. If the locals knew Morrison was married, they'd likely assume Missey was a girlfriend he'd brought up here into the woods for fun, where his wife wouldn't be the wiser.

And the wife wasn't apt to drop by unannounced, because a pair of Ventura's ops were parked in a rented house in Port Townsend on the Morrisons' street, keeping an eye on Mrs. Morrison. You had to assume that if somebody came after the client, they'd probably consider a pass at his wife worthwhile, and while she wasn't the primary client, it was just good business to watch her when she and the client were apart.

It hadn't taken the ops—another male and female team—but a few hours to figure out that Shannon Morrison, nee Shannon Bell, wasn't the world's most faithful spouse. Since they'd begun the surveillance on Monday, Mrs. Morrison had visited a young and well-built leatherworker, one Ray Duncan, and stayed in his shop behind a locked door three times, for more than an hour each visit. It was the opinion of Ventura's ops that judging from the flushed face and big smile when she left, Mrs. Morrison was *not* being custom-fitted for moccasins—unless she was doing that with both feet in the air while lying on Duncan's couch.

Ventura saw no reason to mention this to his client. Ray Duncan, twenty-seven, had been a resident of the town for more than ten years, long before the Morrisons had moved there, and a background check of the man showed nothing more illegal than a couple of traffic tickets and a dismissed bust for a single marijuana joint in Seattle when he'd been eighteen.

Mrs. Morrison's extramarital activities weren't relevant to protecting the client. Yet, anyway.

"Situation?" Ventura asked.

The man to whom he was speaking looked to be about sixty, gray and grizzled, wearing a fisherman's vest and floppy-brimmed canvas hat, overalls, and boots, and a pair of binoculars and a digital cam dangling from around his neck. A battered copy of *Peterson's Guide to Birds of North America* stuck out of a vest pocket next to a small flashlight.

The older man laughed. "Well, let me see. About thirty minutes ago, something that looked like a big rat ran behind the garbage bin over there. Maybe it was a nutria or a possum—zoology is not my strong suit. And fifteen minutes ago, a light went on in the bathroom of unit number five, stayed on for two minutes, then went out. What else? Oh, yeah, a couple of real big mosquitoes buzzed me. That's as good as it's gotten."

Ventura gave him a tight professional grin in return. "You rather be shooting it out with the Mexican drug dealers again?"

"No, but if they were all as exciting as this one, I'd have to start taking Viagra just to keep my attention up. This is going to be a cakewalk."

"You said that about the Mexicans at first."

The older man looked at him. "You expect things to warm?"

"Highly likely, though probably not for a while yet. I'll keep you apprised."

Ventura drifted away, a man out for a late night stroll, meandering toward the next station, a couple hundred yards away.

As he walked, he considered the client and the situation again. He had no problems with what the client was doing, that was his business and not Ventura's, save how it affected the job. Ventura didn't think much about morality. He had his own ethical system, and it didn't match that of most citizens when it came to what they did, or why they did it. From his viewpoint, he was mostly, well . . . *amoral* about most things—when you had killed as many people as he had, the rules just didn't seem to apply to you in quite the same way as they did to normal people. He knew what sociopaths were, and he wasn't one. He had loved, had hated, had felt the usual emotions. He had been engaged once, but she had broken it off because she wasn't ready to settle down. He had fathered a child in South America, and though it had been twenty years ago, he still sent support to the woman and his daughter, whom he had seen several times secretly, but never officially met. There were a couple of people he had deleted that he'd felt sorry for, and wished he hadn't had to do them. So he wasn't mentally disturbed or unstable, he had just gotten into a line of work that involved terminal violence, and had happened to be very good at it.

Of course, he had been in business long enough to re- alize that most governments operated with the same kind of amorality he did in many—if not most—areas. Cer- tainly in those areas where public scrutiny wasn't likely. He had known federal prosecutors who had let multiple murderers go free so that they could make a case against major drug dealers. He had known intelligence officers who had looked the other way and allowed whole villages of innocent civilians to be killed because to do otherwise would have jeopardized some covert operation. He had known boy-soldiers who had cranked up their assault ri- fles and hosed grandmothers and babies into bloody pulp—for no other reason than because they had been having a real bad day. All of these people had convinced themselves they had been working for a greater good, that the end justified the means. That what they had done was, in fact, moral.

Ventura did not try to fool himself that way.

Protecting a man who had created some kind of mind- control device he wanted to sell to a foreign power for a lot of money was not much in the grand cosmic scheme of things. Ventura wasn't going to get any piece of the man's action, nor did he want it. He was hired to do a job, and he would do that. Money was not even a way to keep score, it didn't mean anything, especially if you had enough of it tucked away to live the rest of your life without ever lifting a finger. No, it was the personal challenge, the achievement of goals you set for yourself, that mattered. When he was hired to kill somebody, he killed them. When he was hired to keep somebody alive, he kept them alive. Simple.

Up here in the woods where he could command the lines of fire around his client, keeping him alive would be fairly easy. If another birdwatching group showed up, Ventura wouldn't make any assumptions, but he certainly would consider them a potential threat.

Outright assassination wasn't likely, not yet, anyway. No, the worry would be kidnapping, torture, *then* execution. And it would be a lot harder to protect the man once they went back to civilization.

Well. Worry about that later. A man with his mind too far into tomorrow was more likely to get blindsided by somebody today. You had to consider the future, of course, but you didn't live there. Be in the moment, that was the way of it.

Always.

The second man in the surveillance unit watched Ventura approach him across the parking lot, lit by the yellow bug lights mounted on tall wooden posts. Some of the bugs were apparently too stupid to realize they couldn't see the yellow light, for dozens of them swarmed the lamps, flitting around in ragged orbits, banging against the glass that covered the bulbs.

The op disguised as a birder kept one hand under the

untucked tails of an unbuttoned, oversized, short-sleeved shirt until he was sure it *was* Ventura heading toward him. Good. You never let your guard down when you were working. Never.

13

Michaels could hardly believe it. "Toni! I'm glad to see you."

She nodded. "Can I come in?"

"Oh, yeah, yeah, come in, come in." He reached for her bag.

"I got it," she said.

Inside, there was an awkward silence.

"You want something to drink? Eat?" God, she looked great. It was all he could do to keep the baboonlike grin from taking over his face.

"We need to talk," she said.

His stomach twisted and churned, but he said, "Yes."

"Why did you lie to me?"

"I . . . I . . ."

"You said you *slept* with her!"

"Toni—"

"*She* says you didn't! Which is it, Alex?!"

She was facing him squarely now, and her anger was a tangible thing in the room. "Did you have sex with Angela Cooper or not?"

"No," he said, his voice quiet.

"Jesus *Christ,* Alex! What is the *matter* with you?!"

He raised his hands palms up, then dropped them. "I— It's hard to explain."

"Well, you are *gonna* explain it, right here and right *now!*"

He nodded, and started to tell it.

When he got to the end, she was shaking her head. "Why didn't you tell me that was what happened?"

He had had a lot of time to think about that, too much time. "Because I was ashamed."

"You turned down a gorgeous woman who wanted to jump your bones and you were *ashamed?*"

"I shouldn't have gone to supper with her, I shouldn't have had the beer, and I sure as hell shouldn't have gone to her apartment, shucked my clothes, and let her rub my back."

"All true. Why did you?"

He'd had time to think about that one, too. "You and I were having some problems. I was rattled about the whole British situation, I wasn't in control of work, of what was going on with us, there was all that crap about Megan and Susie and that private eye. Angela is an attractive, competent woman and she was interested in me. I was flattered. I know none of it excuses what I did, but just so you know."

"You're an idiot," she said.

"I know. It never should have come up," he said.

"So to speak," she said. She gave him a small grin, and a great weight left him, as if he had suddenly shrugged off a coat made of lead. "But that's not what I meant. You're an idiot for not telling me."

"When I saw you in the hotel lobby that morning, I didn't think you would believe me. You were certain I had done it, and you didn't want to talk about it, remember? You said you didn't want to hear another word."

She frowned, as if trying to remember. "Did I say that?"

"It doesn't matter. The truth was, I *was* lying naked on a table with a naked woman straddling me and the desire was there."

"But you didn't act on it."

"The thought is as bad as the deed."

She smiled again, shook her head. "Not on my planet, it isn't. You felt guilty because in the moment you *thought* about it? You really *are* an idiot. If they could hang us for thinking, we'd all be pushing up daisies. You can't always control what you think, only what you *do*. You could have saved us both a lot of grief if you had just *told* me, Alex, even if *I* told you not to."

"Yeah, well, I can see that now."

She reached for his hands, took them in hers. "Come here."

"Yes, ma'am."

And just like that, Michaels's life was very, very good again.

Friday, June 10th
Anchorage, Alaska

They were in the airport waiting for the Alaska Airlines flight to SeaTac to board when Morrison's new phone cheeped. He froze for an instant. It was them! He looked at Ventura, then slipped the wireless headset on and adjusted the straw-microphone. "Yes?"

A crisp, accentless voice said, "Good morning. I understand you have a used car for sale?"

Morrison's neck prickled with gooseflesh and he had a sudden urge to visit the nearest toilet. This was the phrase he had told them to use, and outside of the anonymous note he had posted into a security page run by the Chinese, nobody had been given the number of this particular phone, which he'd paid for in cash and registered under a phony name.

He put his thumb over the mike. "It's the Chinese," he said to Ventura.

Ventura looked at his watch. "Thirty seconds," he said, pointing at the phone. "No more. Follow me."

Morrison nodded and stood. He moved his thumb from the mike as Ventura pulled his own com from his pocket and started talking into it quietly.

"Yes, I have a car for sale."

"I would like to see it," the man said. "When can we get together?"

"Is your call number blocked?"

"No."

"I'll call you back."

"I'll look forward to it."

Morrison thumbed the discom button on the belt phone. Ventura said, "My people have scanned the incoming number, we have it. Go in there and put the phone in the trash." He pointed at the men's room.

"Should I turn it off?"

"Leave it on. They probably already know where you are, but it'll give them something to look for."

Morrison headed for the bathroom. Ventura waved, and a pair of college-aged men dressed in shorts and T-shirts and backpacks went into the men's room ahead of him. Ventura stayed out in the corridor.

Making sure nobody was watching him, Morrison shoved the phone into the bin under the paper towel dispenser. Then he went and used the nearest urinal.

When he exited, Ventura said, "There's a car waiting in front of the airport for us. Let's go."

"You think they can get here that fast?"

"They can trace the phone from the carrier sig alone if you don't bounce it—major national intelligence services have access to some very sophisticated equipment. They'll probably send somebody. It won't be a trio of long-fingernailed Chinese dressed in colorful Mandarin silks and sporting Fu Manchu mustaches smiling and bowing and looking like the incarnation of the Yellow Peril. More likely it'll be a busty Norwegian blond nurse helping a little old man with a cane hobble along—the last people you'd look at and think 'Chinese intelligence.' Certainly they have local agents within a few minutes of most major cities. Fortunately, Anchorage isn't that big a town. If you used a decent remailer, they won't backtrack your e-mail for a while, though probably they'll get that soon. I'd expect them to know who you are within a day or two at most, even if you don't call them back."

Morrison swallowed dryly. "The service I used guaranteed confidentiality."

Ventura smiled, looking at that moment like a human shark. "Sure, if somebody calls them on the phone and asks, they won't say anything. But confidentiality goes right out the window when somebody puts the point of a sharp knife into your remailer's back, over his kidney, and asks."

"They would do that?"

"Sure. I would." He flashed the smile again, and Morrison was in that moment as afraid of Ventura as he was the Chinese. Thank God the man was on his side.

"They'll know you're at the airport, but since the phone isn't in your name, they don't know who you are, so they'll look for the phone. When they find that, they'll look for single men traveling alone. You're under a pseudonym, ticketed as part of a group of three passengers, including two women, so they won't get that immediately. With enough computing power, they can strain out all the flights leaving here today, and check on every passenger. Our phony IDs will hold up under a cursory scan, but if they can dig deep enough, they'll figure out they are fake eventually, though that won't really help them except to tell them we were going to Seattle, and that we weren't on the plane.

"We could probably get to your house in Washington before they get who you are. You are dealing with some serious people here, and it's never been a matter of 'if,' but of 'when.' "

"My wife—"

"—is being watched by my people, and I've just sent more ops to back them up. She'll be safe. And we aren't going there."

"Where are we going?"

"To a place where I can control access for the meeting."

"We're going to *drive* there?"

"No, we're going to drive to a private airstrip and rent a plane. We want to be in the air as soon as we can."

Now that he had been put on alert, Morrison regarded the other people in the airport hallway with a newfound suspicion. Those young men with snowboards, that middle-aged gay couple laughing over a laptop, the tall man in a gray business suit carrying a briefcase. Any of them could be armed and out to collect him.

"Frankly, I don't think they will scramble the A-team to grab you, yet," Ventura said, as if reading his mind. "They know about the tests you did in their country, what the effect was on their villages, and they know you *know* about it, but they don't know for certain that you *caused* it. They'll have to check you out. Once they believe you, that's when we'll have to be extremely careful."

Morrison's mouth suddenly felt very dry indeed. He'd known this was coming, but it hadn't seemed so . . . *real* before. The pit of his stomach felt like it did on a roller coaster. Well. There was nothing for it now. He was committed.

"This isn't quite what I expected," Morrison said.

"It never is," Ventura said.

14

The boomerang championships were being held in Washington Park, which Tyrone thought was funny. They'd driven a couple thousand miles from Washington, D.C., to wind up in an Oregon park with the same name. It wasn't like any park in his neighborhood, though. The place was a giant sprawl that contained a lot of hills, tall evergreen trees, the Portland Zoo, plus a forestry center and some other stuff. Up and away from the zoo parking, they had carved a flat field out of one of the meadows, big enough for three or four soccer teams to play at the same time. The field was covered with what Tyrone thought of as winter grass, trimmed short, like something you might find on a golf course, instead of the coarser Saint Augustine grass you found on a lot of lawns back home.

"What a great venue," Nadine said.

"Yeah."

The contest didn't start officially until tomorrow, and their event wasn't until Sunday, but there were twenty or so throwers out on the green practicing. The warm summer air was full of colorful twirling 'rangs, blues and reds and oranges and greens, bright blurs looping back and forth.

Tyrone turned to his father. "Okay?"

His dad looked around, then nodded. "Looks safe enough. Mom and I will be back in a couple of hours."

Tyrone nodded back, already thinking about practice. His dad had rented a car and left the RV parked back at the hotel, a place called the Greenwood Inn. His parents wanted to go check out downtown Portland, but they didn't want to leave Tyrone and Nadine alone until they had checked out the park. Given the numbers of families with small children, the lack of gang colors, or guys throwing beer bottles at each other, Dad had decided that Tyrone and Nadine were probably safe enough here in the middle of the afternoon.

"You have your credit card?"

"Yep."

"You got your phone?"

"Yes, Dad."

"It's on?"

Tyrone rolled his gaze toward the heavens. He pulled the little phone from his belt and held it up so his father could see the display. "Yes, Dad."

What, did they think he was still a baby? This was Portland, not Baltimore. He almost said so, but realized that might not be the smartest thing, so he kept his mouth shut. He was learning that sometimes, that was the best strategy. If you don't say it, they can't nail you for it.

Nadine started unpacking her 'rangs.

"Go already, parental units, we're fine here."

His mom smiled.

Once they were gone, Tyrone and Nadine looked for a place to get started. There were circles drawn on the grass, but most of these were already taken. That didn't matter—they had wash-away chalk; they could make their own circle.

"Over there," Nadine said. "Wind is from the south, but it's almost calm, we'll have plenty of room for hang."

"Hey, scope it. Isn't that Jerry Prince?" He pointed.

She looked. "I think so."

Best MTA guy in the world, the Internationals winner last year, and the world record holder. Word was, he threw eight minutes in practice on *slackwind* days, and had a witnessed-but-unofficial fourteen-minute flight.

"Let's watch him. Maybe we'll learn something."

She laughed. "*You* will, for sure. I *got* style already."

"You got mouth, is what you got. I'm gonna be pushing three minutes here." He waved his stopwatch at her.

"You're pushing a Dumpster full of horse pucky is what *you* are pushing. You are probably gonna trip and *fall* into it."

He laughed. She was funny.

There were several events at most boomerang competitions—accuracy, distance, trick and fast catch, doubling, team throws. Like Tyrone, Nadine's event was MTA—maximum time aloft—and the idea was to put a lightweight boomerang into the air and keep it there for as long as possible. There was no problem with judging this one—you put a stopwatch on them, and the longest time up won. They had dicked around with the rules for a while, trying different things in different competitions—you got two throws but one didn't count, or you got three and you could pick the best—but now it was different. You got a practice throw once you were in the circle, but after that, it was one throw, period. You had to catch it when it came back, and you had to be inside the official circle for the catch, or the throw didn't count. The record for somebody in Tyrone's age group was just over three and a half minutes, but unofficially there were guys who had thrown into freakish wind conditions and kept a bird twirling for a lot longer. The longest unofficial time by anybody was more than eighteen minutes, though that kind of time came out of the professional adult ranks. It was hard to even imagine eighteen minutes aloft.

Tyrone himself had placed third in last year's contest with a time of 2:41, using the Möller Indian Ocean, an L-shaped lightweight made of paxolin—layers of linen and rosin built up and then cut to shape. The winner—Nadine, which is how they'd met—had beaten him by seven seconds, using the same model boomerang as his, so he couldn't blame it on better equipment. Some kid from Puerto Rico with a Bailey MTA Classic had slipped in between his time and Nadine's to bump Tyrone out of second place, but since it had been his first ever competition, he had been happy to have third.

Not this year. This year, he wanted *first*. And Nadine was the defending champion, and he *had* beaten her—in practice, anyway. Of course, if he was gonna do that, he'd have to be better, 'cause they were gonna use the same 'rang. The new Takahashi Silk Leaf he'd bought had added ten or fifteen seconds to their best times, and the blue beast was the way to go, no question. And she had beaten him as often as he had her, so it was not a sure thing. And on any given day, the wind could be hinky, the thermals might go weird, and you could get a great throw or a bad one. No way to tell until the moment of truth.

Nadine put her pack down and started rolling her shoulders. You couldn't throw without warming up and stretching, that was a good way to injure a joint or tear a muscle. Even if you were real limber, you could strain something, and you didn't want to do that in general, and certainly not when you were going to be competing in the Nationals.

"Don't see any Indians or wagon trains," Tyrone observed as he used his left hand to pull his right elbow up and back over his head. His shoulder popped like cracking a knuckle.

"Doesn't look like it's gonna rain, either," Nadine said.

"God, I hope not. That would be awful."

After a couple minutes, they were loose enough. The sun was shining, it was warm, but not too hot, and the wind was mild. A great day for flying.

Washington, D.C.

Michaels might have felt better a few times in his life. His wedding night. The day his daughter was born. Even the first time he and Toni had been together in this very bed, but this had to rank right up there with the best. Toni was back, and the two of them were naked under the sheet. That went a long way to smooth the turbulent waters he had been in lately.

"What time is it?" she asked, sleep still thick in her voice.

"Eight."

"You're late for work."

"I called in sick."

She grinned. "I have to go pee."

"Go ahead. I'll make the coffee. Meet you back here in a few minutes."

"Um."

He had already started the coffee, and was able to snatch a couple of cups and be back in bed before Toni returned from the bathroom.

"That was fast," she said, taking one of the heavy china mugs. She inhaled the vapor. "Mmm."

"So, you want to talk some more about how stupid I am?"

"You'd have to call in sick for a few more days to exhaust that one."

"Okay. How about, what now?"

"We could take a shower together." She smiled over the top of the mug.

"Oh, yeah, I can line up with that. But I meant something a little further ahead."

"We could come back to bed after the shower?"

"Uh, Toni . . ."

"I know, I know. Let's just let everything else wait, okay?"

He nodded. He didn't want to push her. But he also didn't want her to get up and dress and leave, either.

"Enough talk," she said. "Actions speak louder than words, remember?"

"Really? Maybe you better show me. I kinda don't remember."

She threw her pillow at him. "You *better* remember!"

Portland, Oregon

"You think the kids will be all right?" Howard asked.

"You want me to drive?" his wife said. "You know you can't worry and drive at the same time. This is the village of the happy nice people, John. At least compared to where we live. They are in a crowd full of people playing with *boomerangs,* for God's sake, they'll be fine."

They were driving through a tunnel on Highway 26 that led into downtown Portland. The walls of the tunnel were white tile, and they were pristine. Not just white—there wasn't any graffiti painted on them. Clean.

"This is the cleanest town I've ever been in," she said, echoing his thought. "No trash, no beer bottles, it's like Disney World."

Somebody honked, just like somebody always seemed to do in a long tunnel, just to hear the sound it made. He nodded in the direction of the honker. "Yeah, too bad they can't get rid of the morons."

"Stay in the center lane," she said as they exited the tunnel.

It *was* a pretty city. There were more buildings than he remembered from his last visit, and the views of the mountains were not quite as open. Mount Hood still had snow on it, even in June, and to the left Mount Saint Helens did, too. He'd talked to people who'd lived here when the volcano blew its top off, back in the spring of 1980, and it had apparently been quite impressive.

The initial blast had not only blown powdered rock upward, it had spewed outward, knocking down trees, a "stone wind" that had scoured everything in its path. The explosion created ash and snowmelt pyroclastic flows that had filled lakes and rivers, knocked out bridges, buried a tourist lodge—empty, fortunately, save for the old man who ran it and refused to evacuate. Most of the people who died had been inside the safety zone established by the state, and it could have been a lot worse.

According to an old staff sergeant Howard knew who had been in town when it blew, the volcano had looked like a nuclear blast, great clouds of pulverized rock boiling into the stratosphere. The wind hadn't been blowing toward the city that day, so they'd missed the big ash fall, though they got some in subsequent eruptions. It was like living next door to a concrete plant when that happened, the sarge said, fine clouds of gray dust swirling in the streets like powdered snow. Jets had to detour around the city when the ash was at its heaviest; it would eat up the engines otherwise, and car air filters clogged and had to be changed within a few hours. People wore painters' masks to keep from choking on the stuff. It was hard to imagine it.

And you couldn't tell by looking at it now.

"Stay in this lane."

"I heard you the first time. Who's driving this car, me or you?"

"You're driving. *I'm* navigating. Clearly the more important job."

Howard grinned. Was there anything more wonderful than a bright woman? Even if she was shining that brightness into a place you'd rather keep dark sometimes, that didn't detract from her radiance.

"Yes, ma'am, you *are* the navigator."

She smiled back, and looked at the car's dash-mounted GPS. The little computer screen showed a map.

"Stay on this street—Market—until you get to Front Street, then turn left. Immediately get into the right lane, and turn right on the Hawthorne Bridge. The restaurant we want is called Bread and Ink, and it's thirty blocks east of the Willamette River."

"Begging the navigator's pardon, ma'am, but that's pronounced 'Will-*lam*-it,' not 'Will-uh-*met*.' Accent is on the second syllable."

"Ask me if I care."

"Just trying to keep the navigator honest, ma'am."

Howard's virgil chimed. He pressed the receive button. "Yes?"

"Hi, Dad. This is Tyrone. Just calling to check in. We're fine here. Everybody is fine, no problems, and how are you?"

"Nobody likes a smart-ass, Tyrone." He shook his head. "But thanks for calling."

Tyrone put on his airline pilot's voice: "Ah, roger that, parental unit two-oh-two. We'll, ah, be standing by here for, ah, your return. That's a discom."

"He's a good boy," Nadine said when Howard shut off the virgil.

"Yeah, I know. Too bad he's turned into a teenager."

"You survived it."

"Once. I don't know if I can do it again."

"I have great faith in you, General Howard. You are, after all, a leader of men. One boy, how hard could it be?"

They both grinned.

15

A pair of armed guards—heavily armed guards—stepped from a cedar planked and shingled kiosk and waved the cars to a stop at a big wood-and-wire gate. The men were in camouflage clothing, and one of them kept his assault rifle trained on the ground right next to the car as the other man approached. Aside from the rifles, they had sidearms, big sheath knives, and some kind of grenades strapped on.

They must be burning up in that, Morrison thought. It was in the high eighties out here, even in the woods.

"Colonel Ventura," the guard said. He saluted. "Good to see you again, sir."

Morrison's roommate of last night, Missey, was at the wheel. As they drove through the gate in a ten-foot-tall chainlink fence topped with coils of razor wire, Morrison said, "*Colonel* Ventura? What *is* this place?"

"The rank is honorary," Ventura said. "I did some work for the man who runs the place, once. And let's call it a . . . patriot compound."

There was a car in front of them with Ventura's operatives, and one behind them, special vehicles rented at a place Morrison didn't think was going to run Hertz out of business. The guy who provided the cars had been covered in what looked like Maori tattoos, including his face, and the deal had been done in cash.

The drive from there had turned into a ride in the country, about forty-five minutes' worth to this place.

Morrison put two and two together: Idaho, men with guns in paramilitary gear, razor wire. "Some kind of militia group," he said. "Neo Nazis or white supremacists?"

"Let's just say if you were black, it would be a lot harder to call in the favor."

"Jesus."

"These people speak very highly of him, yes, but I doubt he spends much time here."

Morrison shook his head.

"Then again, it is unlikely in the extreme that anybody will sneak in here and kidnap you," Ventura said. "Certainly not anybody of the Oriental persuasion."

"I thought you said the Chinese wouldn't send somebody who looked Chinese."

They passed another trio of armed men in jungle camo sitting on or standing next to a military vehicle, a Hummer or Humvee or whatever. The three silently watched the cars go past, and when Morrison looked back, he saw one of the men hold up a com and speak into it.

"That's only if they want to sneak up on you. The Chinese don't like to delegate certain functions—they don't trust each other, much less round-eyes. If you arrange a meeting with them for something they want, they'll send someone who looks and acts the part. They won't want you to doubt their sincerity."

The narrow dirt road curved through another thick patch of woods, then into a cleared space maybe three or four acres big, with several prefab metal and wooden buildings centered in the clearing, all painted a drab olive green. A big air-conditioner rumbled in the background, spewing vapor into the hot afternoon.

There were more military-style vehicles, more armed men—as well as several armed women—and a pair of flags flying from a tall wooden pole in front of the largest of the structures. There was Old Glory, and under it, a shining white flag with what looked like a pair of crossed yellow lightning bolts over a line drawing of a hand.

"Sons of Pure Man," Ventura said, watching Morrison as he looked at the flags. "Empowered by God Almighty to smite the wicked, scourge the impure, and kick the asses of anybody else who would mongrelize the true race."

"These people are *friends* of yours?" Morrison said.

"*These* people will help me keep the wily Chinese from grabbing you, draining you dry, and then smiling politely as they hand your widow your head with an apple stuffed into its mouth, on a platter. We aren't family here, but allies are where you find them—sometimes you have to overlook a few little cultural or philosophical differences."

Morrison sighed, but didn't say anything else. Ventura had a point. He was about to go into negotiations with people who had been wise in the ways of political and court intrigue for five thousand years. Being ruthless was not a problem for a culture with as much practice at it as they had. And he had hired Ventura for his expertise. As long as he did the job, Morrison didn't care how.

"So now you put in a call to your friend the used car buyer and invite him to drop round for a little chat. He won't like it, but he'll come, especially if he's figured out who you are, and that you might indeed have something worth selling."

"And after that?"

"Well, once they know you are where they can't get to you, then we can leave. Further communication can be relayed through here—the general has quite an up-to-date collection of electronics—and with any luck, we can keep them believing you are still here until the deal is done."

"And after the deal is done—if it is?"

"One step at a time, Dr. Morrison. We'll burn that bridge when we have to burn it. Oh, and by the way, after we step out of the car? Assume that everything we say is being monitored—because it probably is. They can't hear us in here because we're protected by certain devices, but outside, you can book it that somebody will have a shot-gun mike or even a laser reader on us at all times."

" 'Allies,' you said?"

"Trust no one and no one can betray you. Just good tactics is all. Ah. There's the general, come to welcome us."

Jackson "Bull" Smith was no more a general than Ventura was a colonel, save to the bunch of mouthbreathers who hut-hut-hutted around his compound in the Idaho woods. Thirty years ago, Smith had been an Army infantryman, done some fighting in the Middle East, and more ground-pounding in one of the never-ending eastern European wars, but he'd never gotten past master sergeant, and that only when he got tapped to serve in the unit quartermasters, where he spent his last two tours. Still, he knew the Army way as well as any decent NCO, had seen legitimate action—he had a Purple Heart and a Bronze Star— and he was very canny. It was true you couldn't run an army without sergeants, and Smith knew the ropes well enough to organize a bunch of half-assed warrior-wannabes into a fair imitation of soldierly discipline. At the very least, they were good robbers, because that was chiefly how they raised their operating funds. So far, they had knocked over supermarkets, banks, a theater multiplex, an armored car, and a small Indian casino, all without being caught or losing a man, and without killing too many bystanders. Ventura knew their M.O., and he'd sort of halfway kept track. Smith's boys had stolen somewhere in the range of six to seven million dollars in the last year alone, Ventura guessed.

You could buy a lot of Idaho backwoods and MREs for seven million dollars.

As Smith stepped forward to shake his hand, Ventura nodded crisply at the man, a choppy, military bow. "General."

"Please, Luther, it's 'Bull.' "

Ventura suppressed a smile. Yeah, he thought it was bull, too. "I don't want to break discipline in front of the men."

"Understood," Smith said.

Ventura didn't know how much of the pure race crap Smith really believed, if any. The money and power were probably a lot more attractive, since Smith's history, military and otherwise, didn't show any particular contention with or hatred of any of the "mongrel" races until lately, but—you never knew. Pushing sixty, ole Bull here had been at this militia game for about ten years. He was living high on the hog, considering the location. Good food, good booze, women, toys, and the admiration and obedience of a couple hundred men, give or take. There were a lot worse ways to spend your time if you were an old ex-sergeant with no other skills.

Five years ago, when Ventura had still been in the assassination business, Smith had contacted him the usual roundabout way, and they had struck a deal. A certain influential politician in the Idaho statehouse—if that wasn't an oxymoron—had been standing in the way of Smith's acquisition of this very compound, something to do with land use, or butting up against state forestry property or some such. The politician, a state senator, knew what Bull and the boys were up to, and there was too much of that going on in Idaho already, the state was getting a real bad reputation. Tourists didn't want to come and see the boys playing war games—at least, not the kind of tourists the state wanted. It was bad for business if little junior went out picking berries and got mowed down by a bunch of gun-happy paramilitary goons who mistook him for an enemy, or Bambi, as had happened at least once.

If he couldn't stop it legally, there were some shadier ways to get things done, and the senator knew how to do them. This, of course, played right into Bull's conspiracy fantasies.

So. The politician died in what the coroner said was an accident, and Smith got the property he wanted. And Bull was not a man to forget somebody who'd done him a service.

"General, I'd like to introduce Professor Morrison. The

doctor here is doing some secret work for the Navy and Air Force, and naturally we don't trust them to keep him safe for our mission."

"Understood," Smith said. He offered his hand to Morrison, who took it. "There are traitors everywhere."

"Sad, but true," Ventura said.

"I'll have my adjutant show your people where to bivouac, and you and the professor can join me for dinner."

"Excellent idea, General," Ventura said.

When Smith was a few yards ahead of them, Morrison said, "How are you going to explain a Chinese agent coming here to see me?"

"What, a turncoat chink double-agent? We're feeding false information to our gook enemies, Doctor, you know that. The general understands how espionage works. He keeps his ears open." Ventura tapped his own ear, and hoped that the man would remember what he'd said about being watched and listened to.

Morrison remembered. "Ah. Yes, I see you're right. A man in the general's position would know these things."

"Of course. Hell of a soldier, Bull Smith, and a credit to the Race." He turned slightly so that Morrison's head would block any camera that might see his face, and gave the man a quick wink.

He also reached around and adjusted the paddle holster in his waistband. The general's people were probably fairly loyal, not counting the undercover federal ops that must have infiltrated by now; still, Condition Orange applied here, just as it did everywhere else. If need be, he could pull the Coonan from concealment and get off two shots in about a second. Not a patch on John Wesley Hardin out of a hip-slung rig, maybe, but still pretty damned fast from under a vest. And until they got inside with Smith, his people would have his back covered.

So far, so good. Pretty soon, though, it was going to get a lot more interesting.

16

The voice was female, sexy, throaty, and designed so that everything it said seemed like an urgent request to go to bed with it: "Alex? We have a Priority One Com. Alex? We have a Priority One Com. Alex—?"

"All right, I heard you already! Computer answer page off, please."

Next to him, voice thick with sleep, Toni said, "I thought you were going to change that voice."

"I haven't been able to figure out a way around Jay's program."

"And you're supposed to be the head of Net Force."

"Yeah, well, Jay is the best *programmer* in Net Force, now isn't he?" To the computer, Michaels said, "Answer com, visual off."

"Hey, Boss."

Speak of the devil. "What, Jay?"

"Sorry to bother you at home this early, but you said I should let you know if I got something on this, uh, Chinese business. Well, I think you might want to see this."

Michaels looked at the clock. Too early. "All right. You want to download it here?"

"Probably not the best idea, Boss. It needs telling."

Michaels sighed. "I'll be at the office in an hour."

When Jay was off the com, Michaels turned to Toni. "Another crisis."

"I remember them."

"Why don't you come with me?"

"I quit, remember?"

"Your job is waiting for you—I haven't hired anybody to replace you."

"Let's hold off on that. I still need to sort all this out."

He smiled. "I thought we had done that." He waved at their mutual lack of clothes under the sheet.

"No, we resolved the personal issue. I'm still working on the business stuff."

"Come along as a visitor, then."

"No, you go ahead. I think I'm going to sleep in."

"Be here when I get back?"

"Maybe."

They both grinned.

Quantico, Virginia

Michaels leaned back. "Okay, you got me down here. Speak."

Jay said, "Well, I can tell you the theory. Still doesn't *prove* that it works."

"I left a warm bed to come hear this, Jay. I take your point. Go."

"All right. Background stuff: Generally speaking, the human brain operates over a fairly small bioelectrical frequency range, and while there is some overlap, these are usually divided into four parts:

"The mental state Beta, sometimes called 'beta waves,' is from 13 to 30 Hz. This is the so-called 'normal' level of awareness. At the top end, at around 30 Hz or a bit higher, you have states of agitation—anger, fear, stress, etc.—but most conscious human thinking is done in this range.

"Below Beta is the Alpha state, from 8 to 13 Hz, and this is normally associated with a relaxed, mellow state of mind, kind of daydreamy, but with an increased ability to concentrate. This frequency is easily achieved by such things as meditation or self-hypnosis. For more than forty years there have been devices—biofeedback, or 'brain wave synthesizers'—that help produce Alpha, and you can pick up one in any large electronic or new age store. Some people supposedly can do it just by rolling their eyes back in their sockets."

Michaels nodded. He'd read about this stuff somewhere along the way. It sounded vaguely familiar. "I'm still awake."

Jay continued: "Beneath Alpha is Theta, at 4 to 7 Hz, and this is generally a state of very deep concentration, such as advanced meditation or devoted prayer, and it includes intense waking memories, and lucid dreaming.

"Under Theta, we have Delta waves, from 0.5 to 7 Hz, and these frequencies were once thought to occur only in deep sleep. Certain people, however, such as Indian yogi adepts or Tibetan priests, have been able to produce Delta states on demand, and while appearing to be asleep, fully participate in and recall conversations later when they are 'awake.'

"There are some variations, and some people run higher or lower, but that's pretty much the basic model."

"All right," Michaels said. "So now I know about brain frequencies."

Jay nodded. "Over the years, various agencies of various governments have tried broadcasting certain extremely low-frequency radio waves in an effort to alter human consciousness. In the fifties, the Russians had something called Lida, a machine that supposedly rendered people susceptible to hypnosis. The North Koreans had variations of this during the Korean War, used on American POWs. They didn't work very well, but that was not for want of trying.

"For years, back in the old Soviet Union, the Russians beamed microwaves at the American Embassy in Moscow, centered on the ambassador's office. The CIA discovered this in 1962, and some effects on various ambassadors were speculated upon, including a leukemia-like illness, and a couple of deaths from cancer. Nothing proven.

"In 1976, ham radio operators around the world noticed a peculiar signal originating in the Soviet Union that came to be known as the 'Russian Woodpecker,' from the staccato way it interfered with their radios. This signal was thought to come from big Tesla transmitters, and was thought by the CIA to be designed to depress or irritate the recipient."

"Tesla? Like the Tesla coil?"

Jay grinned. "Let me tell you about Nikola Tesla. There are some who believe the Tunguska Event—an explosion estimated in the 10-to-15-megaton range that blew down half a million acres of pine forest in Siberia in 1908—was either a test—or a malfunction—of one of Tesla's giant transmitters."

"I thought it was a comet," Michaels said.

"You probably think Oswald shot JFK, too, Boss. Merely a cover story, according to the conspiracy theorists. Some say it was an alien spaceship, others a runaway black hole, others a speck of antimatter, but, hey, my money is on Tesla. He was a certified genius. Aside from being the guy who came up with and patented the idea of alternating current, thus helping George Westinghouse to become filthy rich, he created working fluorescent lights long before Edison's uncredited lab monkey made the less efficient incandescent bulb. Tesla patented all kinds of stuff. His work was the basis for the X-ray machine. He sued Marconi—and won—for swiping his work to create radio. Tesla came up the ideas that would later become radar and tomography.

"Listen, in 1904, in Colorado Springs, he built a big power generator for his wireless power transmission experiments. Using what he called 'terrestrial stationary waves,' he lit two hundred lightbulbs twenty-five miles away by pumping juice into the *ground,* no wires. He could generate artificial lightning bolts of a couple to three hundred thousand watts that were more than a hundred and thirty-five feet long; you could hear the thunder fifteen miles away in town. He was *waaay* ahead of his time, so he certainly had the smarts and gear to knock down a few trees. It would have been the last in a long line of tests that—some say—included sinking the French ship

Iena by electrical bolts generated miles away."

"Apparently Tesla didn't much care for the French," Alex said, smiling.

"He didn't care much for anybody," Jay said. "Anyway, in 1906, J. P. Morgan financed Tesla, and he built a bigger generator than the one in Colorado, this was on Long Island. Eighteen stories tall, topped with a huge metal globe that weighed more than fifty-five tons. Eventually he and Morgan had a falling out, and he made a couple of bad choices, so he ran out of money before he proved it could work. According to his theory, you could focus the power just right, and turn it into what would essentially be a death ray with the power of a small nuke, and send it anywhere on the planet by bouncing it off the ionosphere."

"Fascinating, Jay. Are we getting to the point any time today?"

"There's a great story about Tesla going to a bridge with a hammer and a stopwatch, tapping the metal at precise intervals, and damn near taking the bridge down with the Galloping Gertie effect. I'm telling you, Tesla was head and shoulders above everybody else of his time."

"Jay. Hello. Earth to Jay?"

"It's the *same technology*, Boss, pumping juice into the air without wires! The HAARP people aren't doing anything Tesla didn't think of a hundred years ago."

"All right, I'm impressed. He was a genius. Get to the point."

"Well, according to my mole in the CIA—and that's for the benefit of any CIA ops listening to our conversation, good luck on finding him—even after the demise of the evil empire, the Russians continued their experiments with ELF radiation, using devices that Tesla would have recognized as his own. Ivan hasn't found the magic combination yet, that we know of. Aside from HAARP, which is the biggest, there are other 'atmospheric heaters' like it all over the world, at least a dozen, not counting any somebody might be hiding in the woods somewhere. And using the ionosphere to bounce off of—like playing pool, you can bank the shot—any one of them could be driving the Chinese bonkers—if they've figured out the correct frequency to do it. And given what we know, it seems as if somebody might have figured it out."

"Sounds like science fiction to me."

"No, *that* is the point, Boss—it's old tech, the root stuff. Anybody with some wire and a lot of time on his hands can produce it. It's the frequency stuff they need, not the hardware. It's like plug-'n'-play; you don't need to be a whiz to get it to work. Tesla did the basics a century ago. Certainly a theory we ought to check out."

"And how do you propose we check it out?"

"Hey, that's the fun part. We go into the wonderful world of VR and hunt it down on the net. I bet that somewhere, sometime, somebody has put something about this into the ether, and even if they hid it, I'll find it."

Michaels nodded. Mind control. A scary thought.

"What about Morrison? Are we checking him out?"

"Oh, yeah. I'm paying his files a visit this afternoon. I'll get anything anybody knows about Dr. Morrison or my name's not Lightnin' Jay Gridley."

Michaels just shook his head again.

17

John Howard watched his son watch the boomerang throwers. The contest was going full steam, several events at once, and the air was full of bright plastic bits spinning in all kinds of flight patterns. Outside of computers, this was the first thing that had ever seemed to really attract Tyrone. Well, not counting that little girl who had broken the boy's heart a few months back. What was her name? Belladonna? It had to happen eventually, of course, and maybe sooner was better than later, but it had been a wrenching experience. And your first heartbreak never went away, not altogether. Howard could remember his own with a clarity he wouldn't have thought possible more than twenty-five years after it had happened. He'd even told Tyrone about it, trying to ease his son's heartsickness. Maybe it had helped. He liked to think that it had, a little.

Ah, yes, beautiful Lizbeth Toland, who had betrayed him at sixteen with his best friend, costing him both of them. It was a lifetime ago, and in the grand scheme of life, it didn't mean much, a tiny bump in the road, but not something that ever quite went away. Even after all the years, he could still summon up the sadness he'd felt, though it had lost the painful sting it had once had.

Ah, well, it was the path not taken, and he didn't have any regrets about the one he had gone down instead. If he'd wound up with Lizbeth, then he'd never have met Nadine, never fathered Tyrone, and he would have missed entirely the life he enjoyed. It was possible that other life could have been better, but he couldn't see how. He wouldn't trade Nadine and their son for all the money, fame, and power in the world.

He smiled at Tyrone and his new girlfriend, and their enthusiasm for this whirly-twirly sport. Fortunately, Little Nadine didn't seem to be evoking the same sexual response in Tyrone that Bella had; they were more like pals, and Howard was happy to see that. Plenty of time to play that game later.

After a career in the service, first the military, then taking over the military arm of Net Force, finally rising even in this bastard service to general, he now felt a need to spend more time with his family.

It seemed like yesterday that he'd gotten married, a few hours ago that Tyrone had been born, and here he was already a teenager. It would be but a blink of an eye before the boy was off to college, getting married himself, maybe having children. One day, Howard would look down, and there would be this little version of Tyrone standing knee-high to him, saying "Grampa! Grampa!"

It made a man stop and consider his life, such thoughts.

"Where did you go?" his wife said.

"I was just thinking about my grandson."

"Oh, really? Something you haven't told me, John?"

"No, no, I meant Tyrone's son."

"Lord, he's only thirteen. Let's give him a few more years before we start asking for grandchildren!"

He put his arm around her. "Okay. Two years, Granny."

She leaned her head against his chest. "Nobody is *ever* going to call me 'Granny,' not in this life, no way, no how."

Coeur d'Alene, Idaho

It sure hadn't taken long, Morrison reflected. He'd made the call yesterday, and less than a day later, here was a black limo carrying a Chinese agent pulling to a stop in the hot Idaho afternoon ten feet away from him. He swallowed, his mouth dry.

Standing a few feet away, Ventura had changed into a green T-shirt, blue jeans, and cowboy boots, and he made no effort to cover the pistol holstered just behind his right hip. He had his thumbs hooked into his front pockets, and looked like a good old boy with nothing to do standing in the sunshine. Morrison couldn't see Ventura's eyes behind the man's sunglasses, but he was more than a little certain his bodyguard was watching the limo with deadly expertise. This had been a good idea, hiring Ventura. He felt a lot better knowing somebody like him was on the job.

Behind them, twenty feet back at parade rest, stood General Smith, flanked by a pair of his men holding assault rifles across their chests.

The limo's door opened, and a small, balding, round-faced Chinese man wearing a white silk summer suit and soft, gray, leather Italian shoes alighted. He smiled at Morrison and bowed slightly. "Dr. Morrison, I presume?"

Morrison nodded slightly and offered a nervous smile in return.

"I am Qian Ho Wu, but my friends call me 'Chilly.' Nice to meet you." From his voice, the man could have been born and raised in Kansas—there was no trace of a Chinese accent.

Chilly Wu? Hardly a name to conjure up visions of water torture, was it? He seemed perfectly harmless.

"Mr. Wu. This is my associate, Mr.—"

"—Ventura, isn't it? Also a pleasure to meet you, sir." Wu extended his hand, as if to shake Ventura's hand. Ventura gave him a broad smile, but kept his hand down.

Wu smiled in return, and it seemed as if something had passed between him and Ventura, though Morrison couldn't tell what it had been.

"Well. Gentlemen. Where can we talk?"

"Why don't we take you on a tour of the facility," Ventura said. It was not a question. "A ride around to see the sights."

"Certainly." He held his hand out toward the limo.

"We have a car," Ventura said. He nodded toward one of the special rental units.

Ventura had told Morrison about this before. Inside the car, Smith couldn't eavesdrop on the conversation.

"Of course," Wu said. "Somewhere shady my driver can park and wait?"

"Over there under the trees by the garage would be good."

Wu leaned back into the car and reeled off a fast bit of singsong Chinese.

The driver responded in the same language.

Ventura said, "Sure, there's a toilet in the garage."

Wu turned back, one eyebrow raised. "Ah. You speak Mandarin?"

"Not really. A few words I picked up in a restaurant ordering dinner."

Wu flashed a careful smile, turned back to the driver, and spoke again, and it sounded different to Morrison, though it still seemed to be Chinese.

Again the driver responded.

"That's okay," Ventura said, "as long as he doesn't wander far from the car, he can smoke and stretch his legs. I'll have one of my people keep an eye on him to make sure nobody bothers him."

"I see you have a few words of Cantonese, too. You must really enjoy Chinese food. Though wouldn't it have been a better tactic to pretend ignorance? Perhaps learn something useful?"

Ventura shrugged. "You weren't going to say anything useful anyway, were you, Mr. Wu?"

"Call me 'Chilly,' Luther. It's always nice to be working with professionals. Makes things so much cleaner, don't you think?"

Still wearing his old birdwatcher costume, Walker drove, Ventura rode shotgun, and Wu and Morrison sat in the backseat of the full-sized Dodge Intrepid. Walker wore headphones plugged into a DVD player with loud music blaring from the phones into his ears, making him effectively deaf. The phones were a precaution. Even though Ventura had worked with him long enough to know Walker could keep his mouth shut, what you didn't know, you couldn't be forced to say.

Ventura had taken his pistol from its holster and laid it on the seat where the men in back couldn't see it. He kept his hand on the weapon. Wu didn't look it on the surface, but he was a dangerous man—Ventura had been around enough of them to know one when he saw one. Something in the eyes, something in the body language. Wu played it down—the silk suit and expensive shoes—and he wasn't carrying a gun big enough to show, but underestimating an opponent was always a mistake. With Wu, it could be fatal in a hurry. It was still early in the negotiations, and probably there wasn't any real threat yet, but "probably" wasn't something you risked your neck on.

"So, what exactly are we looking at buying, Dr. Morrison? Would it be too forward if I call you Patrick?"

Wu was showing off a little, dropping names just to let them know he'd done his homework and that he knew who he was dealing with. They would have squeezed the computer remailing service to get Morrison's ID, no big deal, but knowing Ventura was on the case was a little more impressive. That meant they were working this one hard. Well they should be, too.

"A very useful vehicle design," Morrison said.

"That's it? Just the design? No hardware? No wheels, motor, no chassis?"

"Any electrical engineering student could build you the

hardware, Mr. Wu. Only I can show you how to make it work."

"I see. And how much are you asking for this . . . design?"

"Four hundred million dollars."

Wu chuckled. "A hell of a used car."

"Satisfaction guaranteed or your money back."

"Uh-huh. And what proof do we have that you can deliver?"

Morrison smiled. "Proof? Next time you're in the old country, take a trip to visit the villages of Daru and Longhua and ask the survivors there how things have been lately."

Wu glanced at Ventura, then back at Morrison. "Are you sure you want Luther here to hear the details?"

"I have no secrets from Mr. Ventura."

Wu nodded. "Very well. Anybody with good intel connections, such as Luther has, could have gotten those two names. How do we know you aren't running a scam?"

"What would it take to convince you?"

"Well, you could give us the technology, allow us to test it, and then let us pay you."

Morrison laughed, and after a moment Wu joined him. "Just a thought," Wu said.

"Try a different thought."

Wu rubbed at his chin and pretended to do that. Ventura picked up his pistol and lightly pushed the muzzle against the back of his seat, pointed at Wu. If the man made any sudden moves, the Chinese were going to need themselves another purchasing agent—and at the least, the rental company was going to have to put in new seat covers.

"All right, then. Try this: Let's take it for a little test

spin, shall we? Kick a few tires, rev the engine, drive around the block. This time, we pick the destination. If it works there as it did in Daru and Longhua, then we would be very interested in your vehicle."

"At my price?"

"It seems reasonable—assuming nobody else will be driving the same model anytime soon?"

"They won't be."

"How, ah, big is this car? How many, ah, *passengers* are we talking about?"

"There is a point of diminishing returns. With more power, I could do more, but the limit right now is a circle about ten miles across."

Wu nodded. "I think we've strained the car metaphor as far as we can. I need to get back to my superiors with your offer. We will come up with coordinates for a test. We'll get these to you, you run it, and if it works, then we'll discuss terms. Is this satisfactory?"

"Yes."

"Good. Shall we head back?"

Ventura nodded, and tapped Walker on the shoulder. Walked looked, and Ventura pointed his finger at the car's roof, waved it in a tight circle, then pointed behind them. Walker nodded, and pulled into a dusty field next to the gravel road to turn around.

As they headed back toward the HQ compound, Wu said, "Fascinating place here, Luther. You a believer?"

"No. Parallel traveler. You make do with what you have."

"I hear that. We have similar places in our country, you know. Now and then the government uncovers a nest of malcontents and has to step on it. If you don't, pretty soon you have fools who are willing to walk barehanded in front of tanks. Better to crush them before they get too brave. The difference is that you *know* these people are here, and yet you allow them anyway."

"The price of freedom," Ventura said.

"I've always thought that freedom was a highly over-rated commodity," Wu said. "More trouble than it is worth. Order is much better. Besides, it doesn't really matter to people like us—you and me—does it?"

Ventura shrugged. "Everybody has to be someplace. One is as good as another."

"I suppose." Within the tiny shrug of indifference, there was a flash of something on Wu's face, something cold and ugly, just a fast hint, and Ventura had to fight the urge to pull the trigger and cook the little man right here and right now.

No, he didn't look like much, but Ventura had a feeling deep in his gut that Chilly Wu here would be a formidable opponent in any kind of a fight. With any luck, he wouldn't have to find out. If he did, it was going to end in blood, he was sure. He hoped it wouldn't be his own.

18

Vermillion River, Lafayette, Louisiana

Jay had to smile at the imagery the boss enjoyed. He had
a thing for the swamps—a couple of times Jay had gone
with Michaels's default scenarios and they had been boats
on bayous, like that. They weren't bad, better than a lot
of off-the-shelf stuff, but not as textured as Jay normally
liked to create. He'd added in some pretty neat stuff for
this setting, at least he thought so, even if Michaels might
not notice. Of course, the boss was management, and VR
programming wasn't his real strength.

As he motored along the narrow river in the little
outboard-rigged flat-bottomed skiff, or whatever they
called them down in Cajun country, Jay decided to stay
with this sequence. He had a lot of work to do—places
to go, things to look for—and it was easier to use this
than to create a new ersatz, so he cruised past the Spanish

moss and the alligator and right on up to the . . . Dewdrop Inn.

That name was worth another smile.

Carrying a small satchel, Jay approached the front door. There was a raggy, bearded yehaw kinda guy in nothing but overalls leaning against the door, and Jay walked right up to him, smiling. Yehaw, so the joke went, was the kinda guy whose father might also be his brother or his uncle.

"Ain't open," the man said.

"I know. I just wanted to let you know that somebody is around back trying to break in."

It took a second or three for it to register—probably because Yehaw had some kind of dinosaur-like sub-brain down in his nether regions that had to relay the thought back and forth a few times before he got it.

Yehaw frowned, pushed off the wall, and lumbered away, heading for the back door.

Jay waited until he was out of sight, then slipped the lock on the front door with a thin piece of steel, stepped inside, and relocked the door behind him.

The door guard—in reality a fire wall program for the HAARP computer system to stop outside access—was strong, but not very bright. The guard would amble around back, not see anybody trying to break in, then return to his post in the front. He'd remember that Jay had approached, if anybody asked, but since Jay wouldn't be visible, the guard wouldn't worry about him. He'd never think to look inside; that would be beyond his capabilities.

That was the problem with software. Hardware, too. People didn't upgrade for all kinds of different reasons, and it always cost them something. Shoot, the military arm of Net Force still had—and still *used*—some sub-gigabyte-RAM tactical computers when there were systems with ten or fifteen times that much power you could buy off a department store shelf! Might as well be steam-powered. The honchos-military would mumble, and say that was all they *needed* to run their tried-and-true programs; they were dependable, and shockproof, why bother going for more power with some untested unit or software that might crap out when they really couldn't afford that? Shortsighted of them, Jay thought, but then he wasn't interested in being anywhere except on the cutting edge. A lot of people still thought slow and steady won the race, when *fast* and steady was much better.

Well, that was not his problem at the moment.

Jay found the lockbox under the bar that the boss's report had mentioned. He removed a pair of latex gloves from his satchel, slipped them on, and bent to examine the box. He saw the scratches showing that the padlock had been tampered with. Humming to himself, Jay removed a small aerosol container from the satchel, aimed it at the lock, then sprayed it with a fine mist of dry powder. He blew the excess dust off, then used a second aerosol can on the lock, this one a kind of liquid glue.

Yeah, okay, so he brought maybe a little more attention to detail to his constructs than was necessary. A man had to have *some* standards.

Several fingerprints appeared as the chemical reaction from the two sprays took place. Jay pulled a clear strip of transfer tape from a roll in his handy satchel, carefully pressed it against the lock, peeled it off, and stuck it onto a white plastic card.

Just for fun, he took his pick gun and a torsion tool

and opened the padlock. Took all of about six seconds, a piece of cake.

The lockbox had stacks of papers, money, some coins—all virtual representations of various kinds of electronic files. Jay picked up a couple of papers and scanned them, but he wasn't as interested in what they had to say as he was in who had broken in before him. He closed the box, relocked the padlock, and headed for the back door.

He would take the prints back to the office and check them. Of course, what he would really be doing was back-tracking e-codes and running down servers and all, looking to see who had left traces of their visit. If the thief had been stupid enough to do it barehanded, Jay would have him. Probably he hadn't been that stupid, but you never knew. Generally speaking, if crooks were smart enough so they wouldn't get caught, they were smart enough to make more money honestly than they could by thievery. Not always. Some were smart, but lazy. Some liked the adrenaline rush of doing something illegal. Jay remembered one case where the head of a large computer software corporation got his thrills hacking into private computer systems and copying crap, like employee addresses or financial records, stuff he could have *legally* gotten elsewhere. He didn't even use the material, just stashed it in a booty file. The thief never did any damage, and never took anything of value—it was the electronic equivalent of petty shoplifting, and if he'd wanted, he could have *bought* most of the companies he plundered. When Jay had run him down, the corporate prez had laughed, paid the fine, and was probably back at it the next day. A thrill junkie.

Jay ran into guys like that all the time, hackers who thought they were faster or smarter or better, and who wanted to test themselves. He could understand that—if he hadn't gotten into Net Force, he'd probably be doing it himself. But now it was his job to nail 'em.

Jay had gone up against the best, and while he hadn't always beaten them easily or fast, in the end, he *had* beaten them. Well. At least the ones he knew about. There might be crooks out there who were so good they could commit the perfect crime, that being one that nobody ever realized had happened. But truth be told, Jay didn't believe there were many, if any, who were that good. And he didn't think whoever had broken into HAARP's computer was one of the best, or they wouldn't have left scratches on the lock. This would be a walk in the park.

Now he had to go and find out about Dr. Morrison. If anything, that ought to be even easier.

Saturday
Portland, Oregon

Tyrone and Nadine had spent the morning watching contestants in the various events, concentrating on checking out the MTA seniors. Nobody was coming close to Gorski's unbelievable record, but there were some pretty good hang times.

They decided to practice after lunch, and went to the field set up for that, a little farther up the hill.

Tyrone looked at the sunny meadow with others practicing, then at Nadine. She wasn't a looka'me like Bella, but in this light, here in this green field, she was a lot more attractive in ways that Bella was not. She was a *person*, somebody who liked being with him, somebody who he liked being with for reasons that went past a pretty face.

"What are you grinning at, fool? Your chances of beating me tomorrow?"

Tyrone shook his head. "Nothing," he said.

"Well, come on, let me give you another lesson in how to throw."

"Your ass."

"Yeah, you are my ass, aren't you?"

They both grinned. At that moment, Tyrone didn't see how life could get much better than this. Well. Maybe after he won the championship it could.

Coeur d'Alene, Idaho

"Have you ever fired a handgun, Dr. Morrison?"

They were on one of several shooting ranges at the militia compound. Though it was late, nearly nine, it was still light enough to see the targets, squared-off human torso silhouettes made of cardboard, mounted on wooden stands. There were a dozen of these at various distances from where they stood behind a chalk line drawn on the dirt, next to a beat-up table made of weathered two-by-fours and plywood.

Morrison shook his head. "No. Rifles and shotguns when I was a boy, not pistols. My parents didn't believe in them."

Ventura said, "The principle is the same. You use a sighting device to line the weapon up on the target, press the trigger, the gun goes bang. The main differences are that a shorter barrel is harder to aim well, and most hand-

guns have considerably less punch than a rifle or a shotgun. You trade stopping power for portability and being
able to conceal the weapon."

Ventura pointed to the tabletop, where several pistols
lay. "What we are going to do is let you try several of
these, to see which one you can shoot the best. There isn't
time for you to gain real expertise, and this is for a last-
ditch, enemy-in-your-face situation. If you have to resort
to it, then my people and I will likely be dead, and
frankly, your chances of surviving will be slim and none.
But they probably won't expect you to be armed at all,
so you might surprise them."

Morrison nodded again, feeling a cold rush in his lower
belly. He hadn't thought this far ahead. The idea of being
kidnapped or killed had been more intellectual than real.
Looking at a table full of guns made it all too real.

"Ideally, you would carry the biggest handgun you
could—the larger and faster the bullet, the more rounds,
the better. That's a Glock .40 semiauto, the black plastic
one. Next to it, that's a Taurus .357 revolver. These two
have the most oomph. If you hit somebody solidly in the
torso with one round of either, they'll go down and be
out of the fight better than nine times out of ten."

Ventura shook his head. "I have to apologize, Doctor.
This isn't how you'd learn to shoot if I had time to teach
you properly, but we don't have time. We'll start with
those."

Morrison put on the headphones Ventura handed him.

"The hearing protectors are electronic," Ventura said.
"You'll be able to hear fine until the gun goes off, but
they'll cut out the noise. These two pistols are particularly
loud devices. If you shoot one inside a car without protection, you can blow out an eardrum.

"Hold it like so, both hands. Stand like this, arms out, in an isoceles triangle. Grip is important, hold it tight. The sight picture should look like this." Ventura drew a picture on the table with a felt-tipped pen. "Line the post up inside the notch, put the target right on top. If you need to shoot, you probably won't have time for a clean sight picture, your attacker will be right in your face, so what you'll do instead is point it like you would your finger, and index the whole gun. Here."

He handed Morrison the black plastic pistol. "If you can see the back of the gun against the man's chest, that's good enough for close range."

"How close?"

"Inside twenty feet. In your case, probably more like six or eight feet."

"Okay."

"Glock operates like this. Magazine in here, pull back the slide like this to chamber a round, pull the trigger. No external safety. Point, press. Don't jerk it. Try it, that target right in front of us. Shoot it twice. It will kick some."

The cardboard human torso and head was maybe a dozen feet away.

Morrison took a deep breath, pointed the Glock at the target, and pulled the trigger. The damned gun almost jumped out of his hands, and the second shot went off before he was ready, so it was probably a little high . . .

He lowered the weapon and looked.

There were no holes in the target.

How could he have missed? It was right in front of him!

"First round was off to the right, second was way high and right. Try the Taurus."

Five minutes later, Morrison felt a sense of profound

embarrassment. He had fired ten shots from five guns. Only two of the bullets had hit the cardboard, both of them almost off the target to the right, barely on the edge. *Two.*

"Don't feel bad," Ventura said. "Trained cops miss at this range. Ever see the video of the state cops who stopped a couple of guys in a truck for an expired license? Guys were guilty of other crimes, so they came out with guns. The truck passenger and one cop faced each other from twelve feet, each fired five or six times, nobody hit anything. If somebody is pointing a gun at you, it's a lot worse than shooting at a target that won't shoot back. Adrenaline makes your hand muscles twitch funny."

Morrison shook his head.

"Try this one. Smith and Wesson Model 317, an Air-light."

He handed the gun to Morrison.

"It's not very heavy."

"Aluminum, mostly. Just under ten ounces. Holds eight rounds of .22 caliber."

Morrison took another deep breath, indexed the little gun, pulled the trigger, one, *two*! The revolver jumped a little, but not much, and when he looked at the target, there were two small holes in the center, no more than an inch or two apart. Hey!

"Again. This time, keep pulling the trigger until the gun stops shooting."

Morrison obeyed.

This time, he was able to *see* the holes as they appeared in the cardboard. They weren't very big, but all of them were clustered in the center, except for one, and it was only a few inches above the others. The clicking of the hammer on empty came as a surprise.

"Very good. This is your weapon," Ventura said. "It's light, simple to operate, almost no recoil. It doesn't have any real stopping power, but a solid hit from a small-caliber round is a lot better than a miss from a hand cannon."

Morrison looked at the gun.

"Here is how to reload it, though I don't expect you'll get that far if you need it. If it's one guy, point and shoot until he falls down or goes away. If it's more than one, give them two rounds each, then repeat. We'll practice that, double-taps."

But they didn't get to double-tap practice. The sound of Morrison's cell phone ringing was clearly audible through the electronic sound suppressors.

That would be the Chinese calling.

Morrison removed the earphones and thumbed the receive button on the phone.

"Hello," he said.

"Hey, Pat! What say we take that car of yours for a test drive? I know just the place."

As Morrison listened to Wu, Ventura reloaded the Airlight, then handed it to him. With a cell phone in one hand and a gun in the other, it suddenly seemed to Morrison that the summer evening's warmth had just turned to winter.

19

The helicopter pilot pointed. "Plinck Field!" he yelled over the copter's racket.

Ventura nodded. They were two thousand feet up and easing in for the landing. He looked at his watch. Though it wasn't that far, the hop to the private airfield via chopper had taken forty-five minutes; part of that was for a couple of changes of direction, just in case. And it *was* farther away from Smith's compound than the commercial airport at Coeur d'Alene. Ventura had arranged for the helicopter before they'd arrived, knowing they'd need it once the game was fully engaged. Inside the militia's base, they'd be safe, but once they left, the odds shifted. Even Morrison understood this, once it had been pointed out to him.

"But why a helicopter?" he'd asked.

"Because they know you're leaving. They also know where you are going—unless you can conduct your test by remote control, you have to go back to Alaska to play the tune on your HAARP. I've got people in place there, and anybody who shows up for hunting or birdwatching is going to be considered armed and dangerous. But if I were the Chinese and interested in grabbing you, I'd give it a try here, first. There is only one road leading to this place, and a couple of half-wits in camo with binoculars can cover it. Half my people will convoy out in two of the rental cars an hour before the copter arrives, heading for the airport at Coeur d'Alene. That'll give them something to look at if they are out there. They'll probably expect some kind of subterfuge, so the third car will leave fifteen minutes after the first two, going the other way. Probably this will draw any fire teams that might have been set up. Forty-five minutes later, we take off. They won't be able to follow us in the air without us seeing them, and I don't think they'll expect that anyhow. Even if they manage to footprint us with one of their spysats, we won't stay in range long, so they'll lose us while we're still heading the wrong way. If they have that much going for them, they'll probably figure out we're going to a private airfield, but by the time they can figure out which strip and get people there, we'll be gone. We have a chartered plane waiting for us when the copter touches down."

"What if they've anticipated this and already have people at the private airfield?"

Ventura grinned. The man was beginning to catch on. "If they're that smart, then I'll just have to shoot them."

He digested that for a moment. "This must be costing a fortune."

"Not even a drop in your bucket, if you pull it off. Besides, I haven't even run out of your retainer yet."

Morrison hadn't spoken to that, but Ventura could see the man was scared. Well he should be, dealing with these kinds of players. But at this level of the game, if Morrison got deleted, it was likely that Ventura would be crossing that bridge with him, and he wasn't quite ready to do that yet. He only had to keep the Chinese hopping long enough for the deal to get done. Once the money was transferred and the information was in hand, Morrison would have to disappear, go into hiding permanently, though he didn't know that yet. With enough money, you could vanish completely and live out your life in comfort and security, provided you knew how. Ventura knew the drill and he would advise Morrison, but that wasn't in his own future.

Morrison was probably rationalizing that the Chinese would figure he wasn't going to be telling anybody he'd sold them American secrets, and that once the deal was done, he was no threat. He was only partially right. The Chinese would have the software, but in order to make it work, they'd need the hardware, and that wasn't something you could hide under a tarp. If the intelligence service of any major country suddenly had citizens run amok, killing one another, it would be cause for no small concern. If they could figure out the cause, finding the smoking gun would be relatively easy, big as the gun would have to be, and a couple of Stealth bombers could clean that clock nicely and be home in time to see the results on CNN.

The helicopter landed on the pad, the rotorwash kicking up fierce wind. Ventura slapped Morrison on the shoulder. "Stay behind me."

They alighted from the craft, and Ventura pulled his cocked-and-locked pistol and held it down along the side of his leg. He moved quickly toward an ancient DC-3 parked a hundred yards away. As they moved, the elderly gooney bird cranked its port engine, a chuff of white exhaust smoke erupting from the engine.

Ventura smiled. He had fondness for these old planes; he had flown in them all over the world. The DC-3, sometimes called the Dakota, had been around since the mid-thirties. They were noisy, slow, and wouldn't go all that far without refueling, but they were as dependable as sunshine in Hawaii. Ventura, whose piloting skills were emergency-level-only, had always thought that if he ever got around to buying a plane, this was the one he'd get. No bells, no whistles, but it would get you and your cargo there. It was still the best prop plane in the air, for his money.

The plane's door opened, the little ramp lowering, and Hack Spalding stood there, grinning his gap-toothed grin. He gave Ventura the finger, which meant things were okay onboard. Ventura turned to motion Morrison up the short ramp while he watched their backs. Nobody around.

Well, good. Score another one for the round eyes . . .

Washington, D.C.

The Mall was hot and muggy even this late in the afternoon, no real surprise this time of year, but Toni didn't really care. It was good to be outside moving, good to be back in the U.S., and especially good to be walking next to Alex. It was almost as if the last couple of months had been a bad dream. As if she had just awakened from a troubled sleep, the memory of it fresh but somehow unreal.

He wanted her to come back to her job, and the truth was, she wanted to, but that had been a big part of the problem, working for Alex, and she didn't see how it was going to improve. He couldn't treat her like an employee in the same way he had before they'd become lovers. It made a difference, and there were all kinds of problems that came from that. He had skipped sending her into a danger zone when she'd come up in the rotation, and while she wanted him to be concerned for her as a man for his woman, she did *not* want the same concern from a boss to an employee.

She'd have to do some kind of work, though, and the truth was, she'd already been offered several jobs. A couple of computer companies had approached her to head up their security services, and they'd offered a lot more money than she'd been making at Net Force. There were some nice perks, too: cars, condos, a snazzy title. And she had seriously considered taking one of these. Mostly, she could work from anywhere, though there would be some travel for secure-situation setups. But while she didn't want to work for Alex, she also didn't want to get so far away she couldn't see him.

There was the possibility of a transfer. Alex had never put her resignation into the system. She'd quit, but he hadn't told anybody higher up. She was officially on personal leave, not drawing a salary, but still considered employed. Net Force was more or less freestanding as an operation, but it was still technically part of the FBI. There were people on the other side of the fence at Quantico who would be pleased to have her working in their offices—she had heard from a couple of them, too. Thing was, while that meant she'd be in the same general vicinity as Alex, it also meant she'd be viewed as something of a traitor in Net Force. Just as the CIA and the FBI always had a de facto competition going, and there was little love lost between them, Net Force ops tended to think of regular feebs as dweebs—to be tolerated, but avoided as much as possible.

Alex probably wouldn't like it very much if she jumped into the Bureau mainline.

Then again, it wasn't really his choice, was it? She had to do something to earn her living, and she was already in the system—a transfer to another building would be the easiest thing all around, at least insofar as keeping her apartment, getting to work, and not having to learn new systems. And she could still see Alex for lunch or workouts in the gym every day.

Her phone's attention-beck came on—an odd little piece of music that came from a movie more than fifty years old, a comedy about a super-secret agent named Flint. The little tune was the same as the ring of the special phone belonging to a fictional U.S. security agency, reserved for incoming calls from the President of the United States: Dah dah dah, dah dah dah, dah DAH, dah dah dah, dah dah daaah. This little sting was courtesy of Jay Gridley, of course, who loved such esoterica, and who also loved to program personal hardware when the owner wasn't looking.

She looked at the screen but the caller's ID was blocked. If she'd been carrying a virgil, it wouldn't have been.

"Hello?"

"Hello, Toni. How are you?"

Some bored god must be reading her mind and taking an interest in her life: It was Melissa Allison herself, Director of the FBI. On a Sunday, no less.

"Fine, and you?"

"Surviving. Listen, I understand you are interested in transferring from Net Force into Mainline, is that correct?"

The director, who had gotten her job by knowing where a soccer stadium's worth of political bodies were buried, was not one to mince words.

Indeed, Toni had been considering it only seconds before, but she hadn't made the decision yet. That's not what the director wanted to hear. She wanted a yes or no answer. *Here's the spot, Toni, and like it or not, you've just been put on it. Choose.*

Toni glanced at Alex, who was busy watching a young couple with two small children trying to corral the little critters. The boy, about three, was running around in circles, singing a clock song—"One o'clock, bang, bang, bang/ Two o'clock, bang, bang, bang!" The little girl, maybe a year and half, was running away from her mother at full speed across the lawn in that lurching toddle small children had, laughing as she went. Alex was smiling at the show.

"Toni?"

Toni pulled her attention back to the phone. "Yes, ma'am, I have been considering it."

"Wise," the director said, and Toni knew from that one word that the woman knew about her and Alex. "I have an opening in my schedule tomorrow around one. Come and see me and we'll discuss it."

"Yes, ma'am."

With that, the director was gone. Toni hooked the phone back into the belt of her jeans.

Alex turned away from the children and looked at her, lifting his eyebrows in question: *Who was that?*

Maybe it was selfish of her, but Toni didn't want to kill the rest of the afternoon. If she told Alex it was the director, she'd have to explain the rest, he'd want to talk about it, and she just wasn't up to that. She'd only been back with Alex for a couple of days, it didn't feel as secure as once it had, and if he knew she was thinking about going over to the feeb shop, she was sure he would be upset. He might not say anything, he would cover up his feelings—he was good at that, covering up his feelings—and she just wasn't ready to go down that road.

She slipped her hand around his arm. "Nothing important," she said. "Come on, I want to see the Smith's new Ancient Wheels exhibit."

He smiled at her. "Sure."

All right. It wasn't a lie, if maybe not strictly true, but if anything came of it, she would tell him. Why bring it up and ruin the mood now, since it might not amount to anything anyhow? A conversation with the director was all it was.

As they passed the young parents and children, Alex grinned at the little girl, who had finally gotten tired and plopped upon the neatly clipped grass, where she sat quietly cooing.

"Ever think about having children?" Alex said.

Toni was caught flatfooted. She stopped, as if she had forgotten how to walk. She stared at him. Children? With Alex? Of course she had thought about it. Dreamed about it, even. But before she could gather herself enough to say anything, he shrugged.

"Just an idle thought," he said.

20

Sunday, June 12th
Gakona, Alaska

No Chinese assassins materialized to try and intercept them as they drove from the old pipeline airstrip just north of Paxon toward Gakona. Ventura said it wasn't likely, and he had ten of his people checking possible ambush sites along the route, plus cars in front and behind of theirs. The older man, Walker, drove again, with Morrison in the front and Ventura sitting in the back. "If anybody shows up, they'll probably think I'm you, since the VIP usually rides in the back," Ventura had explained.

"You think they'll be here?"

"Oh, they are here, somewhere. I'm not sure they'll try for you yet; they may be waiting for the test, to be certain you can do as you say before they get really serious."

"You think once we're inside the facility we'll be safe?"

"No. I have a roster of the guards, and if any new faces show up, we'll deal with that, but that fence and a few half-trained guys on patrol won't stop somebody really determined to get inside. I'll have my people watching the roads and the air, so if they show up in force we'll know about it in time to haul ass. I've worked out a few escape routes from the facility."

Again, Morrison was surprised at the man's thoroughness. Everything he did seemed thought out to the last detail.

The trip was uneventful, however—if you didn't count a small elk herd crossing the road—and within an hour they were inside the auxiliary trailer, warming up the system. As Morrison worked, Ventura prowled around like some kind of big cat—alert, watching, listening.

"About ready," Morrison said. He picked up a dog-eared phonebook-sized tome of locations by latitude and longitude and thumbed through it until he found the ones he wanted. There it was . . . 45 degrees, 28 minutes, 24 seconds North; 122 degrees, 38 minutes, 39 seconds West . . . Not the center of the city, but it would take in all of downtown on both sides of the river . . .

Ventura nodded. "Okay."

"It'll have to run for a couple of hours to get the optimal effect. Not as long as it did in China, since the target is closer, and we lose less energy for the beam."

"Fine."

He looked at the control. Flip the cover up, push the button, and it was done. He could go eat or take a nap while it worked. "I feel kind of, I don't know, awkward about this."

"Why?"

"Well, the target being in the United States and all."

"A pang of nationalism?"

"Maybe a little. I somehow didn't think it was going to go like this."

"That's always the way. 'No battle plan survives first contact with the enemy.' You know why it's a deal breaker if you don't do this, don't you?"

"No, why?"

"Because if this works, and if as a result of it a few dozen people die, then you haven't just killed some faceless people nobody cares about a million miles away, you're a multiple-murderer in your *own* country. And the city you were given as a target? It is in a state with the death penalty, did you know that?"

Morrison felt the taste of bile threaten to rise in his throat. "No. I didn't think about that."

Ventura shrugged. "You can only ride the needle once—that's how they do it there, strapped to a gurney by lethal injection. What the Chinese want is more assurance you won't change your mind and go running to the authorities once the deal is done. Once this deal is complete, they don't have to find you and kill you—all they have to do is tell the feds who you are, sit back, and let them do the work. The Chinese wouldn't want a trial, of course, having all this come out, but neither do you. And once you get arrested? Well, then they'd know *exactly* where to find you. It's very difficult to stop an assassin who is willing to die to get the job done."

Morrison felt the ugly truth of this flood into him like liquid oxygen, chilling him to his core. "I—I see."

"Not quite yet, you don't. Before you push that button, let me lay out a few more things you have to know.

"Once you get your money, Patrick Morrison has to disappear. You have to vanish so completely that the best agents in China and maybe the United States and half a dozen other countries can't find you, because eventually they all might be looking. If you had visions of yourself being on the board of directors of some university and benevolently awarding grants to starving scientists or some such, you might as well erase those ideas now. The *only* way you are going to survive to spend that money is to become somebody completely different from the man you are. You will have to sever *all* links to your past— and unless your wife is willing to go along for the ride, which'll get a little bumpy up front—that will include giving up contact with her, too. You'll be a new man, in a new country, with a made-up background and history. You won't even be able to read the same *magazines* you used to read, or practice any of your hobbies, because you can bank on it, somebody will try to track you from something as innocuous as those, and probably be able to do it. Say you subscribe to a small scholarly journal that thirty or forty thousand people get. You better read somebody else's copy, because while it might take years to physically look at everybody on the subscription list, the Chinese are nothing if not patient. You only have to make one mistake, Doctor, and you lose the game. Patrick Morrison will have to die figuratively, or he will surely die literally."

Morrison stared at him. He hadn't thought it through to this end. But as he heard Ventura speak, he knew what the man said was so. For a moment, it took his breath away. How could he have been so shortsighted?

"That's how it will have to be if you want to survive. I can help you do it, point you in the right direction, tell you the steps you have to take, but once you're set, I can't have any more contact with you, either. They might want to convince me to tell them, and better for you if I don't know your new name and face."

"I didn't even think about the risk to you," Morrison admitted.

"Don't worry about it. I've had people looking for me for a long time, and I've managed to stay alive against the best. I came into this with my eyes open, and I've been living on borrowed time for years. But this is what *you* are facing. So the question you have to ask yourself is, Does four hundred million dollars justify you becoming an entirely new man? With that kind of money, there are places in the world where you can live like a king, have luxury, sex, the power of life and death—as long as you don't stick your head up too high and get noticed. There are men who have done this before, men of wealth and power who had to go away for whatever reason, and they survived twenty, thirty, fifty years, some of them. Some of the ones who are very careful are likely still out there. The careless are for sure dead."

Morrison stared at the button, and a realization solidified in his belly like a lump of cold steel. He said, "It's already too late to turn back, isn't it?"

Ventura gave him a thin smile. "Truth? Yes."

Morrison took a deep breath. "Fuck it, then."

He reached out and pushed the button.

PART TWO

All Problems Are Personal

21

At home, Jay came out of VR, took a deep breath, and removed his headset and gloves. It had been a milk run, a visit to a library, and no matter how skilled you were in creating scenarios, sooner or later, reading a pile of material came down to reading a pile of material.

He had all he could find on Dr. Patrick Morrison, and while he had skimmed it as it was being copied, he hadn't begun to take it all in. From what he'd gleaned so far, the guy was legit enough. Degrees, work experience, marriages, the usual living-life stuff. No trouble with the law, no beefs at work, pretty much Mr. Dull N. Boring right down the line.

The only blot on an otherwise white-bread career was at the job he'd had before going to work for HAARP. He'd been doing some kind of behavioral modification experiments on chimps, working with extremely low-frequency radiation, a post-doc research project at Johns Hopkins, and it had apparently petered out. He failed to get the results for which he had been looking. His grant, as the report mildly and politely put it, had not been renewed, and he'd been out of a job.

A small red flag went up in Jay's mind, but when he thought about it, it wasn't that big a deal. Yeah, the guy was into ELF stuff, but that's what a lot of HAARP was about. If you were looking for a plumber, you didn't hire a cabdriver, now did you?

"All work and no play make Jay a dull boy," Soji said.

He smiled up at her. She stood there in a bathrobe. "Look who's talking. You've been so deep into the web I haven't been able to see anything but your back for days."

"Want to see something else?" She undid the bathrobe and held it open.

"Oh, *mama*! Come here!"

Before she could move, however, the phone played the opening strains of Bach's Toccata and Fugue in D Minor. Unfortunately, his phone was programmed so it played that particular tune only if the call was IDed as coming from Net Force HQ or Alex Michaels's virgil.

"Shit," he said.

Soji closed her robe and belted it shut. "He who hesitates stays horny," she said.

"Hey, Boss," Jay said.

"Better get to the office, Jay," Michaels said. "There's been another case of collective madness."

"In China?"

"No," Michaels said. His voice was grim. "Closer than that."

Sunday, June 12th
Portland, Oregon

John Howard watched as his son came up to make his throw. The boy stopped, rubbed his fingers back and forth, and allowed some glittery dust to fall to check wind direction. He held a stopwatch in one hand and his boomerang in the other. The judges waved Tyrone into the circle.

Howard felt more tense than he'd thought he would. It was a big deal to Tyrone, of course, but it was just a game, after all. No reason to be digging his fingernails into his palms.

Off to one side and behind Tyrone, Little Nadine stood, waiting for her turn to compete. She was three contestants behind Tyrone, so she'd know what time she had to beat. So far, the times hadn't been very good, according to Tyrone, and both kids had done better in practice.

The judge nearest the circle held up his hand in a halt sign, then called another judge over for some kind of consultation.

"Come on, come on!" Howard said. "Let the boy throw before his arm gets cold!"

Next to him, his wife said, "Asshole."

He looked at her. "You talkin' to me?"

"Not particularly, I was referring to the judge, but if the shoe fits . . ."

That pissed him off. What was she on the rag about now? He hadn't done anything. He glared at her. She glared right back.

Tyrone stood there for another few seconds, then walked to where the judges were. Howard couldn't hear

what his boy had to say, but apparently the judges really
didn't like it.

The head judge reached out and slapped Tyrone upside
the head.

"Fuck!" Howard yelled. "You see that? He *hit* our son!"
Even as he spoke, Howard ran toward Tyrone and the
judges.

The second judge must have figured the slap was
rude, because he hauled off and punched the head judge
square in the mouth, knocking the man down. Certainly
this was justice, but that irritated Howard even more.

"Leave him!" Howard yelled as he ran. "That bastard
is *mine*!"

Tyrone stepped in and delivered a solid kick to the
fallen judge's ribs. It sounded like somebody dropping a
watermelon, *thoo-wock!*

Even as he drew near to the trio, Howard was aware
of noises coming up the hill: horns honked, metal crashed
into metal. He slid to a stop as the second judge spun to
face him.

"Get off the circle!" the man screamed. "You can't be
here!"

"Oh, yeah?" Howard said. "Hey, pal, I'm *already* here!
What are you gonna do about it?"

Tyrone gave the fallen judge another kick. Not as good
as the first one; it had a flatter sound. *Weak, son, weak.*

The second judge threw a haymaker at Howard, who
ducked it, came up, launched a fast left hook to the face,
then a right cross to the chin, bap-*bap!* That straightened
the sucker out like popping a shoe shine cloth. The guy
sailed backward and to the ground. *Get off* that, *asshole!*

The judge Tyrone was kicking got to his feet and
lurched at the boy, but before Howard could get there,

both Nadines arrived. His wife kneed the guy in the crotch as Little Nadine latched onto his arm and sank her teeth into his shoulder.

Irritated, Howard moved toward them. This was *his* business to take care of, he didn't need the goddamned women getting in the goddamned way—!

A car came across the field, lights on and horn honking, a big, powder-blue Cadillac. It plowed into a group of five men who stood there giving the driver the finger. The men flew like dolls in all directions as the driver gunned the engine.

Not real smart to shoot the bird at a man coming at you in a car at speed.

"Eat shit and die!" the driver screamed. Then he started to laugh.

Four or five other people attacked the Caddy, slamming their fists and feet at it. The driver spun a donut in the grass, still cackling madly.

Something wrong here, Howard thought. He shook his head, then looked at the man he had just decked. What was he *doing*?

He looked down the hill and saw a dozen people fighting. One of them was a policeman. The cop pulled his gun, and a quick succession of shots—*pop-pop-pop-pop-pop!*—echoed up the hill. Gunshot victims fell, and added more screams to the din.

Dazed, Howard looked up the hill. There were people there, too, but they weren't fighting; they were watching, staring in surprise.

Howard's thoughts were fogged with rage, but something was trying to make its way through the anger: This was a bad place. Down the hill it was worse, but up the hill, it was better. Therefore . . .

"Come on!" he yelled to his family. "We have to get up the hill!"

"Fuck off!" Tyrone yelled back.

Little Nadine released her hold on the judge, who was screaming in pain. She stared at Howard. "What is going on?" she said, her voice high and frightened.

"I don't know. Gas, maybe. We've got to get out of here. Help me."

His wife kneed the judge in the nuts again. The man gurgled in agony. Howard grabbed her, pulled her off.

"Leave me alone! He hit my son!"

Howard jerked her backward. "Tyrone!"

The boy turned, and the mask of primal rage on his face slipped a little. He raised his eyebrows. "Dad?"

"Up the hill, son, up the hill. Go, go!"

Tyrone nodded. Little Nadine grabbed his hand and they started running.

Howard had to pin Nadine's arms to her side and he half carried, half dragged her away from the meadow. She kicked and screamed at him for a hundred meters before she stopped. She was a lot stronger than he'd realized.

Finally, when they were two hundred meters away, Nadine came back. "J-John? What—?"

"I don't know, hon. But whatever it is, the farther away we get, the better. Come on."

They caught up to the children, and the four of them kept moving. Howard looked back as they ran. The Cadillac was lying on its side, and a mob had the driver out and on the ground, kicking him. He was a dead man. More gunshots echoed from farther below. Horns honked. Cars crashed. People screamed in voices full of incoherent fury. This beautiful park, what the locals like to call God's country, had gone mad.

It was the Devil's land, now.

Howard reached for his virgil. Who to call? The local cops were down there shooting people. They needed help, and they needed it bad.

Sunday, June 12th
Quantico, Virginia

Toni had come with him this time, and he was glad to have her here. Along with Toni was Jay Gridley. It was seven P.M. on a Sunday, but they wouldn't be going home tonight.

"All right, here is what we have so far," Michaels said. "It's still kind of sketchy. Late this afternoon, people inside what appears to be a rough circle ten miles across and centered in the Westmoreland area of Portland, Oregon, went nuts. So far, there are sixty-seven confirmed deaths—murders, self-defense, traffic and freak accidents. There have been hundreds of people hurt bad enough to require hospitalization, and thousands more lesser injuries. Whatever caused it seems to have stopped, but the city is in chaos. The numbers of dead and injured keep climbing."

"Lord, Lord. How is General Howard?" Jay asked.

Howard had been the one who'd called it in. He'd gotten hold of the National Guard, then Michaels.

"He and his family are fine. They were apparently right at the outmost edge of the phenomenon's effect. A couple hundred meters closer in, and they'd have been in a lot more trouble. What have you got for me?"

Jay said, "If we assume this is coming from some very

powerful broadcast station, then it's a matter of figuring out which one, and who is running it. I played a hunch and put in a call to HAARP, talked to a guard there. They are supposedly on hiatus, except for some calibration tests."

"That's what Morrison told me," Michaels said.

"Well, Morrison is up there right now running one of these tests. And guess what—according to the guard's logs, he was running other 'calibrations' on the same days those two villages in China went bonkers."

"Jesus."

"Yeah. Awful coincidental, ain't it?"

"Toni? What do you think?"

"I think maybe you ought pick up this Dr. Morrison for a serious chat."

Michaels nodded. "I'll get a federal warrant and some marshals on the way."

"You don't want to toss this one over the fence to the mainline feebs?" Jay said.

"Not yet," Michaels said. "This looks like our mess. We should clean it up on our own if we can."

Maybe Morrison wasn't involved with this, but given the situation in Portland, they couldn't afford to take the chance. The next incident might happen anywhere—New York, Chicago, even Washington, D.C. While the thought of senators and congressmen beating each other to bloody pulps sounded fine as a joke punch line, the reality of it was different.

Getting a warrant would be easy enough, and there were probably federal marshals somewhere in Alaska who could serve it. And while he was at it, he would give

General Howard a call. After his personal experience, John might like to go along to have a few words with Morrison himself. In his position, Michaels knew he would.

22

Ventura looked at his watch. It had been six hours since the real test had ended, but Morrison felt he had to play out the fiction of conducting his calibrations. In the end, Ventura knew that wouldn't matter, but Morrison felt the need. It was late, and Ventura, while not tired, was feeling somewhat edgy. There had been no contact from the Chinese, and he didn't much like sitting in one place for so long, not this far into the game. The trailer had a stale smell to it, and the night had cooled some, because an electric heater kept kicking on and off.

As the HAARP system did its automatic thing, Morrison himself was lying on the ugly brown fake-leather couch at the end of the room, fast asleep.

Ventura's com vibrated soundlessly against his hip. He

touched the mouthpiece of the small wireless headset he wore hooked over his left ear. "Yes?"

"We have company. Two cars, four men. They just passed Rim One."

"Talk to me."

"Tan Fords, unmarked, new, blackwall tires, what looks like government fleet plates. Three men, one woman, couldn't get much more than that. Cunningham will get a better view with his digital scope when they go under the rail overpass."

"Got it."

Ventura felt chill bumps rise on his neck, the gooseflesh warning him of danger. Who would come here in the middle of the night? He looked at his watch again. If they were traveling the speed limit, they'd be reaching the overpass . . . right . . . about . . . now . . .

The phone vibrated.

"Go."

Styles said, "From the front, three men, one woman. Clean-cut, mid-thirties, matching dark windbreakers, blue maybe. Hold on, they are going past . . . Angle is bad here, I can't see their backs. I got a flash of what looked like some kind of logo on the jackets from the side, can't get it all, last letters look like H-A-L . . . That's it. Plates are like Zach said, U.S. permanent fleet."

Sounded like feds. H-A-L. Last few letters of "Marshal," as in reflective yellow letters on the back of a windbreaker: U.S. Marshal. Of course, if it was him coming to collect Dr. Morrison, this was the kind of thing he'd do. Disguising your kidnap team as cops or firemen or federal agents was clever. Who stops a fireman on the way to a fire? Or a cop on his way to an accident?

Unless, of course, they were *real* feds.

"Got it. Discom."

Ventura called the leader of the two men watching the gate into the compound. "Let them pass, but see if you can get an ear on the guard at the gate if he lets them in."

"Copy."

Ventura broke the connection, walked to where Morrison lay sleeping. "Wake up, Dr. Morrison."

"Huh? What—?"

"Listen carefully. My people report that there are two cars that look like they belong to the feds on their way here."

The phone vibrated yet again.

"Go."

"Our shotgun mike picked up the exchange. Guys in the car say they are U.S. Marshals, come to serve a federal arrest warrant. They asked where they could find Morrison. The guard told them, and let them pass."

"Got it. Pull back to Rendezvous A, call the other teams and tell them."

"Copy."

Ventura made another call. "Mercury falling," he said.

"Copy. We'll be there."

"Discom."

Ventura looked at Morrison. "These guys convinced the gate guard they were U.S. Marshals. They've come to collect you."

Morrison shook his head. "No way. They can't know I had anything to do with this. I covered myself."

"Convince me."

"Nobody actually took anything from the computer files; it only *looks* like they did. I got into the HAARP system from a Mac store in San Francisco, using a floor demo model connected to the net. I had a password, but I banged on the door a few times to make it look good before I used it. I damaged a few files on the way in. It was a crowded Saturday morning, nobody noticed me, I didn't speak to anybody in the shop. Even if somebody could backtrack it through the store's server, it ends there—I was just another customer browsing the hardware and I used voxax to light the system. No hands, so no prints, no DNA. Nobody could *possibly* connect it to me."

"All right. So if they aren't real feds, then they must be from the Chinese." He shook his head. "But that doesn't scan."

"Why not?"

"The Chinese know I'm with you, and they know who I am, at least partially. But they only sent four people. They must be banking on us buying the trick, and that's too many eggs in one basket. Unless . . . this is a feint. A ploy designed to keep our attention while they try something else. Yes, that makes more sense."

"What are we going to do?"

"Leave. That little scooter is quiet and in the dark; they won't see us. A pickup car is waiting at a spot where nobody will notice it."

"There are plenty of outside lights until you get well away from the buildings," Morrison said. "And the pad is also lit up like a Christmas tree. They'll notice *us*."

"No, they won't. Come on."

As he followed Ventura from the trailer, terror gripped Morrison in its clammy hand. He needed to visit a bathroom, bad, and it was hard for him to breathe without wanting to pant. None of this had been in his plan, none of it. It didn't feel real. It felt like some kind of demented dream.

Since there was no way the FBI or Net Force could know who he was, it had to be the bastard Chinese coming for him. And he had no doubt that if they caught him and put him in a cell with somebody who even *threatened* to pull out his fingernails or crush his testicles, he'd tell them anything they wanted to know.

And it wouldn't take long in the telling, either.

The technique for disrupting the human brain into a temporary psychosis wasn't something easy to figure out, but once it was grasped, it was easy enough to *do*. The trick that had eluded researchers for all those years was that while they had all the pieces to the puzzle, they just hadn't been able to put them together. Or even known they should. The broadcast frequencies had to be varied precisely, they had to run for a very specific duration, and they had to be repeated at exact intervals. It took a computer to run the sequence—it was too involved for a human hand—and if one variable was off even a hair, the technique simply wouldn't work. The odds of happening on the proper code by accident were astronomically high, even to achieve the partial results Morrison had managed. He didn't deny to himself that he had been lucky, as well as good. And the truth was, driving people mad had never been his goal—controlling their actions in a more deliberate manner had been, and he had failed in that. It was as if he had gone searching for diamonds but had found opals, instead. Still valuable stones, but not what he had sought, and— Hey! Where was Ventura going?

"The scooter is over there," Morrison said. "We're heading the wrong way!"

"No, we're not. We need to do something first."

Ventura had his pistol out, and they were moving toward the power building. Morrison had his little gun in the pocket of his jacket, but it offered him little comfort. If they got past Ventura, he didn't believe he was going to be able to stop them. He could *die* here. Tonight. Soon.

The headlights of the approaching cars shined through the trees. They were almost here!

He voiced the thought: "They're almost here!"

But they were at the power building. Ventura said, "You stay put. I'm going to go have a short conversation with the power supply."

Ventura vanished inside the building.

Morrison tried to calm down. He forced himself to take long, slow breaths, but it didn't help. His heart was racing so hard he could feel it pulse all over his body. *Come on, come on, come on—!*

The lights died, and the heavy *thrum* of the diesel generators began to fade.

Ventura appeared from nowhere. "They want lights, they are going to have to crank those babies back up. Let's go."

"What about nightscopes? Won't they have those?"

"I would, but it won't matter if they do. I have a little something for any spookeyes that might go on-line." He patted his pocket. "Come on, time to leave." He smiled. It was the most joyful expression Morrison had seen Ventura make.

It was like a glass of cold water in the face. The realization that came with it was: "You're *enjoying* this!"

"Of course. It's what I do, Doctor. Stay with me."

They ran.

• • •

Ventura felt the adrenaline surge in him, and he didn't try to stop it. Riding the hormonal high was like climbing onto a half-wild stallion. If you could stay there and point him in the right direction, it would be a thrilling trip at breakneck speed. Bend him to your will just enough, and you could fly like the wind. Lose control, and you would surely perish.

This was the zen of life and death, and the part of him he kept hidden from the world. It was the stretch, the reach, the ultimate test, the perfect way to be totally in the moment. The past was dead, the future not yet born, there was only the *now!* Fail, and you die. Succeed, and you live.

Ah, but to make it a real test, you had to level the playing field. Four against one was not fair, not when the one was Ventura. He had the advantage. They had to capture Morrison alive, so they were hobbled. Therefore, he would give them a chance. He could have taken Morrison and fled immediately. Turning out the lights wasn't necessary—they wouldn't be looking for two men on a scooter, they would be expecting their quarry to be in a trailer. Even if they were nothing but a probe designed to keep him busy while the real attack was mounted, Ventura was aware of this possibility, too. He was way ahead of them, he knew it, and in no real danger. So he delayed. Killed the power, which gave him darkness, but which also gave them a warning: I know you are here. Let's play. Come and find me.

There was no joy in slaying an unarmed man. The challenge was in bypassing his trained guards to get to him. It was the stalk that mattered most not the shot, the path and not the destination. Once in the proper position, any fool could pull a trigger. Getting to the proper position was the trick. Always.

"This way," Morrison said.

"How can you tell? I can't fucking see anything!"

The two cars pulled to a halt, and Ventura heard doors slamming and voices raised.

"Trust me," Ventura said. "I know exactly what I am doing."

His phone vibrated.

"What?"

"Another player approaching. Black man in a new Dodge van, Alaskan plates, looks like a rental car. Just passed me."

Ventura frowned. Who was this? Just a coincidence? Some fisherman running late for his hotel reservation, or part of the backup plan? And a black man? That would be unusual. The Chinese didn't much like black people. Of course, they didn't much like anybody who wasn't Chinese. A lot of people in the West didn't realize that Eastern societies were the most racist on Earth. They not only despised and looked down on Westerners, they despised and looked down on each other. The Chinese hated the Japanese who hated the Koreans who hated the Vietnamese, and all variations thereof. The only thing worse than being a foreigner was being a half-breed.

Well. Whoever he was, it didn't matter. As long as Ventura knew where the man was, he was no problem, just one more piece on the board he needed to track. "Keep me advised," Ventura said. He tapped the headset off.

"Let's go for a little ride in the cool summer night, shall we, Doctor?"

Morrison stared at him, and that wide-eyed sense of amazement that arrived when he'd realized that Ventura was having fun here was still on his face.

A man like Morrison couldn't understand it, of course. Men like him never did.

23

Tyrone stood by the Coke machine at the hotel and ran his credit card through the scanner slot. The credit appeared on the screen, and he tapped the button that delivered a plastic bottle of the cola. The noise it made seemed loud in the quiet night.

He was still rattled. Once everything seemed to be okay, his dad had gone off to Alaska, to help collect the man supposedly responsible for what had happened at the boomerang tournament. Tyrone, Nadine, and his mother were at the motel, miles away from the park, and the madness had stopped, but he couldn't forget it. It was like some kind of nightmare. He had wanted to kill people, and if he'd had a weapon—a knife or a gun or a stick—he *would* have killed somebody. And the thing was, it would have felt just great to do it, too.

He sipped at the soft drink. Life had been easier when he'd been into computers. He sat at home, jacked into the web, lived his life in VR. Once he'd discovered girls and boomerangs, things had gotten a lot more complex. Nothing risked, nothing gained—but nothing lost, either. But the thought of going back to where he'd been before, a web-head with butt calluses from sitting in a chair? That just didn't resonate. Data interruptus, Jimmy-Joe would say.

The tournament had been canceled after all the crazy stuff. He'd never even gotten a chance to compete. Given all the other crap, winning or losing a contest like that meant zed, but even so, he wondered how he would have done.

"Hey, Ty."

He looked up to see Nadine standing there. "Hey," he said.

"Couldn't sleep?"

"Yeah."

"Me, neither."

They stood silently for a few seconds. "You want a Coke?"

"I'll just have a sip of yours, if that's okay."

"Sure." He passed her the plastic bottle and watched her sip from it.

She handed the bottle back to him. "You think it's true?" she said. "That somebody did it on purpose?"

"My dad thinks so, and he knows about stuff like this, so, yeah, I think so."

"Why? Why would somebody do a thing like that? Zap people and make them go crazy? Make people hurt each other?"

He shook his head. "I don't know. I can't think of any reason good enough."

"I didn't like how it made me feel," she said. "I was so angry. I *wanted* to hurt people. I didn't care about them at all. I was watching the vids on the news. They showed a Catholic school somewhere. Some nuns beat a janitor to a pulp. How could that be? Something that could make nuns do that, that's really scary."

He could see she was on the edge of tears, really upset. "Yeah. Scares me, too. But it's okay. My dad is going to get the guy. It'll be all right."

"You think so?"

"Yeah. I do."

She gave him a little smile, and he felt better himself. He took another sip from the Coke. He hoped his dad would kick the guy's ass.

Monday, June 13th
Gakona, Alaska

Howard was still peeved. The marshals were supposed to meet him at the airport, but his plane had been delayed an hour coming out of SeaTac, and they hadn't waited for him. He hated being late, but there had been no help for it. He couldn't really bitch about it officially; Net Force didn't have any jurisdiction in the matter per se, even though they had gotten the warrants and the marshals would be delivering Morrison to HQ in Quantico. And as the commander of Net Force's military arm, he shouldn't be out in the field on this kind of errand anyhow, no job for a general, but it pissed him off being left behind just the same. It was no more than professional courtesy—he'd have waited for them.

Howard rented a car and burned the speed limits trying to catch up, but by the time he got to Gakona, he still hadn't seen any sign of the marshals. He couldn't believe he had gotten ahead of them, so they must have already reached the HAARP compound. Probably had already collected Morrison and were on the way back. Well, if they passed him going the other way, he'd spot them, there wasn't that much traffic. He'd seen only a few cars and trucks in the last hour of travel, and nobody in the last fifteen minutes. Of course, it was almost two in the morning, and in the middle of the great northwest woods, too, not exactly the Harbor Freeway in downtown L.A.

The narrow road he was on ran parallel to a tall chain-link fence topped with razor wire and hung with government warning signs. HAARP would be on the other side of the fence, somewhere past the thick forest of evergreens.

The call of nature that had been nagging at him for miles finally couldn't be denied any longer. If he didn't stop and take a whiz, he was going to drown.

He pulled the car over, shut off the engine, and killed the headlamps. He waited for a moment for his night vision to clear, then stepped out of the car.

He watered the plants nearest the shoulder, felt a lot better, and zipped up.

It was *really* dark out here, nothing offering relief save for a clear sky thick with glittery stars and the glowing face of his watch. It was cool, but not cold, and the scent of evergreen, car exhaust, and even urine blended into a not-unpleasant odor. It was also quiet, save for a few mosquitoes buzzing about. There was something very relaxing about being out in the middle of nowhere, nobody else around.

From the last road sign he'd seen, he judged that he was almost to the compound's gate. He started back toward the car when he saw a bright flash of light over the treetops, almost like distant heat lightning, a brief strobe against the night. What was that?

But the light was gone, and once again the fierce darkness claimed the night. And that was odd, because this close, he expected some kind of glow from the HAARP compound bleeding into the sky. He had been on night patrols in the outback where you could see the light from a campfire or a propane lantern for miles. They must keep some lights on, right?

Almost immediately after the light faded, he heard three shots, a stacatto *pap! pap! pap!* followed by two more that resonated with a louder, sharper *crack! crack!* The shots echoed, and it was hard to pinpoint the direction, but it sounded as if they were to his right and behind him. Inside the fence, and not too far off. There was no question in Howard's mind that the reports came from weapons, and they sounded like handguns. Two shooters, close together, using different calibers. The second of them, he was almost certain, was a .357 Magnum, a round with which he was very familiar, having fired tens of thousands of them himself. Two shooters firing at the same target? Or at each other?

Almost reflexively, he reached down to where the new revolver rode back of his right hip, to touch the gun's butt and reassure himself it was still there.

It could have been a lot of things—spotlighters doing some illegal hunting, drunks blasting at beer bottles, maybe even a couple of campers attacked in their tent by

a bear and cutting loose at it—but knowing there were
U.S. Marshals serving an arrest warrant on a man suspected of involvement in multiple deaths, Howard had to
consider that maybe something had gone wrong with the
operation. And what would campers or hunters be doing
inside the fence?

He pulled the door open and slid back into the rental
car, started the engine, and hit the light switch. The entrance gate was ahead of him, and that was the way to
get into the compound, but he spun the wheel and the car
into a one-eighty and headed back the way he had come.
When guns go off, that's where you find the action.

It was half a mile away when things got tricky. Because
it was so dark and he was moving and watching the fence
to his left, and because the black SUV was parked off to
the right in the trees, he almost missed it. A glint of light
off the windshield—the SUV was facing the road at a
right angle—was what he caught, and a fast glance didn't
give him much more. He took his foot off the gas pedal,
but managed to keep from hitting the brakes, so his tail-
lights didn't flare. He kept going, considering his options.

The SUV could have been parked there empty for days,
for all he knew. Maybe it belonged to those hypothetical
campers shooting at the equally hypothetical bear. For
some reason in that moment, an old memory popped up:
An Alaskan hunter he'd known had once told him that if
you had to stop a really big bear, you needed a heavy
rifle or a shotgun with slugs to do it. He said that when
newbies to the tundra asked about which caliber handguns
to carry, they were told it didn't really matter, but that
they should file the front sight off nice and smooth—that
way it wouldn't hurt so much when the bear took it away
from them and shoved it up where the sun didn't shine . . .

Options, John, options!

He could keep going and do nothing. He could keep going, use his virgil, and call for help. Of course he was hours by road or even air from any law to speak of, and that was too long. Besides, until he knew what he was facing, he couldn't risk using his virgil. There was a chance that the perpetrators, whoever they were, would pick up his call. They wouldn't be able to decode it, but they might trace his location—and at the very least they would know he was still out there.

No, it was against SOP, but he had no choice. What he was going to do was keep going until he was around a curve or far enough away so anybody who might be in the SUV would think he was gone, then he would pull over and backtrack on foot. He was dressed in jeans, black running shoes, and a dark green T-shirt, with a dark green windbreaker, so he'd be practically invisible in the trees. He had some bug dope in his kit, though the mosquitoes didn't usually bother him that much. He had his little SL-4 flashlight from Underwater Kinetics, and he had the Phillips and Rodgers with its six rounds, a speed strip with six more rounds zipped into his jacket pocket. What else did he need for a walk in the Alaskan woods at night?

The idea of action filled him with sudden purpose. As the road curved, he killed the lights and coasted off the shoulder. He pulled the car behind a patch of scrub brush—not perfect, but what cover was available. He switched the dome light off before he opened the door, and as soon as the trunk light went on, he grabbed it to block the glow, and collected his kit bag with his free hand. He fished out the flashlight and stuck it into his back pocket, found two more speed strips of ammo and pocketed those. Found the bug dope and a packet of wa-

terproof matches, too. He remembered to shut off his virgil, then started working his way back along the treeline
toward the SUV. It was maybe three-quarters of a mile
back. It would only take a few minutes to get there. He'd
scope out the scenario and see what he could figure out.
He could call Net Force or the local state cops and give
them a sitrep after that.

Man. He'd never expected this, but he was in it now,
and he'd have to follow up and see it through—whatever
it was . . .

Ventura glanced at his watch. Just past 0200. He had
given them the clue by killing the lights, but the kidnap
team still hadn't spotted him. He frowned. Were they really that bad? And where was the genuine attack, if these
four were only faking? Were they that good, that his people hadn't spotted them?

He called the surveillance team. "Where is my black
man?"

"Still heading toward the gate. He passed the Mercury
Falling point a minute ago. Should be there soon."

They'd be long gone by the time anybody came
through the front gate and got here. "All right. Let me
know when—" He cut it off as he spotted the threat.

Two seconds later, Morrison saw it, too. "Look!"

One of the kidnappers had left his vehicle and circled
around one of the trailers. The man was twenty-five,
maybe twenty-eight meters away. Dim as it was, it was
only his darker form against the lighter color of the building that gave him away. Was he sight- or hearing-
augmented? Did he see them? Could he hear the little fuel
cell motor?

Ventura could hear the man, because Ventura was

wearing bat ears—tiny electronic plugs that functioned both as a hearing aid for normal sounds and suppressors for sudden loud noises.

Ventura pulled the flash grenade from his pocket, thumbed the safety ring out and flipped the cover up, then pressed the timer button. He had five seconds, and he wanted it to go off in the air. One . . . two . . . three . . . four—throw, the overhand lob, up and outward . . .

Ventura closed his eyes against the bright flash he knew was coming. It wouldn't make much noise.

He could see the photonic blast through his closed eyelids anyway. It faded, and he opened his eyes at the same time he heard the kidnapper's startled yell. If the man was wearing spookeyes, that would close the automatic shutters for a heartbeat. If he wasn't, his night vision was going to be gone.

Ventura drew his pistol and goosed the little scooter. The kidnapper fired three shots, but from the angle of the flashes, he was shooting way behind them. Probably no spookeyes, then.

Ventura indexed the flashes and shot back, two rounds. His own earplugs cut out the harsh noise within a hundredth of a second, suppressing the hurtful decibel level. He heard the man scream, and heard him hit the ground.

One down.

He circled the scooter away and back toward the fence, along the path he'd decided upon earlier. He did a tactical reload, changed magazines, dropping the one missing a round into his pocket. Something bothered him, something was wrong, and it took a few seconds before he figured out what it was:

Why had the kidnapper shot at them? Two men on a scooter, more than twenty meters away, in the dark? It was a very risky shot; Ventura was an expert with his pistol and he wouldn't have chanced it. Even if the shooter knew which man was which, how could he take the risk of hitting Morrison? He'd have to know that if he killed the scientist, the game was over, and his ass would be fried. Could the Chinese have hired somebody that foolish? Somebody who would panic at a bright light and accidentally cook the golden goose?

It was one more inconsistency that didn't add up. But he'd have to work it out later—there were still three of them running around, and the one who had gotten into range had surprised him. You didn't want to tilt the playing field too far in your enemy's favor. Ventura did not have a death wish.

"You shot him," Morrison said.

"Yes, I did."

"Is he . . . dead, do you think?"

Ventura shrugged. "Who cares? He knew the job was dangerous when he took it. If he didn't, then he's an idiot. Or he *was* an idiot. And he shot at us first, remember? We were just defending ourselves."

Morrison didn't say anything.

The fence was through that patch of woods just ahead, and there was a path through them. They could play Q&A later. One step at a time.

Be in the moment . . .

24

It had been a long time since Howard had done any real hunting, and even the most realistic VR scenario was not the same as creeping through the woods and sneaking up on a vehicle that might or might not contain unfriendlies. In this case, it had to be done by feel—it was so damned dark he ran a real risk of smacking his face into trees if he didn't go slow. He couldn't use his flashlight, that would be way too easy to spot, and he didn't even want to think about bumping into some hungry critter bigger than he was.

His advantage was that if he couldn't see them, they probably couldn't see him. Even if there were a couple of bad guys in the SUV and they had starlight scopes, he'd be hard to spot unless they were looking right at him, and unless they had eyes in the backs of their heads, or just happened to have their scopes pointed at the rearview mirror, they weren't apt to be looking right at him.

Once he'd left the edge of the woods and moved in deeper to circle around behind the vehicle, it took a few minutes to crawl up behind it. He inched his way forward in the old knees and elbows locomotion, until he was only a couple of meters behind the black SUV, a Ford Explorer. The thing had tinted windows so dark he probably couldn't have seen inside even in bright sunshine, much less the near-pitch night out here. Nobody inside smoked cigarettes to reveal themselves with a telltale glow, there was no radio playing, nobody talking. No sign that the Explorer was anything but empty. And wouldn't he feel stupid if it turned out he was stalking an empty car?

Yeah. But worry about that later.

He inched closer, until he was right at the back bumper. He had in mind listening very carefully, maybe making a little noise to see if there would be any kind of response, but he didn't get that far. A man's voice said, "I gotta piss."

"We're supposed to stay in the car until we see the signal."

"Fuck the signal. I can see it just as well taking a leak as I can from in here."

The passenger door opened, but the dome light didn't go on. The door stayed open and the sound of footsteps approaching on dry fir needles got louder fast. The guy was walking around to the back of the truck!

Even this dark, he'd likely see or hear Howard if he tried to crawl away.

Howard flattened himself fully prone and used his knees to push himself under the Explorer.

Three heartbeats later, the sound of a stream of urine

splashing against the side of a tree came loud in the night. It went on for a long time, and Howard could even hear the man's pants' zipper going back up when he was done.

The peeing man was halfway back to the car door when the driver said, "There it is! Come on, get in!"

From his vantage point under the vehicle, Howard couldn't see much, but he was able to catch a glimmer of light from across the road.

That would be the signal.

Who was giving the signal and what exactly it meant, well, that wasn't altogether clear, but the gist of it was fairly evident to Howard. Somebody was on the other side of the fence that surrounded HAARP, and these two were there to meet whoever it was. His money was on that somebody being Morrison, otherwise it was going to be one hell of a coincidence.

The Ford's engine cranked, and that was incredibly loud from where Howard lay, his head directly under it. He heard the *clunk!* as the driver shifted the transmission from park into gear.

If the guy swung any kind of sharp turn when he pulled out, he'd feel a big bump at the same time John Howard felt the back wheel crush him. He took a deep breath—

The driver pulled straight out, and across the road before he wheeled the big SUV into a tight right turn broadside to Howard. The peeing man jumped out and ran around the car toward the fence, Howard could see him in the red glow of the brake lights. He was carrying what looked like a big pair of hedge clippers, and it took a second for Howard to realize that the tool wasn't for trimming bushes but was actually a pair of bolt cutters.

This was definitely a bad business, whatever it was.

Howard came up, pulled his revolver and started across

the narrow road toward the Explorer, crouching low as he moved. There would be at least three of them, maybe more, and covering them all would be a bitch, but what choice did he have? He couldn't just let them drive away—at least not until he knew what was going on.

The *plinks!* of the cutters snipping the chainlinks sounded crisp in the night.

Howard had almost made it to the Ford's passenger door when the driver looked up and saw him.

"Incoming!" the driver screamed. "Incoming!"

Howard zigged to his left, toward the car's rear, just as a gunshot exploded inside the Explorer. An orange tongue of fire reached from the driver, the passenger window shattered, and the bullet passed somewhere to his right, close enough so he heard it whistle by.

Bad guys—no goddamned doubt about it.

The noise inside the SUV must have been deafening. The driver took his foot off the brake, and the brake lights went out, plunging the scene back into darkness.

Howard still had the after-image of the gunshot seared into his retina, and his rods and cones or whatever weren't doing their job. He rounded the back of the Explorer, dropped prone, and looked for a target.

"Move the car," somebody said. They didn't sound the least bit excited.

The driver stepped on the gas. The smell of burned tire filled the air as the Explorer screeched and lurched forward.

Howard's central vision was still fogged, but he turned his head to the left and caught a peripheral movement. They had *shot at him,* therefore they were bad guys. He hesitated for maybe a quarter second, then lined the revolver up on the movement and squeezed the trigger. He

remembered to close his eyes as the shot went off, to save
what vision he had left, and then he rolled to his left as
fast as he could, three complete revolutions.

Somebody screamed, and somebody returned fire. The
dragon's tongue muzzle blast lit the scene just enough for
Howard to see there were two men standing next to a hole
clipped through the fence, a third man lying on the
ground. A bullet spanged off the road where he had been
and the ricochet whined off into the trees.

Howard scraped his elbows on the road as he swung
the revolver sideways and pointed it where he'd seen the
flash—

"Move," a man said, insistent, but not panicky.

Whoever he is, he's a lot calmer than I am—

The scream of brakes forced Howard to glance away
from his target zone just as he cranked off two more shots.
He rolled again, and saw the Explorer's headlights flash
on as the SUV did a rubber-burning one-eighty.

The driver was going to put some light on the subject,
and that was bad—

An answering pair of shots spewed more orange, and
two more bullets hit the road inches away. If he hadn't
rolled, he'd have eaten both of them, and even so, the
shooter had almost anticipated enough to hit him.

Howard leaped up. He had to get off the road before—

Too late. The SUV's headlights found him. He took
three steps then dived for the side of the road, hit in a
sloppy shoulder roll, came up, and ran for the trees. More
gunshots reached for him, but missed. The roar of the
SUV's engine increased as it headed back in his direction.
The driver angled the vehicle, trying to find him with the
light.

Howard slipped on something, fell, and rolled, ending

up on his back, feet facing the oncoming Explorer. He pulled his feet toward his butt, propped the revolver on top of his left knee, got a nice clear sight picture outlined against the oncoming headlights. He aimed at the windshield on the driver's side. The SUV was fifty meters away and closing. He pulled the trigger, one, two, three, four—

The gun stopped shooting after three times, clicked empty, but the SUV slewed off the road and angled into the fence, bowing a big section before it took out a post and stopped.

His piece was empty, and there was still too much reflected light out here; he felt like a bug under a microscope. He scrabbled up and into the trees, managed to run into one with his right shoulder and spin himself around, but at least he was hidden. He dropped to the ground on his butt, thumbed the cylinder latch, shoved the cylinder out with his left hand, hammered the extractor rod with the palm. Empty shells flew. He grabbed a speed strip and started to reload. One, two, three—

The SUV's motor raced, and there came the sound of metal tearing. The motor roared louder, the tires screamed—

He must have missed the driver. Either that, or the other two had gotten to the SUV.

Load, load, come on, come on—!

—four, five, *six!*

He snapped the cylinder closed and crawled toward the road. As he reached the edge of the trees, the Explorer roared past, accelerating away.

"Fuck that!" Howard yelled. He scrambled up, ran into the road, and whipped his gun up in both hands. The SUV was really moving; it was eighty, ninety meters away as he cooked off all six as fast as he could, closing his eyes to avoid the muzzle flashes—

Again the SUV squealed into a one-eighty turn, and the lights came around to find Howard. But the car didn't start back, it just sat there. Ninety meters—okay, okay, he had time to reload again—

The SUV's door slammed shut. Somebody got out?

Howard ejected the empties, reached for another speed loader. Plenty of time—

He saw the muzzle flash, felt the kick in his belly from a heavy boot as he went down, *then* heard the *boom!* from the weapon.

Fuck! He was *shot* and his gun was empty. His side burned, over his right hip. *Get up, John, get up, now!*

He half-crawled, half-rolled off the road and back to the woods. In the trees, he kept moving, his fist jammed over the bullet wound. He got as far as he could before his legs just quit working. He sat, fumbled for his virgil, managed to trigger the distress signal as he felt himself graying out. His last thoughts as he lost consciousness were of disbelief: How could somebody have hit a target at ninety meters like that? With a handgun, and only the headlights of a car in the dark?

Hell of a shot . . .

Gakona, Alaska

"What the hell happened?" Morrison said again and again. "What the hell happened?"

The cool night air whistled through the car from the three holes in the windshield. Morrison, in the back, was

probably in shock, but at that, he was a lot better off than
Ventura's two men. One of them was dead on the seat
next to him, slumped against the passenger door; he'd
taken one right between the eyes. The other man was lying next to the fence back at the pickup point, and he was
just as dead, one to the heart. Nice work.

The black man had done it. Ventura didn't know who
the hell he had been, but he'd screwed things up pretty
good. How had the black guy managed to find them and
set up his ambush? That had been a good trick. Still, it
didn't matter. He was probably dead or dying himself by
now. Ventura had put one solidly into him; he wasn't
going to be causing any more trouble. If he was the Chinese's primary attack, he'd failed, even though he had
caused a lot of trouble. He should have been wearing a
vest. Odd that he wasn't. Ventura had his on.

The client was alive, and they would rendezvous with
more of Ventura's team in a couple of minutes. Nice try,
but no cigar.

"What the hell happened?"

"Relax, it's okay now. They tried, but they failed. We'll
regroup and wait for them to contact us."

"Are you crazy?"

"Listen, you can't take this personally. It's just business. They tried, they missed, so now they'll deal. Nothing has changed."

"I could have gotten killed!"

"And you still could. But none of this matters. What
matters is that you aren't dead *now*. You still have something they want, and they are still going to have to pay
to get it. You move on."

"This is madness," Morrison said.

"Way of the world, Doctor. If you don't want to get

hit, don't step into the ring. You're here now, so we have to make the best of it. Think of it as a great story to tell your new friends someday."

He saw Morrison in the rearview mirror, his face dimly lit by the instrument lights. The man looked as if somebody had just told him there was a rattlesnake in his pocket.

Ventura watched the road, his pistol in his lap. Amateurs just didn't understand how the world worked. They took everything so personal.

25

"Sir?"

Michaels came out of a shallow sleep, blinking. He was in his office, on the couch. What—?

One of the night crew—Askins? Haskins?—stood in the doorway. Must not be time for shift change yet. Michaels sat up. "Yes?"

"We got a distress signal from General Howard's virgil. From Alaska."

"What?" He still wasn't quite awake and tracking yet. Where was Toni?

"Federal Marshals found him, he's been shot. An Alaska National Guard copter is on the way; he's up near Gakona."

He looked at his watch. It was six A.M. He needed to

wash his face and to find Toni. What had John gotten into?

But before he could reach the door, his own com chirped its top-priority tone. He hurried to the receiver and picked it up. "John?"

"No, it's Melissa Allison."

The director. What was she doing up at this hour?

She didn't give him time to wonder: "I just got a call from Adam Brickman in the U.S. Marshals office. One of his men was wounded in a shoot-out in Nowhere, Alaska, attempting to serve an arrest warrant authorized by *your* office. So was General John Howard. They are alive, just barely, on their way to a hospital in Anchorage, but Brickman isn't happy. *I'm* not happy, either, Commander, because when he started chewing me out for not warning his people this was a shoot-sit, I didn't know what the hell he was talking about."

Uh-oh. "I'm sorry, Madam Director, I didn't realize there was any danger."

"You sent marshals and the head of Net Force's military arm to pick up somebody—which is outside your charter, unless there are special circumstances. I'm going to be in my office in forty minutes. I suggest you be there when I arrive."

"Yes, ma'am," Michaels said.

He cradled the receiver. Great. Just great. He had a federal marshal and John Howard shot up and the director of the FBI ready to tear him a new asshole. Great way to start the day, wasn't it? Maybe if he was lucky, a big meteor would fall on him.

"Alex?"

Toni. "Hey," he said.

"What's up? The place feels as if it's about to explode."

He rubbed at his face with both hands. "Walk with me and I'll fill you in."

In the air over British Columbia

Because Ventura wanted to have a few words with the Chinese, he had Morrison's phone when it rang. He used the headset, the engine and wind noise of the DC-3 being enough to interfere with hearing.

"Dr. Morrison?"

"No. Ventura."

"Ah, Luther. How are you?"

"Why, I'm just fine, Chilly. Though I can't say the same for your people. The feint was pretty good, but the follow-through was, well, sad. I expected better."

There was a moment's hesitation. Then Wu said, "Much as I'd like to turn this to my advantage, I have to confess I don't know what you are talking about, Luther."

"Come on, we're professionals here, I don't hold it against you, I realize it was just business."

"Nope, sorry, I'm not tracking."

Ventura considered it. There was no real reason for Wu to be coy. He knew that if they tried to snatch Morrison and failed, Ventura wouldn't care; it was how things were done, they were men of the world here. "So you didn't send people to, ah, have an informal chat with my client?"

"No."

Ventura heard the "Not yet" in that single word, but he also had to stop and think real hard about the implications. Of course Wu would lie if it was to his advantage, that was to be expected. But Wu had to know he couldn't gull anybody into believing that the Chinese were benevolent businessmen who'd never stoop to such a thing as kidnapping and torture. Sure, they'd pay if they had to pay, but if they could get what they wanted for free, they'd do it. They were as cheap as anybody else.

So lying wouldn't serve him at this point—Ventura didn't trust Wu as far as he could fly by flapping his arms, and Wu knew it. And if Wu *hadn't* sent a team, then who were those men?

Had he just shot a couple of *real* federal marshals?

"Dr. Morrison is okay, isn't he?" Wu asked. "No problems with our little transaction? We were quite impressed with the test. We are ready to get down to brass tacks."

"He's fine. Here he is." Ventura waved at Morrison, who was listening to his half of the conversation. He held his thumb over the transmitter mike. "Wu. He's ready to deal. And don't get bent with him—he didn't send his people after you. Those were legitimate feds."

Morrison's eyes went wide. "It couldn't be—"

"You screwed up, Doctor. They figured it out, somehow, and now we have a whole new set of problems."

He handed Morrison the phone and headset. He had to make a couple of calls on his own to verify this, but if it turned out to be what he was now sure it was, he had some serious thinking to do. Very serious thinking.

Quantico, Virginia

Alex had gone off to see the director, and Toni took the opportunity to go to the gym. It wasn't as big as the rooms in the main FBI compound, but she didn't need much space. And early as it was, she was the only person there.

Nobody had gotten around to cleaning out her locker—there was still a pair of sweats and a sports bra folded neatly there, along with her Discipline martial arts shoes, and, by chance, the clothes were still clean, though a little stale. She shook everything out and dressed, then padded into the gym. She could have worked out in her street clothes, she made a point of doing that every so often, but since she didn't have any clean ones to change into afterward, that would have to wait for another time. If you couldn't do it in your ordinary wear, it didn't matter how terrific a move was; if you couldn't use it when you needed it, it was pointless for self-defense. In a streetfight, you wouldn't have time to take off your shoes, get dressed in your gi, nor ten minutes to stretch and warm up. Sweats and limbering exercises saved wear and tear on your clothes, muscles, and joints in the long run, that was why you did them, but they were luxuries, not necessities—

"Toni?"

She looked up and saw Jay. "Hey, Jay."

"Boss around?"

"He had to go see the Dragon Lady."

"Okay, I'll call him." He was in a hurry. He turned and started to leave.

"What's up, Jay?"

He paused. "You knew they found John Howard shot in the woods across the road from the HAARP compound?"

"Yeah."

"He was choppered to a hospital in Anchorage, and it looks like he's gonna be okay."

"Thank God."

"Yeah. He was supposed to be on vacation with his family. How'd he get to Alaska?"

Toni shook her head. Here was another problem for Alex, one he didn't need.

He needed *her*. But she couldn't go back to work for him. She couldn't.

Madam Director Allison was royally pissed. In her shoes, Michaels might have felt the same way, but he wasn't in her shoes, he was in his, and they were getting real damp from nervous sweat.

"And you felt you couldn't pass this along to me? I had to find it out from some other agency?"

He sat in the chair in front of her desk and nodded. "I didn't see the need. Four federal marshals went to pick up one desk-jockey scientist. I met the man. He could hardly stand up without losing his balance. He had no history of violence, no record of having purchased weapons. I asked John to go along to keep us in the loop. It was a milk run."

"Yes, a run that turned into the milkman taking a bullet in the pelvis under the edge of his vest, and your meek scientist disappearing, not even to mention the head of your military arm taking a round." She looked at the flatscreen on her desk. "According to the guards at this HAARP place, Morrison wasn't alone. He was accompanied by a Dr. Dick Grayson. His identity turns out to be bogus."

Despite the situation, Michaels smiled.

"Something funny about that I'm missing, Commander?"

"Dick Grayson is the secret identity of Batman's side-kick, Robin."

"Yes, well, 'Robin' is likely the man who plugged the marshal, along with John Howard, on his way out of town. The rest of the arrest team managed to gather themselves enough to pick up the trail. Morrison and his gun-toting friend took a small cart through the woods, cut a hole in the fence, and were presumably picked up by accomplices. The marshals found an armed dead man next to the hole in the fence, shot in the heart. No ID on the man.

"There were signs that a car had left the road and plowed into the fence fifty yards away. The marshals called in the state police, and a few minutes ago a shot-up Ford Explorer was found at an old airstrip. There were three bullet holes in the windshield, five more holes in the back loading gate and bumper, and another dead man in the front seat. No identification on him, either. Probably Howard's work."

"Huh," Michaels said.

"Oh, you can do better than that, Commander. You are supposed to be playing with computers. You are supposed to be finding and busting pirate ships in the Gulf peddling Viagra and steroids and diet pills over the internet without prescriptions, or hunting down teenaged hackers who post porno in church web pages. You went outside your authority, and I don't know what it is you stepped into, but whatever it is, it is on your shoes and it is *your* responsibility now. I want to know just what the hell is going on—"

His virgil, which he had forgotten to turn off, bleated the opening notes from the old rock and roll song, "Bad to the Bone."

Dah, dah, dah, dah, dah, *dump!*

The director frowned.

"Sorry," he said. He reached for the virgil to shut it off, but saw Jay's face on the tiny screen. If Gridley knew he was here, he wouldn't have bothered him if it wasn't important. "Jay?"

"Looks like John Howard is gonna make it, Boss."

"Thank God!"

"Already sent a few prayers in His direction."

"I appreciate the call, Jay," Michaels said. He discommed, then looked at the director. "Howard is going to pull through."

"That's good news, at least. Why don't you see if you can't add to it?"

26

When John Howard awoke, the first face he saw belonged
to Sergeant Julio Fernandez. With consciousness came the
awareness that he was in a bed, in a hospital room, and
that his right side and belly hurt like hell. He also had a
headache, his mouth was dry, and his arm had an IV tube
running into it. His last memory was of passing out in the
woods, and of all the hoopla before that—he knew what
had happened. He had been shot.

"He's awake," Fernandez said.

"How bad?" Howard asked.

"John!" That was Nadine.

He turned his head slightly—that was a good sign, he
could do that. "Hey, babe. Julio?"

"You're shy a loop of small intestine, but you won't
have to poop into a bag for the rest of your life or any-

thing. Won't even have a bullet scar in the front, they took that out when they went in to fix your plumbing, but you will have one in the back—round went right through, didn't hit anything else worth mentioning. Missed a kidney by a cun—uh, by a hair."

Howard nodded. "Thanks."

Nadine was there then, and there were tears and hugging. After which she called him a few names, the least of which was "stupid."

Man, he was glad to see her.

"Dad?"

"Hey, son."

Fernandez cranked the bed so Howard could sit up. Tyrone came over and smiled at him.

Howard said, "Where's your little friend?"

Tyrone frowned, then saw Howard grin and realized it was a joke. "She's in the waiting room. I'll go tell her you're okay. They wouldn't let anybody but family in."

Howard looked at Fernandez. He shrugged. "I told them I was your brother. They decided it wasn't worth arguing about."

A nurse came in, asked a couple of questions, then looked at the beeping machine to which he was wired. "The doctor will be in to see you in just a minute."

"Uh-huh. Sure. I've heard that one before."

She shook her head and left.

"How long have I been out?"

"Not long," Fernandez said. "Been about six hours since you got here."

"Where *is* here?"

"Anchorage. That's in Alaska."

"Thank you for that information, Sergeant. How did *you* get here so fast?"

"I have a friend in the Air Force who owed me a big favor. You haven't lived until you've done a supersonic barrel roll. Yee-haw."

Nadine said, "Are you okay, John?"

"I've felt better, but yeah, I'm okay."

"Good. I have to go to the bathroom. Stay right here."

He laughed. "Don't do that. It hurts to laugh."

She headed for the bathroom. Howard grinned as he watched her walk away, then looked at Fernandez again. "You want to tell me about it?"

"Why don't you go first? I'll fill in what we know that you don't."

Howard nodded. He laid it out, the whole thing; it was vividly clear in his mind.

When he was done, Fernandez nodded in return. "Ninety yards, huh? Hell of a shot."

"That's what I thought. I wouldn't want to meet this guy one-on-one in the daylight."

"Your tactics could have been better."

"I lie corrected, Sergeant. Your turn."

"Well, you actually did better than he did. The marshals had one wounded, but they collected two corpses, one by the fence, one in the SUV. One in the car was in the passenger seat when they found him, but holes in the windshield and spatter pattern says he got it while driving. How many rounds did you fire at the driver?

"Three."

"All in the glass, four-inch group. And they counted five holes in the back."

"I shot six."

"You missed one. You need more practice."

"Five out of six at ninety yards, in the dark, car going away? I don't think so. I do think I'm gonna keep that

Medusa," he said. "I feel a certain bond with it. Go ahead."

"No ID on the dead men, nothing useful in their pockets or clothes, which makes them pros. Feebs are running prints, nothing yet, but I'd guess we're talking some kind of mercenaries. Our boy Morrison must know he has reason to rent serious muscle. Everybody and his kid sister is looking for him. Some kind of plane took off from an old field not far away, no ID on it yet, but it must have hugged the ground for a ways. Nobody's radar spotted it."

Howard's wife came back from the bathroom, and within a few seconds the doctor came in. He was maybe sixty, iron-gray hair cut short, in a white shirt and slacks and a lab coat. "Good afternoon. I'm Dr. Clements. How are you feeling, General?"

"I'm ready to run a marathon. Right after breakfast."

"Yeah, I bet. Let me poke and prod a little here. Folks, if you'll step outside?"

"Nothing he's got we haven't seen," Fernandez said.

"Humor me," Clements said.

"You heard the man," Howard said. "Maybe I don't want you to see my new tattoo."

Fernandez grinned. "I got a few calls to make, anyhow. I don't know why, but there are people who care if you croak."

As he started to walk away, Howard said, "Thanks for stopping by, Sergeant."

"Hey, no problem. It was a slow day at the office anyway."

Nadine said, "You stupid, stupid, *stupid* men! Would it break your faces to say you care?"

Fernandez looked at her deadpan: "No, ma'am, but I'm pretty certain our balls would fall off."

You really shouldn't laugh after being shot in the gut, you really shouldn't.

Quantico, Virginia

Toni stood outside HQ and stared into the cloudy blue sky. *Going to rain,* she guessed.

Yeah, and maybe if you're real lucky, lightning will strike you.

She sighed. How did she get into situations like this? She had just come from her meeting with Director Allison, and the good news was that she had been offered a job. The bad news was . . . that she had been offered a job. And what a job—a newly created position, special assistant to the director, and liaison to Net Force.

She would be working with Alex, but not for him. And she would be responsible for conveying the wishes of the director to Net Force in such a way as to make certain that the "interface" between the bureau and Net Force would be more "cleanly meshed."

Translation: She would be looking over Alex's shoulder, making sure he didn't screw up.

She didn't have to take it, of course. She could walk away, and she would have, except that it was the perfect job. She'd be in fairly close contact with Alex, she could cover him if he did stub his toe now and then, and she'd still be working for the government. With a grade and pay raise, to boot. Essentially, she would be Alex's equal at work.

The thing was—how was she going to tell him? He

might not see it for what it was, and knowing Alex, he might feel, well, *upset*.

She didn't want to upset him. Then again, it wouldn't really hurt him, would it? And in the long run, it could be better for their relationship.

Ah, said her inner voice, *rationalization rears its ugly head!*

"Shut up," she told her inner voice.

A Marine lieutenant walking past glanced at her, but apparently decided she wasn't talking to him.

She didn't have to take the job. She told the director she'd have to think it over, that she'd get back to her. But she had made up her mind.

Coeur d'Alene, Idaho

Morrison never thought he would be glad to see the gates of a racist militia compound, but as soon as they closed behind the car, he felt a lot better.

General Bull Smith was waiting at the main compound, and as soon as Ventura had alighted, he made straight for the man.

"Everything go okay, Colonel?"

"More or less, sir. We had some problems. I don't want you to get blindsided by this, so I'll just tell you up front—we are going to get some heat because of a few things that went down."

Smith smiled. "Heat doesn't bother us at all. Idaho summers'll give Hell a run for the money sometimes."

"Some of this could be from our own side."

Morrison watched Smith take this in. "That a fact?"

"You'll hear about it on the news soon enough. I lost two men. A couple of federal marshals went down, too."

"No shit?"

"I don't think they know who we are. And they can't know where we went."

Smith nodded. "Well. Revolution might be starting sooner than expected. We're ready, if it comes to that."

"I don't believe it will, General, but I had to bring you up to speed."

"I appreciate it, Colonel. Why don't y'all come on in and have a beer? Got barbecued pork cooking."

"That sounds great," Ventura said.

After Smith was out of earshot, Morrison, mindful of listening devices, said, "Good that you updated the general." What he meant was "Why the hell did you tell him?"

Ventura's answer also carried a hidden meaning: He said, "I expect the general's own intel sources would have gotten it in short order anyhow." And what Morrison heard was "He needed to hear it from us, just in case he ever got a clue."

"What now?" Morrison asked.

"We wait for our friends to get in touch with us as to the transfers on both sides of the negotiation. Since nobody trusts anybody—nor should they—certain safeguards must be put into effect. We'll have to work those out."

"They won't come here?"

"Wishful thinking, Doctor. No, they'll want a place of their choosing. They'll settle for one of our choosing, but it'll have to be a lot more neutral than an armed camp where the shape of their eyes and sallow skin color might get them shot, just for the fun of it. Wouldn't you?"

"I suppose so."

"You suppose correctly. This is where it really gets tricky."

Morrison stared at him.

Ventura chuckled. "We're in the tiger's cage, and he's not made of paper. Any mistakes now, and he eats us. Speaking of which, shall we try some of that barbecue? I'm starving."

Morrison shook his head. The last thing he felt like doing was eating.

27

On the phone, Michaels realized he was all knotted up as he sat hunched forward in his office chair. He tried to relax. Probably an oxymoron, that, trying to relax. Nonetheless, he took a deep breath and let it out slowly, and allowed his shoulders to slump with his exhalation. It helped a little. He said, "So what's your take on it, John?"

Howard didn't sound as if he had been shot and almost killed only hours ago. He said, "Morrison is our boy. No reason for him to resist the marshals otherwise, and damned sure no reason for him to have shooters on hand to resist *with*. If we can keep him away from HAARP or any of the other transmitters like it, we can stop the attacks."

Michaels asked the question that had been bothering

him. "Why would he do this? Drive people to a killing madness?"

There was a pause. "I don't know. Maybe he's crazy himself."

Michaels sighed. The man hadn't seemed crazy when he'd been sitting right here in this office, talking about this stuff. In retrospect, it was obvious that Morrison had been covering his ass, trying to misdirect Net Force, and except for Jay's talking to a security guard, he'd done a good job of it. So he wasn't *that* crazy. He'd known they might come looking for him, known it and thought to head it off in advance. Didn't sound crazy.

Why *had* he done it? To see if he could? Once would have proven that, twice made it certain. Three times was overkill. If he had planned on extortion, he'd screwed up—they knew who he was, and had an idea of what it was he had done, if not actually how he'd pulled it off, so any threat he had in mind was dead—especially since he no longer had the tools to do it at his disposal. This wasn't something you could cobble together with a kit from RadioShack.

So far, Jay hadn't been able to find anything else that directly connected Morrison to the events in China or Portland. Hell, if he hadn't come in, Net Force wouldn't have had a clue about any of this. Maybe the guy was too smart for his own good. What he'd overlooked had been so simple, so basic, that it seemed incredibly stupid on the face of it. Like that mission to Mars a dozen years or so ago where the scientists had mixed up English measures with metric and plowed the little vessel right into the surface of the planet at speed because the calculations had been so basic nobody had even thought about them.

Overlooking something as simple as a security guard's log was the kind of thing a scientist just might do because it would never occur to him. A mistake so basic he never even thought about it.

If Jay was right about the technology and the possibility of using it in such a manner, then Morrison had had the means and opportunity, but what had the motive been?

"Any leads on where he went?" Howard asked.

"Not yet. The mainline ops are on the case, and we've got bulletins out to every state police agency in the U.S., as well as to the Canadian authorities. Flight plans in Alaska and the Pacific Northwest are all being checked."

"I'm going to be out of here in a day or so," Howard said. "I'll get to the office—"

"You will go home, General. We will run this guy down doing the things we know how to do. What we haven't done enough of lately—computer detection."

"I'll be okay to work."

"Not according to your wife you won't. We'll keep you posted as to progress."

Howard wasn't happy with that, but there wasn't much he could do about it. They said their good-byes.

Michaels headed to Jay's office. He tapped on the door and stuck his head into the room. Gridley was off-line. "Hey, Boss."

"I just got off the com with John Howard. He is going to be okay, so the doctors tell him."

Jay relaxed a little. "Good to hear it."

"I trust you are well on the way to catching the man responsible for shooting our teammate?"

Jay smiled. "Oh, sure. Well on the way."

"Which means?"

"We've got all his personal records. We know where

he's been and what he's done that required use of his credit cards, or his driver's license. We have his work records, too, but there are some gaps. He took out a second mortgage on his house and cleaned out his bank accounts, so he has a big chunk of cash, and not everybody requires ID for every transaction. He could have bought a cheap car, rented a private plane, maybe even gotten himself some phony ID for whatever.

"We have a description of the guy who was with Morrison from the guards at HAARP, but 'your average-looking science geek' isn't a lot of help. No surveillance cameras managed to catch an image of 'Dick Grayson,' and it was ole Dick who must have done the shooting—unless Morrison has a stash of guns we don't know about and also practiced his fast draw without anybody we talked to knowing about it."

Jay smiled. "Hey, you know who Dick Grayson is?"

"Robin, the boy wonder," Michaels said.

Jay looked disappointed, but he continued: "FBI field agents have questioned Morrison's wife, and she doesn't know anything. Really. According to the reports I just read, she isn't exactly the brightest bulb on the string—she doesn't know what her husband does for a living, and it is the opinion of the interviewing agents that she wouldn't know HAARP from a harpoon."

"What else?"

"Nothing else. We have a respected scientist who apparently figured out how to drive people crazy using a giant walkie-talkie, then up and did it. We know when, and we think we sort of know generally how, but not why."

"Conjecture?"

"I dunno, Boss. Doesn't make any sense to me. Revenge, power, money—those are the big motivating factors that come to mind."

Michaels said, "Anybody ever screw him over so bad he'd want this kind of revenge?"

"Not that I've seen. His ex-wife lives in Boston. If he wanted to get her, he missed by three thousand miles. No alimony, no kids, and the new trophy wife is a lot prettier, anyhow. He lost his funding on a research project, but got a higher paying job right after. "

"Power?"

"Never had an ambition to run things, far as I can tell."

"Money, then?"

"How does zapping a couple of Chinese villages and then downtown Portland get him rich? Extortion, maybe? But that wouldn't be too bright, 'cause he'd have to know the authorities would be on his tail forever for multiple murder. He'd never be able to relax, it's too high-profile. Too late for that now, anyhow, we have the gun. Ammunition is no good without it, and he can't walk into another of these radio palaces and ask pretty please to use the transmitter, can he?"

No, it didn't make a lot of sense.

Michaels had a sudden thought. "Suppose you wanted to buy a new computer system, something experimental, way ahead of what everybody else had?"

"Yeah?"

"How would you go about buying it if you weren't sure what it would do?"

"Sit down and put it through its paces," Jay said. "Crank it up to high and let it fly, find out what it would do—ah."

Michaels saw that Jay was going down the same path. "Yeah," he said. "Maybe that's what Morrison was doing.

Maybe he was showing it to a potential customer. How much you figure such a thing might be worth, to the right customer? The power to drive your enemies bonkers?"

"Damn," Jay said.

"Yeah. I think we just might have found ourselves an even uglier can of worms. As long as it is Morrison, we get him eventually. But what if he passes it along to somebody else? Somebody we can't get so easily?"

"That could be a problem."

"It already is a problem. Ours. As of now, this is your reason for living. Hit the net. Get all the help you can get. Find this guy, Jay. And find him fast."

"Yeah."

Michaels looked around. "You seen Toni? I kind of lost track of her around lunchtime."

"Uh, no. I haven't, uh, seen her." He looked back at his computer.

Michaels said, "I'm hoping to get her to come back to work. I think she's considering it seriously."

"Really. That's, uh, good, Boss." Something on Jay's desk suddenly seemed fascinating to him. And something in his tone of voice didn't sound quite right.

"What?" Michaels said.

"What, 'what'?" Jay responded, still not looking up.

Michaels realized he was maybe not the most perceptive man in the world when it came to reading people, but Jay Gridley wasn't one of the world's great adepts when it came to hiding his feelings, either.

"You aren't telling me something I need to hear."

"Boss, I—"

"I have a lot on my mind right now, Jay. How about you don't add worrying the unknown to it?"

Jay blew out a sigh. "All right. Last time I was in the

feeb mainframe, I left myself a couple of doors, you know, just in case we had problems like when the Russian got into the government systems?"

"Skip the rationalizations, you're a hacker to the bone. It's what we pay you for, remember."

"Yeah, well, I kind of left myself a door in the director's office subsystem."

"And you found something I need to know but that you don't want to tell me. What—am I going to get fired?"

"No, no, nothing like that. It's just that, well, Toni had a meeting with the director today. At one."

Michaels's immediate urge was to cover and say, *Oh, sure, I knew about that.* But since he hadn't known, and since there seemed to be more, he didn't say that. Instead, he said, "And now you can drop the other shoe."

"You really ought to hear it from her, Boss."

"Maybe so, but I'm *going* to hear it from you."

Jay shook his head. "The director just put in the e-forms for a new staff job in her office. Special assistant. She was offering the job to Toni."

Michaels blinked. "And she took the job?"

"Not that I can tell."

Michaels felt an absurd sense of relief. A job offer, fine, that was no big deal. Sure, she should have told him about it, but, hey, things were busy, and maybe she'd planned to brush the director off before she mentioned it. That would be like her. Nothing to worry about.

Yeah? Then why is your stomach suddenly all twisted and cold?

Anchorage, Alaska

When he used his phone to check his e-mail, Tyrone Howard saw a priority call from Jay Gridley. Huh. What was that about?

It took forever to scroll the message on the tiny screen, but it was pretty straightforward. Jay had put out a call to all his contacts on the web. He was looking for some information, and he was asking for help.

Tyrone stared at the phone. What seemed like a thousand years ago, he had helped Jay chase down a bad guy in VR. He and Jay knew each other from way back, ever since Tyrone's dad had been at Net Force. Of course, that time he'd helped Jay had been when he was spending six or seven hours a day jacked in to his computer, something he hadn't done in a while. These days, he was on-line two hours a day, tops, almost nothing, just enough time to read his mail, run through a few VR rooms, and maybe a few minutes of an on-line game. But if Jay was asking, Tyrone bet it had something to do with his dad getting shot, and he was ready to sit down, plug in, and get the data flowin' fine and fast for that. This was the guy who had pack-pronged Portland, killed people, and ruined the championships, too. A dragfoot juicesucker who needed to be shorted out, no feek. He had his laptop with him, in his pack in his dad's room. He'd get it and get on-line.

Nadine could help him. She didn't know a whole lot about computers, but he could take her along and show her as they went. He was not as sharp as he'd been, but he could still lubefoot the net okay. He'd help Jay and they would catch the sucker who had shot his dad.

28

Inside the car, even with the motor running and the air conditioner going on high, it was warm. It was just the two of them, Morrison in the back, Ventura driving. They passed the odd militiaman on the dusty gravel road as they crept along at just over walking speed.

Over the phone, Wu's voice was silky, relaxed, lulling. He said, "Of course we trust *you*. It's just that some of your . . . ah . . . *associates* seem to have a bias against people of our . . . persuasion. No point in tempting fate, now, is there?"

Morrison nodded at the unseen speaker. Both phones had their picture transmission off, so neither man could view the other. Not that it would have helped Morrison much to see Wu. He wasn't particularly good at reading expressions on Western faces; as far as he was concerned, the Chinese *were* inscrutable. Besides, it didn't matter. Ventura had coached him, and so far, everything the bodyguard had said was right on the button. In theory, their conversation was scrambled, encoded so that it couldn't be understood even if somebody was able to intercept and record it.

"Perhaps the Chinese embassy might be more to your liking?"

Wu had the grace to laugh. "Well, of course, we could arrange that, but somehow I don't think Luther would feel very comfortable under such circumstances. In his place, I would not."

"Let's cut to the chase," Morrison said. "I'll name a place, and we'll meet there."

Ventura had told him they wouldn't like that, getting right to the point. The culture from which Wu came was more patient than America's, by and large, and the Chinese were willing to engage in as much ceremonial talk as necessary to please all the speakers. They viewed Americans' lack of formality and impatience as signs of youth and poor breeding.

"Let them think what they want," Ventura had told him. "The lower an opinion they have of us, the better."

"Perhaps," Wu said. "Where?"

Morrison glanced ahead at Ventura, who saw him in the rearview mirror. He nodded.

"There's a theater in Woodland Hills, California. That's just outside Los Angeles."

"I know where Woodland Hills is, Doctor." His voice was dry, and no overt anger came through, but Morrison smiled. Ventura had told him *that* would irritate Wu, too.

Morrison continued: "The theater is fairly new, an IMAX. It's on the edge of a big shopping center—"

"Ah, yes, on Mulholland, just north of Oxnard," Wu broke in. "I saw the latest James Bond picture there a few months ago. You take the Ventura Freeway."

Again Morrison smiled. "He'll one-up you," Ventura had said. "But it'll be subtle."

"Good, that'll save me having to give directions. Tomorrow at noon."

"Any particular reason for this meeting place?"

"I haven't seen the picture they're showing."

"I see. All right. But there are a few details to which we must attend."

"Such as?"

"Well, you can hardly expect us to show up hauling a suitcase with four hundred million dollars in small bills, now can you? It would take a truck to carry that much."

"I have a secure account in an island bank," Morrison said. "Electronic transfer will do. Bring a laptop with a secure wireless modem."

"Ah, but there is the rub. You expect us to deliver that much money to you, and *then* you will give us the information, is that correct?"

"I'm the only one who can. It isn't written down anywhere." His meaning here was clear enough: If something happens to me before you get what you want, you won't get it. The truth was something else: He did have a copy of it—but only one. Any other references to the sequence had been erased, and he'd done that using a deletion program that made all those files unrecoverable. The remaining file was well hidden, too. Nobody would ever find it. He could not imagine forgetting the sequence, but if for some reason he did, he wouldn't lose it.

That's what you thought about the feds connecting you
ll this, too, remember?

He tried to ignore the thought. He still couldn't figure out how they had done that. He had been so careful.

"How do we know you will deliver?"

"You know I have the information. I've demonstrated it to your satisfaction, haven't I? Once I have the money, why wouldn't I? It doesn't make any sense *not* to, does it?"

"Having it and giving it to us are not exactly the same though, are they?"

"I'll be sitting right there next to you. You transfer the money. I transfer the information. I assume you will have scientists standing by who can verify the information. I can give you the names of some of yours who have the ability to confirm it—Dr. Jang Ji, or George Chen, or Li Hun—"

"That won't be necessary. We know who our scientists are. But can they verify it immediately?"

"If they have a test subject and access to ECG equipment and a couple of basic transmitters, they can be ready to run the experiment as soon as they get the code sequence. They'll be able to confirm it before the movie is over. Only on a small scale, of course, but in this case, size doesn't matter. It will work as well in the field as it does in the lab—you've seen that."

There was a short pause as Wu apparently digested this information.

"That's the deal, Mr. Wu. Take it or leave it."

"All right. I'll see you at noon tomorrow. Have a pleasant trip."

Wu disconnected, and Morrison blew out a big sigh of relief. This had all gone a lot more crossways than he had ever anticipated. A large part of him wished he could turn back the clock and reconsider this whole idea.

"He went for it," Ventura said. Not a question.

"Yes."

"Good. We're in business."

Morrison was worried. "This sounds very risky to me. A public movie theater? It will be too easy for him to bring men with guns in and hide them among the audience. He could have fifteen or twenty of them and we wouldn't know it."

Ventura smiled into the rearview mirror. "Do I tell you how to program your signals? Offer advice on frequencies?"

"I'm sorry, I didn't mean to—"

"Don't worry, we'll know who they are. The theater will be having a special screening tomorrow at noon, for screenwriters, members of the WGA. They'll have to show a card to get in the showing. Everybody else will either be one of ours or belong to the Chinese. We'll let their people in, because we will have the advantage. The employees, from the booth to the concession stand to the guy who tears your ticket in half, will be our people. For every one they get inside, we'll have one in a nearby seat covering them. Everybody our men don't know will be a potential target. If click comes to bang, they will know who to shoot. And if they miss? Well, nobody will notice if there are a few less screenwriters anyhow. Everybody in L.A. is working on a script."

"How can you do this? You know the guy who owns the place?"

the guy who owns the place. Over the years, I've
etty well for my retirement, Doctor. I own that
a bar, part interest in a health club, and a couple

of high-profile restaurants. Plus the blue chip stocks and bonds, of course. I'm not in the same class as you are about to be, but I could live fairly comfortably off the investments and interest without ever touching my principal. If your money isn't working for you, it's just gathering dust." He smiled.

Morrison shook his head. This was incredible. Why would a man of wealth and property risk his life to work as a *bodyguard*?

Ventura must have read his mind. " 'Idle hands are the Devil's workshop.' A man likes to keep busy doing work he enjoys."

Morrison looked away from Ventura.

This was getting stranger—and more frightening—all the time.

Washington, D.C.

Michaels sat at his kitchen table, holding a cup of coffee. It was early, just about dawn, and Toni was still asleep. He drank and stared at the wall, his gaze going through the paneling and Sheetrock and wood and focusing on nothing a thousand miles away.

And how is your life, Mr. Michaels?

Why, just fine, thank you very much. My ex-wife is getting remarried to some Idaho dork and taking my child away from me—unless I want to get into an ugly child custody case that will probably scar my daughter for life, something she doesn't deserve and I won't do.

I *personally* spoke to the man who almost certainly killed scores of Chinese by using some kind of radio beam to drive them crazy, and if I had been on the fucking ball, I would have stopped him before he did it again to scores of Americans. He walked into my office and I smiled and let him walk out.

The head of my military arm was shot and seriously wounded because I wanted him to go along and keep the federal marshals company, and the guy I sent them all after plugged a marshal while he was at it, *got away,* and is still on the loose.

My boss is ready to nail my ass to the nearest wall for not keeping her in the loop.

What else? Oh, right. My woman is back and sleeping in my bed, but she's considering taking a job where she'll be looking over my shoulder at my work and then telling my boss all about it. And she didn't think it was worth mentioning.

He had come home late, Toni had already been asleep, and he'd stewed about this particular problem until he conked out. And he woke up thinking about it.

That it?

Yeah, I think that just about covers it. My life is just *swell.*

He sipped at the coffee. It was cold. He considered getting up to warm it, but it wasn't worth the effort. Sitting and staring at the wall was ever so much more important.

Sure, sitting and whining about how hard your life is, that's the way to go, all right.

"Up yours!"

"Hey. What did I do?"

Michaels looked up. He hadn't realized he'd said it aloud until he heard Toni. She stood there, wearing one of his dress shirts and nothing else, and she looked absolutely gorgeous, even though her face was sleep-wrinkled and her hair was a tangled rat's nest. That didn't help, that she was beautiful and he loved her. He'd thought things were okay when she came back, he'd thought all was right with the world.

Well, think again, pal.

"Nothing, I was just talking to myself."

She took a mug from the dishwasher and poured coffee into it. She inhaled the vapor, blew it out, then drank. She turned and leaned against the counter, looked at him. "You want to talk about it?"

Did he want to talk about it? Goddamned *right* he wanted to talk about it. They could start with *How come you didn't tell me you'd been to see the director to discuss going to work for her? Slip your mind? Not important enough to even mention? Don't want to let me in on little details in your life, like where you are going to work?*

But he didn't say that. Instead, he said, "Not really."

She took another sip of the brew. "Okay."

Fine. Fine. If she wasn't going to bring it up, he would rot in hell for all eternity before *he* brought it up!

He said, "I need to go in early. I'm having a meeting with the mainline SAC to coordinate our investigation to find Morrison."

"Want me to ride along?"

"Suit yourself." That came out a little snippier than he wanted, but what the hell, it was how he felt.

She blew out a sigh, then put the coffee mug down on the counter and crossed her arms. "All right. What's eating you? You're so pissed off you're about to spit. Did I do something wrong?"

"Wrong? No, you didn't do anything *wrong*." He could

feel the acid drip from his voice, feel the rage just barely buried under his words.

"So why are you taking my head off?"

He was not going to say it, he was *not* going to say it! "No reason. I was just wondering, since you are always hammering at me for keeping to myself, not telling you what is going on inside my head, I was just wondering why you didn't tell me you were considering going to work for Melissa Allison, that's all."

Well. So much for his burn-in-hell resolve not to mention it.

She unfolded her arms, put one hand to her mouth, and she had, by God, the grace to at least look guilty. She said, "I . . . I'm sorry. I was going to tell you."

"When? When I saw them painting your name on your new parking space?"

"Alex—"

"No, no, you don't have to explain. You can do what you want, I don't have any strings on you. You want to work for the folks on the other side of the compound, hey, it's not my business. You *are* going to take the job, right?"

Her arms came back up and she crossed them tightly in front of her breasts. She stared back at him. "Yes. I am."

His gut twisted. Well. There you go. Signed, sealed, delivered.

He stood. "Congratulations. I'm so glad we had a chance to discuss it before you made your decision." He stalked past her toward the bedroom. Probably not as impressive as it might have been, since he was wearing nothing but his old ratty bathrobe with the frayed cuffs and torn shoulder.

"Don't do this, Alex! Don't shut down on me!"

"You have *no* room to say that right now," he said. "No room at all. I'm going to work."

"If you do, I won't be here when you get back!"

"Fine, you're going to do what you want anyhow— why bother to tell me!"

And that pretty much ended that conversation.

29

In the cab on the way to the rental car place, Toni fumed. Why did Alex have to be such a horse's ass?

All right, yes, she should have told him about the job interview, and that she was seriously considering taking the offer. But, really, when did she have the chance? After she had seen the director, Alex had been out of his office and busy. He hadn't come back to his condo until late, and she'd been in bed. The first time she could have reasonably brought it up was this morning, and before she had a chance to say anything, he'd jumped down her throat. How fair was that?

Uh-huh. You can make the case that way to him if you want, but let's not bullshit ourselves, okay? You could have mentioned it before *you went to the meeting. And you were only pretending to be asleep when Alex got home because you didn't want to talk about it. Try again.*

All right, yes, yes, it was true. But even so, he still didn't have any right to blow up like that. He wasn't her father!

No, but he's the man you love. And he was right about one thing—you did to him what you absolutely hate to see him do to you—you kept him in the dark about what was going on inside your head. And all that business about you not being there when he got home? What was that?

Toni sighed. She hated these arguments with her inner self. She always lost. She could rationalize to somebody else, but she couldn't fool herself—not for long, anyhow. Alex's anger had ignited her own, and when they'd both had a chance to cool down, they'd be able to discuss things more rationally. He did love her, she knew that, and just because they'd had a fight didn't mean all was lost forever. She hadn't had much practice at that, fighting with somebody you loved, and every time it happened, she had a belly-twisting fear that it would be the end. One cross word, blap! they'd go their separate ways. Maybe you got over that, in time. She hoped so.

All right. So now the question was, Should she wait and hash this out with Alex? Or should she go to Quantico, see the director, and tell her she was going to take the job? Her ego said to hell with him, do what you want. But her heart said she should at least sit down and explain to him why she wanted to do it. Okay, so he was pissed off at her, he was busy, and he had a lot on his mind, but they could find a few minutes to work this out. This was more important than anything else in her life, she couldn't just turn and walk away from it.

"Here we are, lady," the cabbie said.

Toni blinked. The trip had been a blur, she couldn't remember any of it.

"Thanks," she said.

Her mind was set. She would get the rental car, drive to the office, and find a time and space to talk to Alex. She could make him understand. She knew she could.

New York City

The bar was a rat hole—shoot, a self-respecting rat would think twice about sticking its nose in here, and if it had two neurons to spark at each other, it would decide not to risk it. The lighting was mercifully dim, but you could still see the knife scars in the wooden bar, the initials carved in the tables and stools. There were flats and holographs on the walls lit by neon beer signs, the posters of mostly naked women perched in various poses on Harley Davidson motorcycles. On a couple of the pictures, certain portions of the women's anatomy had been worn through to the dark wall underneath, caused by somebody rubbing or kissing the images. The mirror behind the bar was cracked in two places, held together with glass-mend strips, and few of the liquor bottles on the shelves behind the bartender were more than half-full.

The bartender was six and a half feet tall, probably weighed three hundred pounds, and he wore a leather vest and oil-stained jeans that presumably went to the tops of his big old motorcycle boots. He had tattoos all over what was visible of his body, everything from Li'l Hot Stuff to naked women with large breasts—and large fangs. The centerpiece was a Harley logo on his chest, partially obscured with thick patches of graying hair.

Lined up at the bar and seated at the tables were other bikers, men and women, and none of them looking what you would call . . . *wholesome* . . .

On a raised platform off to one side of the bar, red and blue lights played over a listless dancer. She was naked, save for several rings piercing various body parts, and a few small but interesting tattoos of her own, including a flame-colored one shaped like an arrow that pointed at one of the more intimate piercings—or what was being pierced. The music was some bump-and-grind number with saxophones and a lot of drums, and the dancer could have phoned in her performance. From her face, one could see the dancer was well past her prime; from stretch marks and scars, one could guess that she'd had children, cosmetic surgery, and probably an appendectomy. The overall effect was as erotic as a chunk of concrete, and nobody was watching the woman dance.

Jay Gridley, wearing a sleeveless blue denim jacket sporting colors from the Thai Tigers Motorcycle Club—TTMC superimposed over a growling tiger's face—stood between two bruisers a foot taller than he and probably half again his weight.

One of the bruisers accidentally tapped Jay with his elbow as he turned to speak to a mama on the other side of him.

"Watch it," Jay said.

The biker turned back to Jay, death in his eyes, but when he saw Jay, he blinked and said, "Sorry, man."

Jan grinned. Well, what the hell, it was his scenario, wasn't it? If he was gonna be in a bad biker titty bar, he might as well be the baddest guy in the place, right? Jay knew he had the moves to wipe up the virtual floor with anybody in the place, and even in VR, people could sense a real expert from his moves and stance.

It probably said something about his fantasy life that he would come up with such a scenario, and was able to flesh it out as well as he had, but hey, if you can't have fun, what *is* the point?

The bartender came over, and Jay pointed at his empty glass. The giant nodded, reached behind himself, and pulled a bottle of tequila off the shelf. When he poured, the worm sloshed into the glass with the fiery liquid. He looked at Jay.

Jay shrugged. "Leave it. It adds texture."

The bartender started to turn away. Jay said, "I'm looking for somebody."

"Yeah?" He locked gazes with Jay.

"Yeah. A shooter." He pulled the smudged drawing from his jacket pocket. This was the composite put together by the computer artist, based on the HAARP guards' description of "Dick Grayson."

The bartender never took his gaze from Jay's. "Don't know him, ain't seen him," he said.

"Look at the picture."

"Don't need to. Won't matter."

"So that's how it is."

"Yeah. That's how it is."

Jay grabbed the bartender by a clump of chest hair and jerked him against the edge of the bar. With his free hand, he pulled an automatic knife with a five-inch blade from his jeans. He put the point against the bartender's throat, just under his chin.

In the real world, Jay had grabbed the home address of the guy playing bartender and force-fed the generating computer a virus-laced cookie. If he didn't pull the knife away, the guy's system was going to go belly up in about ten seconds after he "cut" him.

"Look at the picture or I give you a new smile."

The bar patrons hadn't noticed the action, save for those closest to Jay, and they quickly edged away. The dancer continued her sleepwalking shuffle.

"Okay, don't get twitchy." The bartender glanced down at the image.

Jay grinned. This visit to a mercenary chat room on VR was a lot more interesting than running facial points of comparison against the image files of the NCIC, NAPC, or the FBI, looking for a match—which he had already done, and come up with zed-edward-roger-oliver.

"Jeez," somebody said from the doorway. "Jay?"

The voice sounded familiar. Jay released the bartender and turned.

Tyrone Howard stood there, looking around the inside of the biker's hangout.

"Tyrone? What are you doing here?"

There were a few people to whom Jay had given his forwarding code, so that if they needed to contact him electronically, they could in essence meet him on the net wherever he was. It wouldn't work in a high-classification security area, but any hacker worth three bytes could follow the line into anything as simple as this kind of public access site if Jay allowed him past the fire wall. Tyrone Howard had been very helpful during the mad Russian thing a few months back, and Jay had added him to the list of people who could contact him in a hurry.

Might have been a mistake, considering the overlay.

Apparently Tyrone had decided to let Jay's scenario be the default, and it wasn't one you particularly wanted to have a thirteen-year-old boy see you in. He might get the wrong idea.

"Yeah, I seen him," the bartender said.

Jay turned back to the giant biker, breaking character: "Really?"

"Yeah. He's been in once or twice."

"Where can I find him?"

"I dunno. But the guy over by the pool table, the one in the Army shirt, drinking boilermakers, he's had some dealings with him."

Jay nodded.

Tyrone walked into the place toward Jay.

"Gimme a second here, Ty, I'll be right with you."

"No hurry, Jay. I'll just . . . enjoy the ambience. Jeez, this is as bad as Jimmy-Joe's strip joint."

Great. All he needed was Tyrone telling his father about *this* scenario.

Worry about that later, Jay. Let's go see the man who likes boilermakers.

But the man who enjoyed dropping a shot glass of whiskey into his beer stein, depth-charge style, wasn't really there—he was a proxy.

While it was true that none of the people in the ersatz biker bar were really "there," some were less so than others. A proxy was a shell, little more than a link to another location, something to mark a place, and not somebody you could interface with directly. A ghost of a shadow.

Jay was able to get a location, but a quick pulse in that direction did a reverb with nothing more than an RW street address, somewhere in the District. Apparently Mr. Boilermaker here didn't like to reveal too much on the net, and if Jay wanted to speak with him, he was going to have to drop out of VR and go RW.

Huh. Who did that anymore?

He wasn't a field op, he was a netjet, so he could pass this along to one of the staff investigators to have them look up Boilermaker here and have a face-to-face chat with him.

Jay shook his head. That might take days, given the way the field ops took their sweet time about such requests. Even if the boss put a rush on it, Jay didn't altogether trust the shoe skidders—some of them weren't particularly sharp, and it would be his luck to get a dull one who'd mess up the interview.

Soji had been after him to get out more. No reason why he couldn't drop by and do the interview himself, was there? It wasn't as if he was afraid of going outside.

He looked around for Tyrone, but the boy had vanished.

"Tyrone?"

A biker with the physique of a competition bodybuilder whose monthly steroid bill was higher than his house note smiled at him. "Hey, Jay."

"Nice suit," Jay said, waving at the mound of muscle.

"I thought it was a good idea. It's a modified pro wrestler, all I had to do was change the clothes and add a couple of tattoos. I didn't want to stand out."

"Come on, let's leave this pit. I've got a private room." He rattled off the password and headed for the door.

As he reached the exit, the exotic dancer's music changed, and the first notes of Destroyers' version of "Bad to the Bone" rumbled its bass beat from the speakers. Jay grinned. For a second, he'd forgotten he'd programmed that in. *Yep, that's me. Jay Gridley, better not step into my path, 'cause I'm b-b-b-b-bad!*

30

Wednesday, June 15th
Woodland Hills, California

Ventura wiped a thin film of sweat from his forehead as
he stood outside the theater, smiling into the parking lot.
It was probably almost eighty degrees, and it was not yet
nine A.M. Hardly a surprise that the sun came up bright
and hot here this time of year. The Los Angeles basin
pretty much had two seasons—hot and real hot. Ventura
could remember going to the beach in January, and getting sunburned lying on the sand, watching girls hip-roll
past in bikinis. He grinned again. *That* had been a long
time ago.

He and Morrison had been here for almost two hours,
and of course his people had been in place since before
Wu had called yesterday. The regular staff had been given
three days off with pay and told that a special training
session for employees of a different theater was being

conducted. If anybody had wondered about it, the free days off were apparently enough to keep them from asking.

Wu would expect Ventura to get there early, of course, and he wouldn't know who normally worked there, but he'd figure Ventura hadn't chosen the place because he liked breathing hot smog.

Like a game of chess or *go*, any move in this level of play, no matter how innocuous it might seem, could have a major impact later on. You had to be very careful, always looking ahead.

Only a fool would choose a neutral meeting place if he could pick one that would tilt the playing field in his favor. Taking the high ground was an old and battle-tested adage. The Chinese knew this—their culture had been steeped in war for thousands of years, and it made for a pungent, bitter drink. They knew this brew.

Within three hours of the call, Chinese agents had put the theater under surveillance, and a couple of them had tried to con their way inside. Ventura's people had kept the place secure, though they really couldn't do anything about the watchers outside. Well. That didn't matter.

The arrival of an ostentatious stretch limo in the front two hours ago had likely drawn most of the outside attention while Morrison and Ventura slipped in the back door, bracketed by four of his best shooters. The guy having coffee in the Starbucks all morning would have seen them and reported it, but Wu wouldn't want to risk a shoot-out in broad daylight next to a major street—it would be too easy for Morrison to take a round, and nobody wanted that. Yet.

Once inside, Morrison felt a lot safer, and Ventura let him believe that, though the truth was, it didn't much matter. If Ventura screwed up, the client was in deep shit no matter where he was.

Still, Ventura knew they had the advantages: He had chosen the time and place, he controlled the building, and they needed Morrison alive, whereas Ventura could pot anybody on their side he wanted. And when it got right down to it, he was pretty sure he was better at strategy and tactics than Chilly Wu.

Of course, that was the crux of it—"pretty sure" was not the same as "absolutely certain," which you could never be in such an encounter. And in that was the secret shared by serious martial artists everywhere. If you were a warrior—a real warrior—there was only one way to test yourself. You had to go into battle, guns ready, and face the enemy. No amount of virtual reality, no practice with targeting lasers against others, nothing other than the real thing mattered. In the end, the only way to know you were better when it came to life and death was to pull the triggers, rock and roll, and see who walked away when the smoke cleared.

That instant of truth, when the guns and knives came out, that was as much in the moment as a man got. That was the ultimate realization that you were alive, when you stared laughing Death in the face and backed him down. Death always laughed, of course, because he knew that in the end, he always won. That was Death—but life wasn't about the destination, it was about the trek. Playing the song was about the flow of the music, not about reaching the end.

If a man spent years, decades, perfecting a skill, no matter how awful the skill was in application, some part of him wanted to test it. To know.

So, part of this was protecting his client. And part of

it was, if necessary, defeating the one who would harm his client. You stepped up and knocked the other guy's dick into the dirt, and thus you knew that in this instance, however briefly the moment lasted, you were better than he was.

It was not the best measure of a man, to pit yourself against another, but it was a method that gave at least a partial answer right then and there.

Ego, and no way around that, but Ventura had come to terms with his ego a long time ago. Yes, he had to accept that there were likely better assassins out there now than he was—younger, stronger, faster. And while old and devious beat young and strong most of the time, that didn't happen when it was quicker reaction time that made the crucial difference.

So, yes, there were better assassins, but he was pretty sure that Chilly Wu wasn't one of them. If the deal went smoothly, well and good, but if things went sour, well, then they'd see.

They'd dance the dance, and then they'd know for sure.

Ventura looked around the parking lot, which was still mostly empty. The first showing in the theater was usually noon or later; most of the stores in the shopping center didn't open until nine or nine-thirty, so the sub rosa ops fielded by the Chinese had to work a little to hide. In the parking lot of the mall, broadside to the theater, there was a supposedly empty delivery van purporting to be from a carpet store, but Ventura would bet rubies to red rust that somebody was hidden in the back watching every move he made. Maybe through rifle sights, though he didn't think they'd shoot him.

Another smile. During the American Revolution, there had been a British sniper, a crack shot, who had once

lined his rifle sights up on George Washington. From the
reports, it would have been an easy shot, but the sniper
hadn't taken it. Washington had been standing with his
back to the shooter, and a true British gentleman wouldn't
shoot an officer in the back, now would he? Could have
changed the whole course of the war, that one shot un-
taken, but that wasn't the issue. There were rules, after
all. Otherwise, what was the point?

A public works–type truck was parked next to a man-
hole cover nearby, orange rubber cones and blinking
lights blocking the area, with three men in hard hats in-
dustriously pretending to be working on something down
under the street.

A telephone truck was backed up to a junction box
across the street at the pizza place.

There were also joggers, dog walkers, women pushing
baby carriages, bicyclists, and little old ladies in tennis
shoes strolling to the stores for their daily mall walks.
Ventura figured that any or all of them could be other
than what they seemed. Probably some of them were legit,
but he couldn't make that assumption about any particular
one—that kind of thinking got you killed. That old lady
might be a kung fu expert; and instead of little Mac, that
baby carriage might hold little Mac-10. If you were prepared for the worst, then anything less was a gift.

He smiled as he headed back toward the theater. He
liked films, but he had always found those movies hilar-
ious where the bad-guy kidnappers or extortionists
showed up to collect their money and never looked twice
at the wino on the park bench, or the young couple holding hands, or the priest feeding the pigeons, all of whom
might as well have had big flashing neon signs on them

saying "Cop!" Crooks who were that stupid deserved to get shot—it was good for the gene pool.

Of course, good people were always hard to find, in most any line of work. Ventura himself had only a dozen pros he'd personally let watch his back when the bullets started to fly, and it had taken twenty-odd years to find that many he trusted. They all worked for him on and off. There were another twenty or thirty second-tier shooters who could do things like the theater setup today, who would follow instructions and hit their marks if push came to shoot. Past that? Well, most of the people he'd met who played at being soldiers of fortune or freelance bodyguards or hitters were okay at best, coffin fodder at worst. He figured the Chinese would send the sharpest they could round up on short notice to play here today, but how many they could get inside was tricky. Too few and they wouldn't feel covered properly; too many, and it would alert anybody half-awake. If he had to trade places with Chilly Wu, he'd be a little concerned about that.

Morrison stood by the concession stand, nervously sucking on a straw stuck in a cup of fizzy orange drink.

He's going to ask me if everything is okay, Ventura thought.

"Everything okay?"

Ventura smiled. "Under control."

"I'm worried about this screenwriter business," Morrison said. "Aren't you concerned that the Chinese might know about it, slip some ringers in?"

"Not really. The op in the ticket booth is checking membership cards. He'll scan those into our systems. I have a man in the manager's office with links to the WGA database. He'll match the names on the cards against a list of members, and the faces on the closed-circuit se-

circuit security cam in the booth against those in the guild's database—those are new, the pictures—and also against California driver's licenses. Anybody who shows up to sneak in using a friend's card had better not sneeze at the wrong time."

"You aren't worried at all? Wouldn't a hidden metal detector or X ray be wise?"

"No point. They know we chose this place for a reason, and they know we're here several hours early. I figure they'll try to slip a minimum of eight men in with Wu, a maximum of twelve. I am assuming they will all be armed. I have twenty men on call, but I probably won't use all of them. Remember, the idea here is not to get into a shooting match, but to keep the balance of power even. It's our place and Wu knows that. If he gets his people in, he'll be a lot more comfortable. If he couldn't get them in, then it might make him twitchy; and that's not what we want."

"No?"

"No. A nervous man might do something rash. They'll take what you have for free if they can get it that way, but if they realize they can't, they'll pay for it. What we want is a nice smooth negotiation in which the Chinese get what they want, and you walk away a rich man, everybody's happy, a nice win-win situation."

"But if they try something—"

"—they won't live to regret it, Doctor. Then we have to start all over again with a new negotiating team. Nobody wants that."

But secretly, a small part of Ventura wanted exactly that.

C'mon, Wu. Show me what you got. Reach for your pocket—and let's see who goes home.

31

Michaels stopped at Jay's office, but didn't see him. He saw instead one of the techs, Ray DeCamp, carrying a stack of hardcopy printouts. The man always wore thick, round computer glasses while at work, so of course he had a nickname appropriate to that:

"Hey, Owl. Jay around?"

"Commander. Nah, he said he hadda go into town, said he'd be back inna couple hours." Owl had a strong Boston accent, so the last word came out "ow-wuz."

That surprised Michaels. Jay seldom left during the day for any reason. A lot of times, before he'd hooked up with the Buddhist girl Soji, Gridley would stay in his office for days, sleeping on the couch and showering in the gym dressing room. There were jokes that he was a vampire, that exposure to sunlight would cause him to burst into flames. And coming from other ghost-white computer geeks who spent a considerable amount of their own time in semidark rooms, that was saying something.

Oh, well. Given everything else going on around here lately, Jay leaving the building during the day was no weirder than the rest of it.

"Hey, Alex."

He looked up and refocused on Toni. "Hey," he said. He repressed a sigh. He'd flown off the handle this morning. Sure, she had provoked him, but he expected better of himself. A man who couldn't control his temper was weak—losing it almost always got you in more trouble than it solved.

"You want to talk to me?"

He nodded. "Yeah. Come on, we can go to my office."

"Kind of stuffy there. How about the gym?"

He had to smile. His office, his advantage. The gym was where she was stronger. He said, "Why don't we go to the conference room instead?"

She smiled back at him, and he knew she understood what he'd been thinking. What they had both been thinking. God, he loved smart women!

Washington, D.C.

Maybe this wasn't such a good idea coming here, Jay thought.

"Here" was a kind of Army-Navy surplus store, though that wasn't strictly true—there were odds and ends from other branches of military surplus for sale here, too, including some stuff from what looked like the Coast

Guard, the U.S. Marine Corps, and the Russian Air Force. And on one scratched glass counter next to a rack of moldy uniforms from some unrecognizable African army, there were even Net Force buttons and insignia.

The whole place had a sour odor, like unwashed cotton socks mixed with damp wool, and instead of air-conditioning, a pair of large and loud metal fans mounted on seven-foot-tall posts circulated the too-warm and fetid air without doing much to cool it, or the people inside. Some of the patrons looked familiar—maybe Jay had seen their pictures on the post office's Most Wanted website—and none of them were what you would call savory.

Still, he was Jay Gridley, a master scenarist. He'd built uglier scenarios in VR.

The guy perched on the stool behind the counter next to the old-style mechanical cash register was the least appetizing character in the place. He was fat, bald, and wore an eyepatch made of what looked like rattlesnake skin over his right eye, and vaguely green Army-style fatigues that had probably been unwashed since the Spanish-American War.

As Jay watched, a customer who looked old enough to have been a veteran of that same war shuffled to the register. The old man was in baggy green parachute pants and a stained and ratty green T-shirt over untied combat boots, the laces dragging along the floor. The man plunked a bayonet onto the counter. "How much for this here baloney slicer?" the old man said. He cackled, amused at his own poor joke, a laugh that ended in a dry wheeze.

Jay took a step backward, so he wouldn't have to share too much of the man's air. Surely the guy must have something contagious.

"That's for an '03 Springfield," Eyepatch behind the counter said. His raspy voice sounded as if it had been pickled in high-proof whiskey, then left out in the desert to bleach for a few years.

Jay made a mental note of the sound. He could use it in a scenario. This whole place was great research; he could get all kinds of material from it.

Patch picked the bayonet up. It was rusty, the wood handle cracked and worn. "Don't see a lot of these around much anymore."

"I know what it is, sonny. I just need to know how much it costs."

"I could let it go for . . . eighteen."

"What, cents?"

"Dollars."

"Sheeit, sonny, you cain't get ten for it. Look at it. It'll take me a week to scrape the rust offen it. And lookit the handle."

"I can sell you some naval jelly that'll eat the rust right off. I might take fifteen."

"Eleven."

"Twelve."

"Now you're talking."

The old man pulled a clump of greasy-looking bills from his voluminous pants and peeled a dozen ones off a wad that would choke a rhino.

Patch rang the sale up. "You want a bag for it?"

"No, I'm gonna walk down the streets of D.C. carrying it where the cops kin see me and shoot me fulla holes. Yes, I want a *bag* for it. I'mona track me down a couple of cats been diggin' in my garbage and give um a new haircut."

Patch pulled a purple plastic bag from under the

counter, with the store's logo printed on the side: "Fiscus Military Supply," it said under a pair of crossed rifles and stylized lighting bolts.

When the customer shuffled out, Jay watched to see if he was going to trip on the untied bootlaces and break his neck, but the old man achieved the door without incident.

"Old fart couldn't track an elephant herd across a football field covered with fresh snow. What can I do for you?" Patch said.

"You Vince Fiscus?"

"That would be me, yeah. And who wants to know?"

"I'm Jay Gridley. I called earlier." Jay pulled out his Net Force ID card.

Fiscus took the card and looked at it carefully, turned it over and examined the back. The hologram flashed a rainbow reflection under the overhead lights. "You want to sell this? Tell 'em you lost it, they'll give you another, but I don't have any Net Force ID." He waved one flaccid arm to take in the store.

"I don't think so." He took his ID back. He wanted to wipe it off, but thought that might not look too good.

"All right. What it's about, Mr. Net Force Agent?"

Jay kind of liked the sound of that. He tendered the picture of the mystery man. He said, "You know this guy?"

Fiscus looked at the picture. He grinned, showing a gap where a front eyetooth had once been.

"That's ole K.S., sure I know him."

Jay felt a sudden surge of excitement. *Aha! Gotcha!* "K.S.?"

"Yeah, stands for 'Killer Spook.' Ain't seen him in a while. He never give me a real name, so I just called him K.S."

"How is it that you know him?"

"Oh, he's been coming around for—must be five, six years now. We first did a little business back in, what? ought-four or ought-five. Sold him some fourth-gen spookeyes—starlight scope image intensifiers, Army Ranger surplus, off an old SIPEsuit. He's bought a few things since then, some of it in person, some of it over the wire. What are you looking for him for? He's not into computer stuff."

"I am not at liberty to say," Jay said. "It concerns an ongoing investigation."

Fiscus shrugged.

"Why 'Killer Spook'?"

Fiscus showed the tooth-gap again. "I asked around, some people I know. Rumor was, this guy made a living doing odd jobs for various folks, including a few guvamint ones. Black bag ops, wetwork, stuff you don't want to show up on the books, you know what I mean?"

This was getting better by the minute. Colorful ole Vince here was giving him all kinds of information. This exterior investigation stuff was a walk in the park—why did the field ops make it sound so tough? Must be worried about job security.

"What kind of weapons you guys carrying now?" Fiscus asked. "I heard that issue was some kinda pansy stun-gun."

"Kick-tasers," Jay said. That was true. Jay did have a compressed-gas electric dart gun. His was in a drawer somewhere at home. Or maybe at the office—he hadn't seen it in a while. Since he wasn't a field agent, he didn't have to qualify with the weapon, and he had only fired the thing once, a long time ago. He did all his shooting in VR.

"Now about this K.S. guy," Jay said. "Where might I find him?"

"Well, I'm afraid I'm gonna have to ask you why you need him again," Fiscus said.

"Like I said, I can't tell you that."

"You wanna bet?" Fiscus raised his whiskey-soaked voice a couple of notches. "Vic, Rudy! C'mere!"

Two fairly young men in green-on-green camouflage shirts and pants tucked into gleaming combat boots seemed to materialize from nowhere behind Jay. The pair of them were huge, five, maybe six hundred pounds combined.

Uh-oh.

Jay had seen enough vids to know he was maybe in a little trouble here. He was alone, unarmed, and it looked as if he was about to make the unwilling acquaintance of Vic and Rudy. Maybe it was time to see if discretion was indeed the better part of valor. He smiled nervously and started to head for the door.

"Whoa, hold up there, Mr. Net Force Agent."

Jay looked at Fiscus and saw that the man held a big, dark metal pistol. "You aren't supposed to have that in the District. It's illegal."

"Do tell. Take your hands away from your belt and put them where I can see them." He waved the pistol.

Jay had another sudden flash. The only reason Fiscus had told him any of this stuff about the man he'd come looking for was because he didn't expect Jay to be able to act on it—or tell anybody else.

He had seen a lot of vids.

Jay suddenly had a vacuum in his belly that must rival deepest space. This was not VR. He couldn't just ax a command and drop back into his office. That gun was real.

He was turned slightly so Fiscus couldn't see his right hip. He double-triple-pressed the panic button on his virgil—one-two-three, one-two-three—then slowly moved his hands away from his body.

"Take it easy," Jay said. "Let's be reasonable here."

"That's real good, Mr. Agent. Now, let's mosey on into the back room, and have ourselves a little talk, hey?"

Woodland Hills, California

Morrison leaned against the counter in the bathroom, staring at himself in the mirror. His face had a psychedelic cast to it—it was as if he was seeing a stranger.

He washed his hands, bent, and rinsed out his mouth. He had the little gun in his sport coat pocket, but the small weight of it bumping against his right hip was not comforting. He was scared, frightened to the point where all he wanted to do was to take off at full speed and run until he couldn't keep going. He wanted to find a place to hide when he got there and sleep until all this somehow went away.

He looked at the frightened man in the mirror again. Running and hiding wouldn't do any good now. It was too late. In a few minutes, an agent for the Chinese would arrive—already some of his people were probably lined up outside the theater waiting to get in—and Morrison was going to have to sit and negotiate a deal with the man who called himself Chilly Wu.

Morrison stood there for what seemed like a long time,

staring into the mirror, but not really seeing himself any longer.

Ventura came around the corner behind him, and Morrison jumped.

"Wu just pulled up. You ready?"

"I—Yes, as ready as I can be."

"Don't worry. My man in the projection booth has an Anschutz Biathlon rifle that will be lined up on the back of Wu's head the second he takes his seat. The shooter can hit a quarter ten for ten at that distance. Every one of Wu's people will have somebody watching him. We have this covered."

Despite just washing out his mouth, it was dry again. "Listen," he said, "there's something I want you to know. I have a hidden copy of the data. If something happens to me, I want you to have it. Sell it, give it away, whatever you want, I don't care, but—sell it to anybody but the Chinese."

"Nothing is going to happen to you."

"I believe you. But just in case. This is the only original research I've ever done that amounted to anything. It's important work. I don't want to see it lost."

"If it makes you feel better, fine. I'll see that it gets to a good home."

"It's not here," he said. "The copy."

"All right. Where is it?"

Morrison told him. When he was done, Ventura smiled. "That's pretty clever."

"Maybe the Pakistanis, they hate the Chinese. They'd find a use for it."

"This is all moot. I can guarantee you, the Chinese will not be walking out of this theater with you as their hostage. At the first sign of trouble they will all become past tense. This is what I do, Patrick."

The use of his first name rattled him even more. Morrison took a ragged breath, let it out, then took a larger one and held it for a moment. Deep breaths. Calm down. "All right."

The movie wasn't scheduled to start for another thirty minutes—but it was definitely show time.

32

Toni had planned to sit down and tell Alex what she felt, to apologize for losing her temper, and to try to get him to see her side of things.

It seemed like it would work out, because the first thing he said was "Listen, I'm sorry about losing my temper."

That was a great start. She said, "Me, too."

But that was as far as it got. Alex's secretary opened the conference room's door and said, "Commander, we just got a distress call from Jay Gridley's virgil."

"What?"

"District police are on the way. Here is the location."

Alex came to his feet.

Toni said, "I saw Jay earlier, he was here—"

"He went into town," Alex said. He headed for the door in a hurry. To his secretary, he said, "Get the helicopter

warmed up and get the GPS location to the pilot. I want
to be in the air in three minutes."

"Alex?"

"This place is falling apart," he said. "Nothing is going
right!" He looked at her. "You coming?"

She nodded.

Washington, D.C.

"Hit him again," Fiscus said.

Rudy nodded. He threw a short uppercut that slammed
into Jay's belly like a steel brick.

Jay doubled over, the pain overwhelming. He couldn't
breathe, couldn't see for the tears clouding his vision,
couldn't believe how much it hurt! He would have fallen
if Vic hadn't been standing behind him, holding him up,
his huge paws meaty clamps on Jay's upper arms.

Nothing in VR had ever come close to this, nothing.

"Catch your breath, Mr. Net Force Agent, and think
about it a second."

Jay managed to breathe again after a few seconds. He
felt like puking, the urge was almost impossible to resist.

"You feel better? Good. Now tell me—why are you
looking for K.S.?"

How long had he been here? It felt like years, but it
couldn't have been more than a couple of minutes. He'd
tried to stall them, but Fiscus wasn't buying it, and after
the second punch, Jay didn't know how much longer he
could hold out. One more, maybe.

"Fuck you."

"You're not my type, but maybe Rudy will take you

up on that later, hey? Boys, girls, sheep, cows—doesn't
matter to him. One more, Rudy."

Jay went out with the third punch, at least partially.
The intense flash of pain went from red to gray, and time
seemed to ooze lazily, like tar on a hot summer street.

"—got all day," Fiscus was saying. "And Rudy ain't
even broke a sweat. I seen him work the heavy bag for
ten, fifteen minutes, four, five hundred punches. You ain't
a bag full of batting, son. How long you figure you'll
last?"

Jay's blurry vision was enough to let him see that gap-
toothed smile, and he knew that Fiscus and his two apes
could and might beat him to death. "Okay," he said.
"Okay, I'll tell you."

"Sheeit," Rudy said.

"See, I told you he was just getting warmed up. Don't
worry, Rudy, you can throw a couple more if Mr. Net
Force Agent gets too sluggish. Okay, let me hear it."

Jay took a raspy breath. The guy didn't know, so it
didn't matter what he said. Jay could create scenario, and
writing the description and background and dialog was
part of that. He could spin it, and how would this guy
know different?

"Okay. We came across a computer break-in, in New
York. A stock trading company, and—"

"Rudy."

The punch took Jay under the armpit on the right side,
a left, hooking move, and he felt, and thought he heard,
one of his ribs crack under the impact.

"Uuuhhh! Ow, ow, what did you do that for?! I'm *telling* you!"

"Nah, you ain't. You're lying. I might look stupid, but

I didn't fall off the turnip truck yesterday, kid. Every lie buys you another slam. Try again. "

Jay felt a great wave of despair wash over him. He was going to die. He knew it. No matter what he told them, in the end, they were going to kill him.

Washington, D.C.

"That's it, that surplus store," the cop said.

In the big tactical van, Michaels nodded. According to the protocols for Net Force distress calls established with the police, the local cops had arrived Code 2—fast, but without sirens. They set up a perimeter and the local version of SWAT or SERT or whatever was ready to go in, but Michaels had gotten there before they hit the building, and he wanted to go along.

The police lieutenant in charge of the scene looked at Michaels's taser and shook his head. "Not a good idea, Commander. We know who this guy is that runs the store. We're pretty sure he's got enough illegal hardware in there to equip a third-world army, and he's usually not alone. Your little zapper won't cut it."

"I'll stay behind the team. That's my man in there."

"I'm going, too," Toni said. She held her own taser.

"What is this, a goddamn parade? Where's the marching band and the baton twirlers?"

"I can make some calls, Lieutenant, and get the heavy hitters into it if I have to. My boss can call yours. You want me to do that?"

"Shit. No. Put masks and vests on and stay in the back

and the hell out of the way, you understand? If you get killed, don't bitch about it to me."

"All right."

He looked at Toni. This was not the time to tell her to stay behind, he could see that, but it was the first thing he wanted to say. Maybe she was right. Maybe she couldn't work for him. Maybe he was too protective. He did not want her in there.

"Heads up, people," the lieutenant said into his com. "We're going in thirty seconds. And we got two feebs riding the caboose. Don't nobody shoot them by accident."

The lieutenant pulled a pair of spidersilk vests with ceramic interlock armor and the initials D.C.P.D. stenciled in reflective yellow on the backs. "Put these on. They'll stop handgun rounds and a lot of rifle bullets. Grab a gas mask and helmet. We're going in with flash-bangs and puke gas."

Michaels nodded.

"Fifteen seconds," the lieutenant said into the com. "Go get into position. Behind Sergeant Thomas over there. And *stay* behind him."

Michaels glanced at Toni, and they jumped from the back of the mobile command post and ran.

Woodland Hills, California

Morrison and Ventura were in their seats in the theater when an "usher" walked Wu down the aisle. The section they were in had been roped off, so that they sat in the middle of a block of four rows alone; the other seats in the block were all empty. There were maybe forty people already in their seats, with a few others trickling in.

Wu carried a fold-out laptop computer slung over one shoulder—and a big tub of popcorn.

Ventura smiled at that. Had to give the man credit for style.

Ventura and Morrison both stood, and Wu moved to join them. He slipped under the velvet rope to sit between Ventura and Morrison. While he was talking and concentrating on the scientist, Ventura would be behind him.

Wu held up the tub of popcorn. "Want some? I think it's got real butter on it. It should be real, it cost four bucks."

Ventura was tempted to dig around and see if there was a pistol hidden there—he'd have a small one under the popcorn—but both he and Morrison declined the offer.

Ahead of them, the huge screen was still dark. There wouldn't be any coming attractions or ads run today.

"What time does the movie start?"

"We have a few minutes," Ventura said.

"Good, good, we can get this business taken care of and enjoy the picture. Same people did this who did *Quinton's Revenge,* and it's gotten good reviews."

He sounded relaxed enough, and that was a good sign. He'd brought in ten people, who were scattered around the theater with their own tubs of popcorn or boxes of candy, so he ought to feel as if he was in control of the situation, or at least be on a par with Ventura. He either couldn't sense the sights lined up on his skull from the projection booth, or he really was a chilly character not afraid to die.

"Now you know we Chinese like to dawdle and make

polite small talk before we discuss business, but this is America and I like to fit in, so what say we get down to it?" He slipped the computer off his shoulder and unrolled the flexible pop-up LCD screen, locked it into place, and then unfolded the keyboard. The computer came on with a small chimed chord, and the screen lit up.

Morrison's computer was already up and running, on the seat on the other side of him. He picked it up.

"Ah, here we are," Wu said. "Your bank account number?"

Morrison read off a fifteen-digit series of numbers and letters.

Wu typed it into his computer. He looked up at Morrison and smiled. "And that was for . . . three hundred million dollars, U.S.?"

"Four hundred million," Morrison said quickly.

"A small joke, Doctor." He tapped in the numbers. He said, "It's a fair-sized transaction, but nothing huge. It'll take only a few seconds for them to verify the account we're transferring from, and acknowledge the credit."

Ventura did a sweep of the room. It seemed as if this might come off with no problems. His team was on alert. If anything that looked like a gun, or a canister of gas, or any kind of weapon, made an appearance in the still-well-lit theater, things would happen fast. Nobody was going to be yelling "Drop it!" or "Don't move!" At the first sign of aggression, his people were to cook the Chinese—all of them—no hesitation, no questions. Any screwups, and Wu's people were all history. It was a harsh response, but the only way to go here. One guy blasting away indiscriminately with a small subgun or even a pistol could do a lot of damage—and it wasn't going to happen.

"There you are, Dr. Morrison. You should see it on your machine."

Morrison tapped keys. "Yes. It's in and verified." He typed in another sequence. "The account number and password are both changed."

"Then you have it. We can deposit but we can't take it back. You're a rich man. Now it's your turn."

Morrison nodded. He still looked like a man sitting in an electric chair, waiting for the current to flow.

"Here is the address for our people," Wu said. He held the computer up so Morrison could see the screen. "You send them the data, they say they can have it tested in less than two hours. They work, we watch the movie, everybody goes home happy."

Wu turned to look at Ventura. "You know, Luther, if it had been left up to me, I expect I would have tried for a—how shall we say?—*cheaper* offer."

Ventura gave him a small smile. "Such an offer couldn't have been . . . *acceptable,* Chilly."

"You don't think so?"

"I know so."

Wu's smile matched Ventura's own. "It would have been very interesting to see whose opinion was right, wouldn't it?"

"Yes."

The two of them held gazes for another moment.

Wu said, "Well. Another time." He looked away, back at Morrison. "Doctor, if you would?"

Ventura was victorious. His smile broadened.

Morrison nodded and started to type in the electronic address.

"Gun!" somebody screamed—

—and sure enough, guns started to go off.

33

Toni was right behind Alex. The gas mask had big, wide lenses that left her peripheral vision clear, but there was an annoying clicking sound every time she inhaled. And she was breathing pretty fast, too. She forgot about her breathing and the noise fast enough when the first of the six-man team ahead of them crashed through the door into the back room of the surplus store. Bright flashes of actinic light strobed her, but the mask's polarizers kicked in and blocked the glare within a hundredth of a second or so. She should have worn earplugs, she realized, because the noise was loud inside the building. A misty cloud of green gray vapor boiled up with the explosions and lapped against the walls with the racket.

She heard a triplet of quick, smaller explosions—*pap! pap-pap!*—gunshots, she was sure—and Alex doglegged to the left. She followed him. Somebody yelled something she couldn't make out, and somebody retched so loudly it sounded as if he was turning his guts inside out.

Alex looked back at her. "You okay?"

"Yes, I'm fine."

Then it was all over.

The mist, which felt greasy on her bare skin, started to clear, and the police team spread out enough so Toni could see four men who weren't cops. Three of them were on their hands and knees, vomiting. One was on his back, blood oozing from holes in his side and one leg. He had his head sideways and he was throwing up, too.

One of the men on his knees enjoying the purging benefits of emetic gas was Jay Gridley.

"Thank God," Toni said into the mask. The sound was muffled, but she saw Alex nod.

"Yeah," he said.

Woodland Hills, California

Wu was quick. He dropped from his seat onto the sticky floor and tossed the tub of popcorn into Ventura's face as he fell.

Ventura was able to hear the rifle shot from the projection booth, was aware even as he pulled his own gun that the flat crack of the small-bore longarm was distinct from the duller, louder handgun sounds—

Wu came up with a gun—it must have been *underneath* the popcorn tub—and jammed it at Ventura. He fired twice—

Quick and good, too—

The bullets hit Ventura square in the chest, but the titanium trauma plate in the pocket of the blended Kevlar/spidersilk vest under his shirt stopped the rounds, even though they felt like sledgehammers against his sternum—

Ventura cleared his own weapon and brought it around—

Morrison was up and running, screaming wordlessly—

Wu cursed and got off another round, higher this time, right on the edge of the trauma plate—

More gunshots blasted in the theater—

One-handed, Ventura fired—*one-two-three!*—letting the recoil raise the muzzle each time, so the shots walked up Wu's body, in case he was also wearing a vest, so the hits were chest-throat-head—

"Stop, stop, stop—!" Morrison screamed.

Ventura looked up from Wu, saw that Morrison had his own little .22 revolver out and pointed in front of himself as he reached the aisle—

One of Ventura's best shooters—the ex-SEAL, Blackwell—moved to grab Morrison, to pull him down and out of the line of fire—good, good!—but Morrison was panicked, and he thrust his weapon out at the man—

"Morrison, no!" Ventura screamed. "Don't—!"

Too late. Morrison pulled the trigger. Blackwell, coming to save the scientist, was five feet away, and even Morrison couldn't miss every time at that range. At least two or three of the six shots chewed into Blackwell. The vest he wore stopped a couple, but one went high, hit him in the jaw, and Ventura saw a tooth explode from the torn mouth in slow motion as Blackwell's head jerked to one side—

Ah, *shit*—!

And he saw with razor-edged and expanded clarity

as Blackwell did what any really good trained shooter instinctively did if somebody pointed a gun at him when the situation went hot—

"No!" Ventura screamed, trying to bring his own gun up around, but he was mired in subjective slow-time, and too late.

Blackwell knew Morrison was wearing a vest, and Blackwell didn't want to die. So even as he fell, wounded, Blackwell lined his pistol up on Morrison and stopped the threat—

He shot him right between the eyes.

The back of Morrison's head blew out in a spew of brains, blood, and bone.

Washington, D.C.

He was going to be okay, Jay realized. The doctor had taped him up, given him a shot to counteract the puke gas, and another for pain. Every breath he took still hurt his ribs a little under the tape, and his stomach was sore from vomiting, but he was real happy to be feeling anything at all.

It was sure better than the alternative.

The boss said, "What on Earth possessed you to go into the field on your own?"

Jay started to shake his head, but that made him dizzy, so he stopped. He said, "I dunno. Pure stupidity would be my best guess. Not ever gonna happen again, I guarantee that. Reality sucks."

They were in the hospital's lock ward, where one-eyed Fiscus had been transferred after they'd patched him up.

He'd been hit twice after firing at the cops, in the side and in the leg, but neither hit was life-threatening once they stopped the bleeding. He was awake, and the boss had flexed his Net Force muscle to get in and question the guy before the mainline boys and the D.C. detectives got there.

Jay and Toni were with Michaels as he walked into the room, and they all nodded at the cop sitting in the chair next to the bed.

"We want some information," Michaels said to Fiscus.

Full of IV tubes and things clipped to his fingertips or taped to his chest, Fiscus flashed his gap-toothed grin. "People in Hell probably want ice water, too," he said. His snakeskin patch was gone, and the eye it had hidden had a milky film over it.

"Which you'll find out all about if you don't tell me what I want to know," the boss said. "Way I figure it, you have kidnapping, assaulting a federal officer, attempted murder of a policeman, and a shitload of illegal weapons charges staring you in the face, at the very least. A man your age? You're going to die in prison."

That seemed to get his attention.

"And so why the fuck should I help you, I'm gonna die in prison anyhow?"

"It's real simple. I can make the federal charges go away. No kidnapping, no assault, no visits from the BATF about all that hardware. I might even be able to convince the locals to cut you some slack on the shooting, since you didn't hit anybody. You could be out in five, six years, maybe."

Fiscus hesitated for a moment.

Jay could almost see the wheels going inside the man's

head. *Don't do it*. Jay beamed his thoughts at Fiscus. *Go and rot in jail forever, asshole!*

"I can get you a lawyer if you want," Michaels said.

"No, no lawyers. I'll take the deal. What do you want to know?"

Michaels nodded.

Woodland Hills, California

"What a mess," Ventura said to himself again. He was on the freeway with the same name as his own, driving in the general direction of Burbank. "What a fucking mess."

And it was, too. Back in the theater were ten shot-up Chinese agents, all of them either dead or well on the way by now. Two of his men had taken stray bullets from the Chinese, but neither were fatal wounds. Four screenwriters had been hit, one was dead, another one pretty bad, two fairly minor. Blackwell was in bad shape, but he'd probably live, even if he wouldn't be eating any caramel apples for a few months.

Wu was absolutely dead.

And Morrison was also gone, killed by somebody on his own side.

What a pisser that was.

The wounded civilians were being hauled by cars to the nearest hospital, where they'd be dropped off, the drivers not staying to answer questions. Ventura's men would be taken to a doctor who was paid to take care of people and keep his mouth shut. The remaining unwounded screenwriters, twenty-three of them, had been stuffed into a storeroom and locked in. Probably half of them were already working on their next movie, one involving a shoot-out in a theater. They wouldn't starve; there were a lot of candy bars and hot dog buns in there with them.

Outside, team members had distracted the Chinese surveillance team where feasible—a pepper bomb in the carpet truck, a sap of lead shot against the head of the coffee drinker in Starbucks, like that, but thankfully, no more guns.

Everybody else had taken off on prearranged escape routes.

Ventura realized that he could kiss the IMAX theater good-bye. Too bad. It had been making a profit for the first time in three years.

What a crappy, stinking, rotten piece of work this had been. Not only had he lost the client he was supposed to protect, but one of his own men had done it. No choice, really. In Blackwell's shoes, he'd have probably done exactly the same thing.

I never should have given Morrison that gun.

Yeah, 20/20 hindsight there. Too late to think about that now.

Though there never would be a way to be absolutely sure, Ventura knew what had happened. One of the Chinese agents had gotten careless, since his own people were more adept than to show a gun that was supposed to be hidden. One of the Chinese agents had gotten careless. Whichever of his people who saw the piece must have felt it was being brought into play. All of his shooters had been told to stay cool—unless a weapon came out. The shout of "Gun!" had been the agreed-upon signal for his shooters to take out their targets, and once that happened, all bets were off.

Had the Chinese intended to take the shortcut? To grab
Morrison instead of paying for the data?

Well, it didn't matter. Done was done, no point in crying over it now. Still, there were consequences to consider. The Chinese were going to be most unhappy, and
they might well decide that Morrison and Ventura had
ripped them off for their four hundred million and decide
to try and get it back, and that was real bad. Morrison
wasn't going to be giving anything back, and Ventura
didn't have it.

He changed lanes, and a fat man in a black Porsche
honked at him for cutting in. Ventura had a sudden urge
to pull his Coonan and put a round into the fat man's
windshield. Honk at somebody else, dickhead.

He resisted the urge. That wouldn't help matters, to
start shooting morons on the L.A. freeway. Once you
started, you'd run out of ammo quick. Probably couldn't
carry enough extra rounds in a moving van to get them
all . . .

He giggled at the thought. He was stressed out, yes,
better just take a few deep breaths and think this through.

He did just that. Three deep breaths, in and out, and
now think about it calmly.

Well. The first thing was, the couple of million he had
tucked away didn't seem like all that much money anymore. The way he figured it, he was going to have to
disappear, just as he had told Morrison he would have to
disappear, forever. Yes, he was living on borrowed time
and had been for a long time, but the truth was, he wasn't
quite ready to check out yet.

If the deal had come off, he'd have been safe enough
from the likes of Wu. They'd have gotten their money's

worth, and pros didn't need to take each other out for doing their jobs.

But it hadn't come off. The Chinese were out that money; they didn't get what they wanted, and too bad for them. This was certainly going to make them *real* unhappy.

Morrison hadn't given Ventura the account number, so he couldn't get his hands on it, either. Too bad for everybody.

The fat man found an opening on the outside lane, whipped the Porsche around Ventura, and zipped past. He waved his middle finger at Ventura as he went by, and though he couldn't hear him, Ventura could read the man's lips easy enough. A fourteen-letter word.

Maybe he could shoot just the one and stop?

The Porsche accelerated and gained away, and Ventura forgot the fat man.

The Chinese money was out of reach, but—there was more where that had come from. Because if he had been telling the truth—and Ventura had no reason to doubt that he had been—Morrison had told him where to find the secret that had just caused more than a dozen people to die. And the Chinese weren't the only oysters in the ocean who had pearls.

Yeah, okay, it was a bad deal all around, a major disaster, a perfect example of Murphy's Law. But now that it was done, Ventura had to get on with his life. That moment was past. If you drove down the road looking only into your rearview mirror, you were going to plow into somebody ahead of you. Time to look forward.

Somebody could still benefit from all this, and it might as well be him. He could even drop the price a little. He

didn't need four hundred million, he could get by on half
that. No point in being greedy, was there?

He drove toward the airport in Burbank. He had a flight
leaving in an hour. It would probably take the screenwriters longer than that to figure a way out of the storeroom. Yes. He had a course of action now. He knew what
he was going to do.

34

"I just got a call from Julio Fernandez," Jay said. "John Howard is home."

"That was quick," Toni said.

Michaels nodded at her. "Yeah. Old soldiers never die, but they don't hang out in hospitals tempting fate if they can help it."

They were in the conference room at HQ. Somebody had put a pot of coffee and a box of assorted pastries on the table. Michaels picked up a bear claw, examined it, and put it back. He selected a glazed donut instead. A nice sugar rush and a little caffeine, just what he needed, so he could rot his teeth, court diabetes, and raise his blood pressure all at the same time.

Hell with it. Given the way things had been going

lately, what difference would it make? He took a big bite of the donut.

"Julio says Howard's ready to come back to work now."

"He can take a few days off and heal. So can you."

Jay shook his head. "I'm fine. I want to be here for this. It'll be a lot less strenuous in VR. I can ride the net here, or I can do it at home, but I'm gonna ride somewhere."

"All right," Michaels said. "Let's review what we have. According to your Mr. Fiscus, the man we are looking for used to be some kind of freelance hired assassin who supposedly got out of that business and into bodyguarding a few years back. Aside from 'Dick Grayson,' he uses a variety of names, among them Diego, Gabriel, Harbor, Colorado, and Ventura. Is he Hispanic, do we think?"

Jay laughed, then said, "Ow." He pressed his hand against his sore rib.

"What?"

"I shouldn't laugh. I don't think he's necessarily Hispanic or Latino, Boss. Those are all names of Los Angeles freeways."

Michaels nodded. "Okay, so he knows about Batman and the SoCal highway system. What else do we have?"

"Zip. I looked in the phone directories," Jay said. "He ain't listed, and we haven't been able to get a facial-points match on any police agency computers. Man has a very low e-profile."

Michaels looked at Toni. He had to ask. "You're going to take the job with mainstream, aren't you? Working for the director?"

"I—yes."

"So is the information flow going to be both ways?"

"That's what the job description says."

"Okay. See what you can get from them on this."

If they could find out who this Ventura character was, if they could background and history him, they might be able to track him down. And if they found him, they'd find Morrison.

The intercom blipped. "Yes?"

His secretary said, "Sir, we have an incoming call from the director for Toni Fiorella."

Michaels frowned. He waved at Toni, who picked up a handset on the table.

"Yes, ma'am?"

The director said something, and Toni nodded. "Yes, ma'am, I have decided." She glanced at Michaels. "I'll take it."

His gut twisted a little at that, but she was a grown woman, she had to make her own choices.

"Yes, ma'am, go ahead."

Toni listened for what seemed like a long time. Neither Michaels nor Jay made any pretense they were doing anything other than listening to her end of the conversation.

"I see. Yes, I'll tell them. Yes, ma'am, I'm glad to be onboard."

She cradled the phone, looking disturbed.

"What?" Michaels said.

"Sheriff's deputies in Woodland Hills, California, were called to a disturbance at a movie theater there a few minutes ago. Inside, they found more than a dozen bodies, all shot dead, plus a locked storeroom full of screenwriters."

"Corpses and a room full of screenwriters? This concerns us how?" Jay put in.

"One of the bodies was IDed as a man named Qian Ho

Wu, a registered foreign lobbyist who the FBI Counter Espionage Unit has tagged as a probable spy for China."

"Uh-huh?"

"One of the bodies has been identified as Dr. Patrick Morrison."

"Oh, shit," Jay said. Then he thought about it a second, and said, "But that solves our problem, doesn't it? Dead men don't generate radio broadcasts."

Toni said it before Michaels had a chance to say it: "You're assuming he didn't tell anybody how he did it before he died."

"Well, he probably didn't tell the Chinese. Maybe they were after him because they figured out he was responsible for what happened to their villages. They caught up with him, there was a shoot-out, end of story."

"Too easy," Michaels said. He tapped the com. "Get me on the next flight going to Los Angeles."

"You're not a field agent, Alex," Toni said. "The FBI will take care of this, you can't—"

"But I can," he said, cutting her off. "Portland got zapped with some kind of death ray, the leader of my strike team is in bed nursing a gunshot wound, and my top computer whiz just got the crap beat out of him—not to mention I had the guy responsible for all of this *in my hands* and I let him walk away. This has been a FUBAR from the word go."

"You didn't know—"

"But I know *now*. You want to tell your new boss I'm overstepping my bounds, fine, go ahead. I can take some vacation days myself if I have to."

"You don't have to," she said. "And if you want, I'll go with you."

He considered his next words carefully. He considered

not saying anything, but decided he needed to: "This is Net Force's problem, Toni, and I think Net Force should take care of it."

She blinked at him. "And I'm not part of Net Force anymore, is that what you're saying?"

"You said it, not me."

She nodded. "I see."

He didn't like the way it made him feel, didn't like the distress on her face, but it was going to come out eventually, and better sooner than later. Maybe they could salvage their personal relationship; he sure hoped so. But the job had already changed. It wasn't going to be the same as it had been. If Toni didn't work for him anymore, okay, fine, he could learn to deal with that. If she was going to report about what he did to somebody else, he needed to have some control as to what he let her see and hear. If the director wanted to keep tabs on him, all right, that was her prerogative. Nothing said he had to make it easy for her.

Toni had made her choice. Now they'd both have to live with it.

In the air over northern California

Ventura glanced around, uneasy. There was nobody looking at him, and he hadn't seen anybody following him, but something felt . . . *off*, somehow. He was in full-alert mode, scanning, listening, being aware, and he hadn't spotted anything about which to be worried, but even so, something was not quite right.

He glanced at his watch. Maybe it was the flight. He

was concerned about being in the jet's first-class cabin—

"Can I get you anything?"

Ventura gave the young flight attendant a polite smile. "No, thank you." He had booked a business-class e-ticket, using one of a dozen fake IDs he always carried, but the flight had been full, and by the time he'd checked in, the only empty seats remaining had been in first class. Normally, he didn't fly first class; it was harder to blend into the herd when you were up front. But demanding to sit in the tourist section would really make you stand out—who refused a free upgrade?—and the idea was to be as anonymous as possible. You wanted to be just another middle-aged businessman, do nothing to stick in somebody's memory, and hope you didn't remind the stewardess of her favorite uncle.

The attendant moved on, and Ventura turned to stare out at the terrain. The flight from L.A. to Seattle took about three hours. He'd rent a car at SeaTac and drive to Port Townsend, probably another three or four hours—you had to allow for the ferry ride, plus he wanted to do a little circling for his approach. That would put him there in the evening, but it didn't get dark up this far north in the summer before maybe nine-thirty or ten. So there was no real hurry, since night was your friend. Plenty of time to stop and have supper, get set up, do the job.

He looked out through the jet's double-plastic window. There was a big snow-covered mountain below and in the distance. Shasta? Must be.

Ventura figured the local authorities in L.A. had uncovered the mess in the theater by now, and if so, they had certainly identified Dr. Morrison. As hard as the feds would have been looking for Morrison after the shootings in Alaska, they'd be on the case quickly. He had considered hauling the corpse away, disposing of it, but since the man was dead and no longer his responsibility, it was tactically much smarter to let him be found. He'd made sure that Morrison's wallet was still in the dead man's pocket, to speed things up. That would certainly stop the direct search, and maybe the feds wouldn't be all that interested in looking for accomplices.

It wouldn't slow the Chinese down. Surely Wu had passed his intel along to somebody higher up the food chain—Ventura couldn't imagine that the man's stingy government had given him hundreds of millions of dollars to spend without knowing every detail of what they were buying. The Chinese would very much like to speak to anybody connected to the deal. Once they found out Morrison was dead, they'd really have their underwear in a wad. Ventura would be at the top of their list of people to see.

The feds would have dropped their surveillance of Morrison's house as soon as they realized what had happened to him—dead men didn't move around a lot on their own, and the only way he'd be coming home would be in a box. Ventura's team was, of course, long gone, pulled off as soon as he'd realized the man he'd shot in Alaska was a marshal and not a Chinese agent, and that more feds would thus be coming to have a little chat with Morrison's spouse. He hadn't told his client, who thought his young trophy wife was protected—no point in giving him anything else to worry about.

The feds would probably want to have a few more chats with the widow Morrison, and certainly the Chinese would pay the young lady a visit, but since she didn't know anything, she couldn't tell either side anything. She might be joining her late husband by the time the Chinese figured that out, but that wasn't his problem—as long as he wasn't there when the Yellow Peril came to call.

The Yellow Peril. He smiled. He wasn't a racist. Sure, he played that card for people like Bull Smith, to allow them to believe he was simpatico with their beliefs, but he didn't care one way or another about somebody's skin color or gender. He'd worked with people of every race, male and female, and the single criterion that mattered to him was how well they could do the job. If you could pull the trigger when it came to that, and hit your mark, you could be a green hermaphrodite with purple stripes for all he cared. He'd learned the term "Yellow Peril" from the old Fu Manchu books, material that had been written in an age where racism was the default belief and nobody thought much about it.

Normally for this kind of work Ventura would have wanted to take his time. He'd get to know the territory, learn the patterns, who went where, when, and how, and not move until he had everything pinned down. The more you knew, the fewer chances for surprises. He didn't have that luxury now. He needed to move quickly, get his business done, and leave this behind him. He had his money cleared, clean IDs, and safe places where he could hide until he had a chance to work out his longer-term plans. Being in the moment didn't mean you couldn't *think* about the future; it merely meant you didn't *live* in the future.

He was, he figured, in a fairly good position. Still there was that nagging uneasiness, that sense of being a bug on a slide. As if a giant eye could appear in the microscope at any time, staring down at him. He did not like the feeling.

Well. You did the best you could, and that was that; nothing else mattered.

They were still an hour or more away from SeaTac. He'd get some rest. It might be a while before he had another chance. He took a series of slow, deep breaths.

In three minutes, he was asleep.

35

Toni went to the small gym to work off the tension and anger she felt. There was a guy in steel-rimmed glasses, a T-shirt, and bike shorts doing hatha yoga in the corner, otherwise the place was empty. She hurried through her own stretching routine, bowed in, and began practicing *djurus,* working the triangle, the *tiga.* Half an hour later, when she was done, she started footwork exercises on the square, *langkas* on the *sliwa.*

The moves were there, automatic after so many years, but her mind was elsewhere.

Alex was upset with her, that was obvious. Well, what had she expected? That he would smile and pat her on the head and offer his congratulations? She tried to see it from his viewpoint, but she knew she couldn't have it both ways, not this time. This was the best thing. Working for him had become a sore point even before they had gone to London; he wasn't treating her like he did the other members of the Net Force team, he was shielding her, and she didn't want that, not in the work. So, okay, there was going to be an uncomfortable period while he adjusted to her new job. She didn't like it, but that was how it seemed to be working out.

In the long run, she kept telling herself, it would be better for them. They'd be able to relate to each other more like equals, the personal relationship wouldn't be bogged down in the professional one.

Yeah, but in the long run, we're all dead, aren't we? So what happens after a couple months of nobody having a good time if you or Alex get hit by a bus crossing the street? How is that going to fit in with your "long run" plan, hmm?

Toni stopped moving and stared into the mirror at the end of the room. *Crap. I really don't need this.*

But—what help was there for it? What else could she do? She had to make a living!

She sighed, went back to her footwork.

A few minutes later, she was aware that the yoga guy had finished his routine and left, but that he'd been replaced by a trio of other men. Two of them were in karate uniforms, the third wore dark blue FBI sweats. One of the karate guys wore a brown cloth belt tied around his waist to keep his *gi* shut, the other a black belt. They were watching her. Watching and smiling. Then the guy in sweats leaned over and said something to the other two.

Pentjak silat wasn't a flashy art; a lot of what went on in it didn't look particularly impressive to the uninitiated. The last time a martial arts player from another style stood here and watched her practice, he had made the mistake of making some ignorant remarks out loud. She had been having a bad day when that happened—not nearly as bad as this one—and she had demonstrated to the loudmouth that what she was doing was in many ways superior to what he knew about fighting. It had been a painful lesson for the man.

The lesson she had learned was pretty painful, too.

She didn't want to think about what had happened with—and to—that man later, but she couldn't avoid it. Rusty had become her student, then her lover, however briefly, and as a direct result, he was dead.

Given the day so far, the opportunity to offer a correction to any—or all—of these three if they spouted off would feel pretty good. It wasn't part of a self-defense mind-set to entertain such thoughts, but *silat* wasn't primarily a self-defense art, it was a *fighting* art, and there was a big difference in your level of aggressiveness.

Toni stopped what she was doing and walked toward the trio.

"Afternoon," she said. "Can I help you with something?"

The guy in sweats was the oldest of the three men; he had short and curly gray hair. He smiled and gave her a small bow. "No, ma'am," he said. "We were just admiring your art, guru. *Silat Tjimande?*"

That surprised her. He got the subset wrong, but he knew it was *silat* and he had enough appreciation and understanding to call her "guru," as well. Damn.

"It's *Serak*," she said, the "k" silent. "But it's Western Javanese, like *Tjimande*. I'm surprised you recognized it."

"I used to work out with an old Dutch *kuntao* teacher in San Diego," he said. "He had done a little training in *silat* as a boy. My JKD teacher also had some training in *Harimau*, tiger-style."

Toni nodded. JKD—jeet kun do, the way of the inter-
cepting fist—was the style created by the late Bruce Lee.
It was a hybrid system, and while they weren't big on
forms, many of the moves were based on *wing chun,*
which to some people looked at least superficially like
silat. At least the WC players knew in theory what the
centerline was, even if they didn't cover it adequately according to *Serak* standards . . .

If Curly here knew enough to recognize and respect
what she was doing, he probably wouldn't be interested
in trying to deck her to impress his friends. *Silat* fighters
didn't go in much for point-sparring, and for that matter,
neither did JKD players.

Well. Too bad. Kicking somebody's butt would feel
pretty good about now.

And she was going to have to do something or she
would explode.

But—what could she do?

Woodland Hills, California

It was dark by the time Michaels got to the theater, and
there really wasn't much left to look at by then. Truth
was, there really wasn't any good reason for him to be
here, except to see things—such as they were—for himself. Anybody involved with this who was still alive was
undoubtedly long gone.

The bodies had been removed, the screenwriters released after giving their statements, and the local police
still puzzled as to what had happened. The mainline FBI
op who showed up to meet Michaels was a junior man,

not the special-agent-in-charge, but he was willing to say what he thought. His name was Dixon.

Michaels and Agent Dixon ducked under the yellow crime-scene tape covering the doors and went into the building.

"Here's what we know," Dixon said. "The dead men, all thirteen of them, were shot in the theater proper. We have identification on six so far"—he looked at his palm computer—"Wu, Morrison, a screenwriter named C. B. Shane, and three men with criminal records: two Vietnamese-Americans, Jimmy Nguyen and Phuc Khiev, and a man named Maxim Schell. Nguyen, Khiev, Schell, and Morrison were armed with handguns. Nguyen's was in his hand, Khiev's on the floor under his body, Schell's still tucked into his belt. None of them got a shot off, though some of the other dead men did fire their weapons.

"Morrison's gun, a little .22, was locked in his right hand in a death grip, and shot empty. Nobody got hit with a .22 that we can tell. We haven't come up with IDs on the other dead men yet, but all of them had guns, too."

Michaels said, "So what do you think happened here?"

"No way to tell for sure. The dead guys were mostly shot in the back or back of the head, so what it looks like is some kind of ambush. You have to figure that if you have a dozen armed men, most of whom didn't do any shooting before they got taken down, there were a lot of other guys in here blasting away, too. Forensics hasn't gotten the blood all sorted out, but a quick prelim says there were a few who got hit hard enough to bleed, but who didn't stick around."

"Jesus."

"We'd take his help if he offered. You must have some ideas. You got anything for us?"

Michaels thought about it. Toni would tell the director anyway, it was her job now, so it didn't matter if Dixon knew. He said, "Morrison had some kind of valuable data and he used it against the Chinese. We think maybe they were after him. Maybe they caught up with him."

"What kind of data?"

"Sorry, that's need-to-know only."

Dixon shook his head. "Doesn't seem right. The dead guys were all sitting down when the shooting started. And according to the interviews with the screenwriters, everything was quiet until somebody yelled 'Gun!' At which point, all hell busted loose. It sounds more like a negotiation than a face-off."

"It must have been an ugly scene in here."

"Yeah. Though a couple of the screenwriters were more pissed because they didn't get to see the movie than they were upset about all the corpses. Welcome to L.A."

Michaels considered what Dixon had said. A negotiation. Yes, it did, didn't it? Why would the Chinese be negotiating with a man who had wiped out a couple of their villages?

Maybe they wanted him to tell them how. Maybe they were willing to pay for it?

Well, if Wu was the guy negotiating, he hadn't done too good a job of it, had he? And Morrison wasn't going to be pedaling anything, either.

Paris, France

Jay sat slouched in a wicker chair at the Cafe Emile, looking out on the Champs Elyseés, not far from the Arc de

Triomphe. He sipped black, bitter espresso from a tiny china cup, and smiled at the couples who strolled past. The war was over nearly two years, the Nazi occupation history. Postwar Paris in the spring was a much nicer place than a military surplus store in any season.

Henri, the waiter, approached. He had in his hand a small paper tablet. He gave Jay a nod that was both servile and arrogant and offered him the tablet. " 'Ere iz ze list you wanted, Monsieur Greedlee."

"Merci." Jay took the tablet and waved Henri away. He looked at the list, scanned down the row of names— no . . . no . . . no . . . wait!

Jay sat upright, bumped the table, and sloshed espresso from the cup. Yes! There it was!

He snapped his fingers loudly, caught Henri's attention. *"Garçon! Voulez-vous bien m'indiquer ou se trouve le téléphone? Je désire appelez faire!"*

Henri rewarded Jay with a sneer. "Bettair you should work on ze pronunciation and ze grammar first, monsieur!"

The arrogant prick knew he wanted to make a call, but he had to correct his French first.

"Montrez du doigt, asshole!"

Henri shrugged off the insult and did as Jay requested— he pointed toward the café.

Jay stood and hurried to find the phone.

Wednesday, June 15th
Woodland Hills, California

Michaels had supper at the hotel, and when room service brought him the chicken sandwich, it had bean sprouts on it. Well, of course. This was L.A.

He ate the sandwich mechanically, not really tasting it. He was screwed, there was nowhere to go from here. Toni had been right, he wasn't a field agent. He couldn't just hop on a plane, fly to a crime scene, and expect to spot some crucial clue that the local police and FBI forensics team had somehow missed. He knew better. But he had needed to see the place for himself, hoping it would somehow jog something in him.

Well, it hadn't. And here he was in a hotel in La-La Land, eating a chicken sandwich with bean sprouts, without a clue as to what he should do next.

On the bedside table, his virgil lit, telling him it was bad to the bone. That was probably Toni, calling to tell him what an idiot he was. At the moment, he was inclined to agree with her.

The tiny screen on the multipurpose toy didn't show Toni's face, however. It was Jay Gridley.

"What's up, Jay?"

"I think I got him, Boss."

Michaels stared at the virgil. "What? How? Where?"

"I crunched all the commercial airline flights leaving SoCal in the last twelve hours. Burbank, LAX, John Wayne, in Orange County."

"And you found Ventura?"

"No. But I did find a Mr. B. W. Corona."

"I don't see—"

"It's another freeway name, Boss."

"Kind of a reach, isn't it?"

"Maybe not. Guy booked a ticket two days ago, a round-trip to Seattle. He was originally scheduled for this evening, but he called and changed it to an earlier flight. Return is open-ended."

"I don't see how that makes it any more certain."

"Okay, look. He planned to leave tonight, but there was some kind of a problem, a shoot-out, so he had to take off early."

"But he's planning to come back, your Mr. Corona."

"If you're on the run, you don't buy a one-way ticket, that's a red flag, first thing cops look for."

"But why would he use a name we might know?"

"Because he doesn't know the freeway names have been compromised. He doesn't know we picked up his pal at the surplus store in Washington, so why would he throw away perfectly good ID?"

"Still sounds like a stretch."

Jay did an imitation of a late-night infomercial: "But wait, but wait, don't order yet, listen to this!"

The virgil's screen was tiny, but it had good resolution, and Michaels could see Jay's grin easily enough.

"I checked the car rental places at SeaTac. A Mr. B. W. Corona walked into Avis, no reservation, and rented a midsize Dodge ten minutes after the flight from L.A. landed late this afternoon. You got a computer terminal there in your room, Boss?"

"Yes."

"Plug your virgil into it, I want to show you something."

Michaels opened the terminal, lit the screen, and tapped the infrared send-and-receive code into his virgil. Jay's face appeared on the hotel's computer screen. "I've got your visual on the hotel's computer," Michaels said.

"Stand by."

The image of Jay was replaced by a digital line-by-line image. It was a close-up of a California driver's license.

"This came from the counter scanner at Avis. They log all licenses."

The man in the hologram had short hair, but a full beard. Could that be Ventura?

Michaels couldn't tell. "I don't see the guy in our sketch."

"No law against growing a beard, having your picture taken, then shaving. But forget the picture."

Michaels was already scanning the information on the license. He got no farther than the name. "Son of a bitch! Why didn't you tell me this in the first place?"

"C'mon, Boss, you always save the best part of a story for last. You want me to call the Washington state police and have him picked up?"

"I suppose you know where he is, too, huh?"

"Sure."

"Oh, really?"

Jay laughed. "You are really gonna love this part. Avis has theft-recovery devices installed in their fleet. Somebody decides to keep a car instead of turning it in? They can dial a number and turn on a little broadcast unit wired into the car's battery. The unit sends a GPS signal to the nice folks at Brink's, and they can tell you exactly where the vehicle is." He shifted back into the infomercial announcer's voice: "*Now* how much would you pay?"

"Son of a bitch." Michaels looked at the computer's flatscreen. The name on the license was the final selling point: The "B.W." stood for "Bruce Wayne." And everybody who read comics, watched television cartoons, or went to action adventure movies knew that Bruce Wayne was the secret identity of Batman, mentor and elder partner of Robin the Boy Wonder, aka Dick Grayson.

If this wasn't the guy they wanted, it was one hell of a coincidence.

"All right, Jay, I'm impressed. What will it take to get the car rental company to give us the tracking information?"

"Already done, Boss. You want to guess where he's going?"

"Surprise me."

Jay laughed again.

36

It was almost nine P.M. when Ventura rolled into the small tourist village of Port Townsend. And though he had the GPS maps his ops had sent in with their electronic reports, he spent thirty minutes driving around, getting a feel for the place. Situated on a fat, semi-hook-shaped isthmus jutting into Puget Sound, the sleepy town had once upon a time been the gateway to the U.S. Northwest via the Straits of Juan de Fuca. Those glory days were long past, and now the tourists came to see some of the prime examples of Victorian-style houses left in the country. Ventura had been here in the daylight, and it looked almost as if somebody had gone back in time, grabbed a section of San Francisco just before the Great Earthquake of 1906, and dropped it up here. Some of the larger and more ornate old houses were now commercial businesses or bed-and-breakfast lodgings, but many of them were still in use as regular housing. There was a paper mill still working down on the waterfront as you got to town, but other than that, not much industry.

The main drag downtown was Water Street, where most of the old buildings were pre–turn-of-the-century. There was a restaurant and marina at the end of the street, and a lot of nicely kept wooden boats moored there.

Above downtown, overlooking a bluff, Lawrence Street was the parallel uptown road. Here were stores, a theater, and other odds and ends. From Lawrence Street, Taylor Street ran up the hill to Foster, which was where Morrison's house was. A bit farther to the north was the old Fort Warden Military Reservation, now a park where you could rent an officer's or a noncom's old house and spend a few days hiking and exploring the long-empty bunkers. Morrison hadn't snagged one of the Victorian homes, but a more modest stone house built in the 1920s. It hadn't been cheap, according to his operative's research, but it wasn't outrageously expensive, since he'd bought it just before the big real estate boom hit here. Houses that had been going for two hundred thousand three years ago now went for half again that much. The town was in the Olympic rain shadow, and while they did get some rain and wind, it was a lot less wet than much of northern Washington state. A lot of the baby boomers had decided this was a good place to retire and enjoy their golden years.

After his reconnaissance patrol, Ventura found a restaurant still open and had a late supper. He took his time, and when he was done, he parked downtown and located a busy pub. He bought a beer and nursed it, killing more time. It was after ten-forty-five P.M. when he left, having spoken to nobody but the waitress.

At this time of night, given the lack of traffic—there was almost none—Ventura didn't drive past Morrison's house even once. If the Chinese had people watching, or if some laggard fed had hung around, a car passing by would certainly be an object of interest if it was the only one they'd seen for an hour or two. He knew where the house was, knew how to get there, and he would be a lot harder to spot on foot, as long as he didn't walk down the middle of the road waving a light.

He had made some purchases when he'd gotten here. There was a big grocery-department store complex on the highway into town, not quite a Wal-Mart, but big enough. He stopped there and bought black jeans, a black long-sleeved T-shirt, and a navy blue windbreaker, as well as a pair of thin-soled black wrestling shoes. He'd changed clothes in a public rest room downtown after he left the bar, putting the new clothes on under his pale gray slacks and white shirt. The rest room was not far from the police station, which appeared to have all of two people manning it.

He parked the car five blocks away from Morrison's, in a line of other cars at the curb. If some sharp-eye local patrol cop happened to notice a vehicle that didn't belong to anybody he knew on the street, likely he would think it was somebody visiting. A rental car with Washington plates wouldn't exactly scream "trouble."

He had the Coonan under the windbreaker—it was chilly enough to justify a light jacket, if not two shirts and two pairs of pants—and he carried a set of lock picks and spare magazines in one windbreaker pocket, a small flashlight in the other. Probably nobody would notice him at this hour. In his mind, he was B. W. Corona, married, two kids, up to meet his family for a holiday. He was staying at a local B&B down in town—he couldn't remember the name, but it was that big Victorian place on the corner, you know?—and he was out walking because he couldn't sleep.

Subterfuge was in the attitude. A cop might stop somebody skulking from shadow to shadow if he spotted him, but a tourist out walking had a different look, a different feel to him. Until he got closer to his destination, that was what Ventura was going to be, a tourist. A local cop would see nothing more. And when the bars started to close, that was probably where the local patrol car would be—looking for drunks.

Once he was within a block or so of his destination, Ventura would shuck the white shirt and light slacks and become a ninja, part of the night. He would be invisible in the darkness, but if a cop did somehow miraculously see him, then it would be the cop's bad luck.

At this stage of the game, he couldn't leave anybody behind to tell tales.

He'd find a quiet spot and wait until it was late enough for the widow Morrison to get to sleep, then he would move.

The rental car waiting at the Port Townsend Airport was a six-year-old Datsun that was badly in need of a tune-up. Only thing they had available, the guy from Rent-a-Beater had told him. Somebody had rented the good Dodge only half an hour earlier. The contract had been done over the phone, the rental place was closed, and the keys were over the sun visor.

Trusting souls up here. Then again, somebody would really need a ride pretty bad to swipe this hunk of junk.

The Datsun chugged and rattled along, ran ragged, and

nearly stalled several times. The dash GPS was broken, but there was a worn and greasy paper map in the glove box, and between that and his virgil's GPS, Michaels was able to locate the address he wanted.

He knew that Ventura had been headed here. Jay had gotten the GPS readings from Brink's, and Port Townsend wasn't really on the way to anywhere else, unless you planned to catch a ferry to the San Juan Islands. By nine, Ventura's rental car was in the town, and it was still here now, at eleven, but Michaels had to hurry, he might already be too late.

It wasn't that outlandish, when you thought about it. This was where Dr. Morrison had lived, and within an hour of his estimated time of death, a man going under the name of Corona, who was in all likelihood the late doctor's bodyguard, had gotten on a plane headed this way. He *could* be going somewhere else in this town, that was true, but this was one more coincidence that didn't play.

There must be something in Morrison's house that Ventura/Corona wanted, something worth taking a hurried flight here for. And what did Morrison have of value? Well, that was pretty obvious.

Maybe it was something else. Maybe he was coming here for some other reason entirely, but Michaels couldn't think of any offhand.

Michaels could call the local police, get some backup from the county sheriff, and maybe a few state police officers for good measure. Surround Morrison's house and grab Ventura when he showed up. Simple.

He *could* do that, but he didn't want to scare the guy off. If there were a dozen local cops tromping around this quiet little burg in the middle of the night, Ventura would have to be blind to miss them. So what Michaels had in mind was to find the house, hide somewhere he could watch it, and wait. When Ventura showed up, *then* he'd call in the cavalry. Give him time to find what he came for, maybe, to save Net Force having to look for it themselves. If Ventura was already there, as soon as Alex saw him come out, he'd make the call. Ventura might be able to run, but he couldn't hide, not as long as he drove his rented car. And that car, according to Jay, was parked not far from here, and had been there for at least fifteen minutes.

Michaels certainly didn't plan to try and take the guy down on his own. This was the man who had outshot John Howard, and the general was no slouch when it came to guns, a lot better than Michaels was. He didn't even *have* a gun with him, only the issue taser, and while that would knock a man on his ass with a single hit, you had to be pretty close to get that hit. He had no desire to go up against a highly skilled killer who was certainly better armed and more desperate than he was. No, Michaels had a strike team in place, five minutes away—as close as they could get without risking alerting their quarry— ready to move on his signal. He'd watch, make sure the guy showed up, and then get all the help he needed. At least Net Force would get partial credit for the capture. And if they were lucky, maybe the workings of the mind control ray as a bonus. That would go a long way to making up for all the mistakes.

He looked at the map. He was still a couple of miles away. Might as well make the call he had been putting off. He pushed the button for Toni's phone. Her message came on before even one ring.

"Hey, you've reached Toni Fiorella. Leave a message and I'll get back to you soon as I can."

He frowned. Was she not taking any calls? Or just not taking *his* calls? Well, okay, it was the middle of the night here, so it was the wee hours in D.C. Maybe she was just asleep and had turned off the ringer.

"Toni, it's me. Just calling to see how you're doing. I—well, look, I'm sorry about everything. I'll be back in town tomorrow, let's sit down and talk about it, okay? We can work all this out."

He thumbed the discom button, tucked the virgil back onto his belt. After he collected Ventura, that would give Toni something she could pass along to her new boss.

He had to hatch this egg before he could count it as a chicken, though.

37

Ventura had studied the overview maps his ops had done
of the neighborhood when he'd taken on Morrison as a
client. He knew as much about the houses and inhabitants
for a block in either direction as a team of good surveillance ops could learn in a short time. He knew which
houses had dogs, which houses had kids, which houses
had night owls who stayed up watching vids until all
hours. And, fortunately, there weren't a lot of any of these
close to Morrison's.

So it was that Ventura now sat in the backyard of the
house behind Morrison's, nestled into a gap between a
small metal utility shed and a couple of cords of firewood.
From the look of it, the wood was fir, alder, and madrona,
a good combination. The fir, when dry, would burn very
quickly. The alder could be used without seasoning, and

the madrona would burn longer and hotter than oak, once it got going.

Odd, the things you learned along the way.

Ventura glanced at his watch. Almost twelve-thirty. The lights had been off in Morrison's house for more than an hour, so the widow was likely asleep by now. What was her name? Ah, yes, Shannon. That sounded like the name of a teenaged starlet, or somebody who was a cheerleader for some NFL football team. Hardly the name one would connect to a scientist who had been twice her age.

Ventura looked around carefully. It was quiet, cool, and he hadn't seen anything to worry him as he had sneaked to this hiding place. If there were other watchers here, they must be working the street out front. Good and bad, that. If they were there, he hadn't been able to see them, which meant they were adept. Then again, if they were out front, they wouldn't see him as he went to the back door.

He took several deep breaths, inhaling and letting them out slowly, oxygenating his blood, trying to relax. He would go at one.

Michaels had left his beat-up Datsun at the bottom of the hill, half a block away from where Ventura's rental was parked, and hiked up toward Morrison's house. It had been a while since he'd done any covert surveillance in the field, a long while, and his skills were not as sharp as he would have liked. A lot of it came back as he worked his way toward his target. He used trees for cover, went through backyards when possible, kept low, listened carefully for dogs. He moved steadily when he left cover, and he stayed in the shadows as much as possible. That nobody seemed to notice him was probably more a testament

to the hour than any real skill on his part, but, hey, he'd
take it.

His hormones were flowing pretty good, too. He sometimes had to remember to breathe. He *had* remembered to
shut the ringer off on his virgil. It wouldn't do to be skulking in the bushes somewhere and suddenly start chiming
out "Bad to the Bone."

As he drew closer to the house, Michaels wondered
exactly what he was going to do once he got there. He
knew that Ventura's rental car was still parked down the
hill, so unless he missed him in passing, he was out here
on foot somewhere. Maybe already in the house.

There was a streetlight up ahead on the right. Michaels
crossed the road, to stay in the darkness.

One A.M., straight up, time to go. Ventura ran in a crouch
toward the back door. It was only a ten- or twelve-second
trip, but it seemed to last for hours. He kept expecting to
feel the impact of a bullet in the back, even though he
knew that wasn't likely—there was no point in shooting
him on the way in.

The trip ended; the bullet had not come. He tried the
doorknob. Locked. And the dead bolt would also be
locked, if Shannon had been doing what her husband told
her.

Ventura took the leather pouch with his lock picks and
torsion tools from his jacket. The button lock on the doorknob would be a snap, and that was all he needed. He
had a key for the dead bolt, since his people had overseen
that lock's installation.

He put the torsion tool into the key slot on the doorknob, used a triple triangle pick to rake the pins. Might

as well try it the easy way first, before picking each tumbler separately . . .

The torsion tool rotated the barrel mechanism on the second rake. Maybe six seconds from start to finish

Ventura grinned. He still had the touch.

He slipped the key into the dead bolt, turned it, and came up from his crouch as he opened the door and stepped into the hallway that led to the basement and the kitchen. He closed the door silently behind him.

The alarm keypad was on the wall just past the light switch. He could see the red On diode gleaming. The only other light was from instrument glows in the kitchen, no help this far away, so he flicked on the flashlight and covered most of the lens with one hand, allowing only enough illumination to see the keypad. He punched in the four-digit number—1-9-8-6—the year Shannon had been born. Morrison had said she wasn't very good at remembering numbers, so he'd wanted to keep it simple.

1986. Ventura had *shoes* older than that.

The hard part was done. The master bedroom was upstairs, and the living room/study was just on the other side of the kitchen/dining room. That was as far as he needed to go. If he didn't bump into the furniture or sneeze, the young widow would likely continue her beauty rest. He'd reset the alarm and relock the door when he left. Shannon would never know he'd been here.

He moved through the kitchen. There was enough ambient light from the digital LCD clocks on the stove, microwave oven, and coffeemaker for him to keep the flashlight lens covered completely. He didn't like to use a flashlight on a hot prowl; it was a dead giveaway to anybody who might be passing by or watching a place. Unless there was a power outage, residents normally didn't move around their own houses using flashlights. But he didn't want to use the overheads or a lamp in here, either. Watchers would at the very least be alerted that somebody was up and about. And some people had a hypersensitivity to light, even when they slept. It was as if they could somehow feel the pressure of the photons on their bodies, although they couldn't see them. It wouldn't do for young Shannon to come yawning and padding down the stairs in her birthday suit, wondering who'd left the light on. If she saw him, it would have to be the last thing she saw, and while killing her didn't bother him per se, finding her corpse would give the authorities pause to wonder why it had happened. Whoever had done it must have wanted something, they'd figure, and Ventura reasoned they would figure out what pretty quick. Right now, they didn't know that Morrison had passed on anything to anybody. Best to keep it that way until he was in a safe harbor.

He let a thin ray of the flashlight peek from between his closed fingers as he stepped into the dining room, just enough to avoid the furniture. He crouched low and duck-walked toward the study. There was what he wanted, just ahead and to the right.

Michaels was prone in a clump of bushes, across the street to the east side of Morrison's house. The plants were evergreens, big junipers of some kind, trimmed into wind-blown bonsai shapes, but thick enough to crouch beneath and be mostly covered. He had worked his way there through the yard from the east, so he hadn't been visible from the street or, he hoped, from Morrison's house.

He had just gotten settled when he saw the man all in black scurry in a crouch to the back door.

That must be Ventura. A minute later and I would have missed him!

The man fiddled with the lock, and in what seemed no time at all, he'd opened the door and slipped inside. Either the door had been unlocked, or this guy was an expert with picks. Long ago, Michaels had covered that in his training, picking locks, but it had taken him half an hour to open even simple locks, and complicated ones were beyond him. His teacher had told him it was a thing of feel, that you either had the touch or you didn't. If you didn't, you could get better, but you'd never be a master at it.

Well, enough ruminating on old training classes. Time to call in the Marines.

Michaels pulled his virgil from his belt and hit the button. Five minutes, tops, and the cavalry would arrive. All he had to do was remain alert until they showed up.

Unless his young wife had unknown sensibilities, Morrison had been quite the classical music fan. A CD/DVD rack above the Phillips/Technics R&P held a couple hundred titles. The titles tended to favor the Baroque composers: Bach, Handel, Vivaldi, Telemann, Heinichen, Corelli, and Haydn.

And Pachelbel, of course.

Fortunately, the man had been meticulous in his cataloging. The titles were alphabetized, so it took only a few seconds to find the DVD Ventura wanted: *Pachelbel's Greatest Hit.*

He grinned at the name and turned the case over. The disk was a compilation, several versions and variations, of the contrapuntal melody *Canon in D,* a total playing time of 41:30. You'd have to be a real fan to listen to what was essentially the same simple tune played over and over again for that long.

He opened the case to make certain the disk inside matched the title, and the silvery disk gave off a rainbow gleam in the flashlight's narrow beam.

The markings looked genuine to Ventura, the little RCA dog and Gramophone, the cut titles and numbers. Maybe an expert could tell the difference; he couldn't.

Put this disk into an audio player, and you would get forty-plus minutes of variations on a musical theme. Put it into a computer and look in the right spot, using the right binary decoder, and you would get something else. Between the end of "Canon of the Three Stars," by Isao Tomita and the Plasma Symphony Orchestra, and the beginning of "Pachelbel: Canon in D," by The Baroque Chamber Orchestra, led by Ettore Stratta—if Morrison had been telling the truth—lay a secret the Chinese had been willing to pay nearly half a billion dollars to get their hands on.

He grinned again, put the disk back into the case, and slipped it into his inside windbreaker pocket. He looked at the stairs.

No sounds drifted down from the sleeping widow. Good. Always good to avoid complications when possible.

He retraced his steps to the back door. He keyed in the alarm code, cracked the door open a hair, and set the button lock on the door. He had thirty seconds to close the door behind him before the alarm kicked on. It only took one of those seconds for him to draw his pistol and slip the safety off. If somebody had been watching him, it made more sense for them to wait until he left with whatever he had come for before they took him down;

otherwise they might never find it. If somebody was watching.

He held the pistol down by his leg. He took a deep breath, released half of it, and stepped outside.

38

Michaels was watching the house when the whole situation suddenly changed. Whatever Ventura had gone into the house for, either he knew where it was, or he'd changed his mind, Michaels thought. He was in and out in maybe two minutes. And the cavalry was still at least three minutes away.

Michaels watched as the man did something one-handed with the dead bolt lock. Save for a quick glance, he did it without looking at the door—instead he scanned the yard, his gaze sweeping back and forth, seeking. His other hand was hidden behind his leg.

Even though he knew he was pretty much invisible on the ground under the bushes across the street, Michaels froze. His pucker factor went right off the scale.

Ventura finished his manipulation with the door's lock,

glanced around again, and started across the backyard.

Michaels gathered himself to get up. He was going to follow Ventura, come hell or high water, but he was going to be *real* careful doing it. His hand hovered over the call button on his virgil, but he didn't press it. Hitting the distress signal now would bring the cavalry with full lights and sirens, and he still couldn't risk alerting Ventura.

He was on his hands and knees about to crawl out from under the evergreen when two men stepped out from behind the shed and pointed guns at Ventura.

"Hold it right—!" one of them began.

He never finished the sentence. There were several bright flashes and terrific explosions, and all three men went down. But Ventura rolled up, hardly even slowing, ran to the two fallen men, and fired his pistol twice more.

It all happened so fast and unexpectedly Michaels wasn't sure what he had seen, but his brain raced to fill it in: Two men with guns braced Ventura, who was either the fastest draw who ever lived or already had his own gun out. One, two, *three* shots, yes, three, two from Ventura, one from one of the dead guys—and they were surely dead because Ventura sprinted over and put one more round into each one, looked like the heads, but it was hard to be sure about that, the after-images from the first shots had washed out Michaels's vision some, and—

Ventura didn't stop to examine the pair he'd shot; he took off at a run, straight to the street.

Michaels scrambled from under the bushes and followed, but he stayed crouched, using cover. He did not want Ventura to look back and see him, no, not after that display. Not only was the man a killer, he was expert at it. To take out two men with guns already pointed at you? That was either great skill or great luck, and Michaels didn't want to test either.

Lights started to go on in houses along the street. They probably didn't get a lot of gunfire up here on a weeknight. No, probably not.

Michaels ran on the darker side of the street, and he had his taser in his hand. He hoped he wouldn't have to get close enough to Ventura to have to use it.

Ventura smiled to himself as he ran. He did a tactical reload, changing magazines, dropping the one missing three shots into his windbreaker pocket. Those had probably been Chinese agents—feds would have yelled out their ID, and there would have been more of them.

Speed was the most important thing now. Gunfire in a quiet neighborhood would wake people up, somebody'd call the police, and even if they were slow, it would only be a few minutes before cops got here. He'd have a little while longer before the locals unraveled things, enough time to get clear of the city, but he had to figure they might have spotted him earlier, noticed his car, so a different vehicle was going to be necessary. The sooner he found one, the better.

He was going to have to get rid of this Coonan, too—he hadn't had time to stop and pick up his expended brass here, and this gun already had two shootings on it, in Alaska and in California. Under better circumstances, he would have dropped the pistol into a lake or ocean after the first time he'd used it, but there simply hadn't been time. Only a fool would hold on to something that would get him the death penalty if he was caught with it. He had other guns, and as soon as he could get to them, he'd lose this one.

There was an old pickup truck parked on the street half a block ahead of him. That would do. He could break the window, get inside, crack the ignition for a hot-wire, be gone in another two minutes.

He glanced behind him. No sign of pursuit, no men chasing him with guns. Maybe those were the only two. Maybe.

But even as he ran, that part of him that feasted on danger grinned and smacked its chops, looking for more. There was nothing like an adrenaline rush, the immediate sense of danger and possible death. He should be afraid, but what he felt was closer to orgasm than fear. He had the prize, he was on his way, enemies were down. All around him, life was crystalline, razor-sharp, throbbing with triumph.

He lived, they died.

It didn't get any better than this.

Here was the truck. Try the door—hah! not even locked! He reached up over the visor, just in case—and lo! the keys!

He laughed aloud. No. It couldn't get any better than this!

He put the gun down on the seat and shoved the key into the ignition slot—

"Going somewhere, Colonel?"

Surprised, Ventura jumped, started to grab the Coonan—

"Don't! You won't make it!"

Ventura froze. He looked up.

Standing six feet away, a shotgun aimed at Ventura's head, was General Jackson "Bull" Smith. Smiling.

This was not in Ventura's game plan. "General. Odd running into you here."

"Not odd at all, Luther. Me and a few of the boys have been waiting for you to show up."

"Those two were yours?"

"They were."

"Sorry."

"Don't worry about it. They deserved what they got—it was a bonehead move, going at you face-on."

Smith smiled again, and the shotgun didn't waver a hair. Ventura was looking right down the muzzle. *Twelve-gauge,* he noted. *Modified choke.*

"There was a pair of other guys here before us, commie agents, near as we could tell, but they . . . went away."

"I thought there might be. Thanks."

"Don't thank me yet. I had a couple other boys tailing you, but you lost 'em after that mess in Los Angeles. Lost your client, too, that's a real shame. Figured you'd show up here sooner or later."

"You continue to surprise me, General. How?"

"Because there are better surveillance gadgets than the ones you had in your car at the compound, that's how. You think because we live up in the woods and stomp around in the bear shit we don't have access to modern technology? You get a flunking grade for underestimating folks, Luther. Especially your friends. You should have cut me in, instead of trying to bullshit me with that story of yours."

Ventura smiled and shook his head. "I sit corrected, General. Real impressive work. Not too late to make amends, is it?"

"I'm afraid it is, Colonel, I'm afraid it is."

• • •

When he saw the man with the shotgun point the weapon at Ventura where he sat in the truck he was presumably going to steal, Michaels slid into a front yard and behind a thick-boled Douglas fir tree. He was across the street and they were busy enough with each other that they hadn't noticed him. Reaching down, he hit the alarm button on his virgil. It would take them a minute or two to react, but he was no longer worried about alerting Ventura.

Now what? Who was this guy? Was he connected to the two dead men at Morrison's? What the hell was going on?

Michaels was sixty, seventy feet away, and the taser was accurate for fifteen or twenty feet, if you were lucky. But he'd only get one shot and then he'd have to reload, and as John Howard and Julio Fernandez had pointed out to him, the fastest taser reloader in the world could not outpace a handgun with multiple rounds. Net Force computer and management people were supposed to be desk jockeys, they didn't *need* guns, that's what the military arm was for.

If he got out of this alive, Michaels planned to start carrying a real gun.

Yeah. Unfortunately, the military arm was not here, he didn't have a real gun, and a taser was what he did have. So—who to shoot?—assuming he could get close enough to shoot either one of them?

He couldn't hear what they were saying to each other, but he was able to hear what the shotgunner said next, because he said it loudly: "Bubba!"

A shaven-headed bodybuilder in dark camo approached the truck from the passenger side, a long-barreled pistol in his hands. He was careful not to come in straight on, but angled slightly from the back. Good move—that would keep him out of the shotgunner's line of fire if things started cooking.

Nothing like another little complication to make his life harder.

Even if he'd had an assault rifle instead of the taser, Michaels didn't like those odds. And he didn't know who these new players were—in theory, they might even be on his side.

Maybe he should wait a second and see what happened before he stood up and commanded everybody to drop their weapons. Maybe a couple of seconds.

Ventura felt the adrenaline pop and bubble in him, heard its siren song calling him to action. *You're invincible,* it said. *Nobody has ever been able to beat you. You're the best there ever was! Kill them!*

"All right," Smith said. "Here is how it is gonna go. You give me whatever it was you came here to collect. Then you can be on your way, your life for the data. I figure that's an even trade. If anything that looks like a weapon comes out of your pocket, we take what we want off your body. This pump's carrying eight rounds of number 4 buckshot. I don't have to tell you what that will do to your face at this range."

"No."

Smith might not be a real general, but he had been a real soldier, and he did have a shotgun pointed at Ventura. Bubba, on the other side of the truck, had a handgun. But if Bubba fired first, he would have to shoot through the glass, and his angle might partially deflect the bullet. If Ventura ducked suddenly, Smith would probably pull the trigger, and with any luck, the charge of BBs would go right over his head and through the passenger window. It would take half a second for Smith to rack the slide for a second shot, and while a full-sized American pickup truck's door would not stop a deer or sabot slug from a twelve-gauge, it would stop a load of number 4 buck, or most of it.

Ventura weighed his chances. This was it. He had assessed the situation as best he could. As soon as he handed over the disk, he was a dead man anyway. Smith couldn't let him walk away and expect to sleep nights, because sooner or later, he'd know that Ventura would come for him. And a wire enclosure full of men playing soldier wouldn't be enough protection, Smith knew that. The only reason he didn't shoot him now was to make sure he had the data, and to find out what he could about it.

Here was the moment. No past. No future. Be here now.

He smiled and made his decision. The only one he could make.

"All right, General. We'll play it your way—"

—but as fast as he could move, Ventura ducked and grabbed for his pistol—

39

As it sometimes did when things turned violently dangerous, time narrowed and slowed. Michaels saw Ventura
disappear from sight, and the blast of the shotgun was a
tremendous *boom!* immediately after that—

Bubba fired his pistol, a thin and almost quiet *crack!*
crack! and two holes appeared in the truck's windshield—

Somehow, amazed at himself, Michaels found himself
on his feet, running *toward* the shooting, his tiny, insig-
nificant taser stretched out in front of himself at arm's
length—

Ventura's hand came up inside the truck like a peri-
scope, a pistol in it, and he fired at the shotgunner,
twisted, and fired at Bubba—*blam! blam!*—that quick—

The shotgunner went down, hit in the body, but Bubba
had dodged as soon as Ventura's pistol came up, and he

fired his own gun wildly, six—eight?—times; it sounded almost like a full-auto, one continuous *crackcrackcrack-crack!* and it must have run empty because it stopped—

Ventura sat up, and he shoved his pistol toward the shotgunner, but the man rolled and came up and pointed the shotgun at Ventura again and fired—

Michaels saw Ventura take the blast in the chest and bang into the steering wheel, but he managed to get off another shot that seemed to hit the shotgunner without major effect. The shotgunner let go a third blast—

Ventura disappeared from view—

Michaels realized he was screaming, as the shotgunner turned his head and stared at him in surprise. He started to bring the shotgun around, and it was too far for a taser shot, but Michaels triggered the thing anyway. Twin silvery needles lanced at the shotgunner—he could *see* the electric darts—but they hit the shotgun, one in the butt, one in the forestock, and that wouldn't do shit—

The shotgun's muzzle came around, slowly . . . *slowly* . . . and it was almost lined up when the shooter realized Michaels was about to barrel into him at a dead run, so he fired—

Too soon! The blast went past Michaels's right ear; he felt a tug and a quick burn, but that was all, and then he slammed into the shooter at a dead run and they both went down—

The impact stunned them both, but Michaels recovered first. He rolled up and kicked at the other man's head. He missed, but caught a shoulder as the shotgunner tried to roll away—

The shotgun was on the street five yards down the hill.

Michaels was aware that Bubba was on the other side of the truck, probably reloading his pistol, and that he didn't have time to fool around here. The shotgunner came up, groggy, hands rising in a defensive posture, and Michaels didn't wait, but leaped in and snapped his elbow right at the man's temple, as hard as he could. There was a damp *snap!* and the man went down bonelessly limp, but Bubba was coming around the front of the truck, Bubba and his pistol, and Michaels knew he was screwed—

He was going to die—

Somebody flew out of nowhere and slammed into Bubba from behind, knocking his pistol loose as he went to one knee. His attacker dived and rolled up, two yards past Bubba, spun to face him—

Michaels stared, unable to believe what he saw.

Toni?!

The big man went down to his knee, and she had too much momentum to stop, so Toni stretched out into a shoulder roll, hit the road hard enough to clack her teeth together, but came up mostly unhurt. Shoulder was gonna be real sore—assuming she survived that long.

The big man was up, coming at her. He swung a punch that would have flattened a horse had it hit, a hard right cross—

Toni ducked, double-tapped the man's thick and muscular arm with her left palm and right backhand, used the momentum of the second tap to cock her elbow, and stepped in at an angle to her left—he was too big to meet head-on—then slammed her right elbow into his ribs.

She felt the ribs go, heard him grunt and slow his advance a little, but it wasn't enough to stop him; he kept coming. He was too big, too strong—if he grabbed her, that would be bad—

Too close for the foot sweep, she had to use her thigh. She caught his upper leg with hers, snapped her knee upward, and shoved with her right hand at his belt line—

The seesaw lever worked. He lost his balance and sprawled facedown on the street, hands outstretched to absorb his fall—

Toni followed him. When he lifted his head, she kicked for his chin, but he fell away and blocked at the same time, and her shin met his left forearm bone—

His arm was weaker. The ulna snapped—

Damn, he was tough. He grabbed at her foot, missed when she dodged back, and used the grab's moment to regain his feet. He jumped in again and fired a hard straight punch, using his good right arm—

Toni was in the zone, fighting in a righteous rage, no longer thinking, blending with her attacker. She punched her right fist at his head, stretched out over his punch, and blocked with her left at the same time, deflecting his arm just behind the elbow. Her punch hit his ear, no big impact, but she was in position for the *putar kepala*—the head twist. She scooped inside his right elbow with her left hand, caught his neck with her right, and circled her hands, left up, right down, pulling them close into her body as she dropped her weight. The motion twisted him around clockwise, and she grabbed his head with both hands.

A twist alone was a neck crank, painful but not damaging.

A twist and pull, putting an arch in his back, was a break.

She twisted sharply counterclockwise and pulled at the same time—

The sound of the vertebrae cracking seemed louder to her than the shotgun blast had been.

The man fell. He might survive, but he wasn't going to be getting up on his own. Not now, and maybe never again.

The fury left her as she turned, looking for more opponents.

There were none. Only Alex standing over the downed shotgunner, staring at her in amazement.

Sirens approached, growing louder, and neither of them could find words. Finally as the flashing lights of the first police car strobed them, Alex said, "What the hell are you doing here?"

"Nobody moves!" a cop nervously clutching his pistol yelled.

No problem. Alex and Toni stood very still—and nobody else there could have moved anyway.

40

Wednesday, June 15th
Port Townsend, Washington

The sleepy little scenic tourist town was certainly wide
awake up on the hillside now: City police, firemen, deputies, and most of the neighbors all stood in the glow of
headlights and emergency flashers, trying to figure out
what was going on. It was noisy, bright, and hectic.

It didn't take all that long to get it sorted out. Michaels
explained who he and Toni were, and when their Net
Force/FBI identification checked out valid, that made
things a lot less tense.

There were two dead men in Morrison's backyard, and
their IDs indicated that they were members of some paramilitary group based in Idaho.

The shotgunner was alive, with a fractured skull, and
it seemed *he* was the leader of that same group, a general.
He had been hit twice by bullets from Ventura's pistol,

both of which had been stopped by his body armor.

Bubba the bodybuilder had a broken neck.

And Ventura? He had taken two blasts from the general's shotgun, and unfortunately for him, he hadn't been wearing body armor. The first shot apparently hit him in the chest, the second in the face. Either would have killed him, the fireman-paramedic said, the head shot faster than the one in the pump.

Michaels and Toni went through Ventura's personal property. He had the gun, extra ammunition, flashlight, lock picks, car keys, and, inside what was left of his windbreaker pocket, a DVD disk inside a plastic case. Both had been shattered into tiny bits by the shotgun blast, some slivers of which had been driven into the dead man's heart by the impact.

"Want to bet that disk is what he stopped by Morrison's to find?" Toni said.

"No bet," Michaels said. "You think the FBI lab could put this thing back together?" Some of the bloody pieces were the size of needles.

She shook her head. "Enough to retrieve whatever was on it? I doubt it. If the secret to the crazy ray was on that disk, it's gone."

Michaels nodded. "Probably just as well. I'm not sure I'd want our government getting its hands on it any more than anybody else." He looked at her. "You're the one who got the good car from the rental place, aren't you? Just before I got there?"

"Yes."

"How did you know where to find me? Was it Jay?"

"No. You left a public trail. You weren't trying to hide. I'm not totally inept on the net."

"Why did you come?"

She looked at him. "Are you sorry I did?"

He shook his head. "I'd have to be a fool to say that, given the circumstances. I can't remember the last time I was so glad to see somebody as when you knocked Bubba down. Thank you."

"I was acting in my capacity as liaison, you know."

"Uh-huh."

"Why are you so pigheaded, Alex? You know that I love you. And you love me just as much."

"Yeah."

"It was going bad for us. And work was the problem, you know that, too. I'd rather lose the job than the relationship."

He nodded. "Yeah. Me, too."

She looked at the firemen hauling away Ventura's body. "It's going to be a long night before we're done here. Do you have a place to stay?"

"No."

"I've got a room at a bed-and-breakfast at the far end of town. What say we go there and take a long nap when this is done?"

He thought about it for a second. She was right. He did love her, and he would rather save their personal relationship than either of their jobs. He gave her a small grin. "Okay," he said. "You twisted my arm."

EPILOGUE

Friday, July 29th, 2011
Washington, D.C.

Michaels walked into the condo, saw that the snail mail was on the table in the kitchen. "Toni?" he yelled. "You home?"

"In here," she called back.

"Where is 'here'?"

"The living room."

He walked into the room. She was sitting on the couch, folding towels.

"I dried the laundry," she said. "You mixed the dark towels with the light ones again."

"What can I say? I'm evil through and through. Shoot me."

He moved to where she sat, bent, and kissed her. "How was your day?"

"Not bad," she said. "I had to do a presentation on what

a wonderful job Net Force is doing for Senator Bogle's staff."

"Sounds easy enough."

"Balancing a dozen spinning plates on the end of sticks *sounds* easy, Alex. Since I left, Net Force has trouble finding its ass with both hands."

He laughed. "Got any plans for supper?"

"I could microwave some burritos," she said.

"How about I order Chinese takeout? My treat."

"Fine by me."

He took a deep breath. It had been on his mind a lot lately, how to do this, and he was nervous about it.

"Listen," he began, "things have been working out okay for us lately, haven't they?"

"You have to ask?"

"No, no, I mean, *I* think they have, but I don't want to take anything for granted. We're okay, aren't we? I mean, we're doing all right on a personal level, right?"

"Except for you mixing the darks with the lights in the wash, we are terrific."

He nodded. Here was the hard part.

She stopped folding the towels. "What is it, Alex? Something's on your mind. Tell me."

He sat down on the couch next to her. "Okay, look, I'm not the most romantic guy in the world, but—do you want to get married?"

Her eyes got wide and she grinned. "Yes, of course."

He blew out a big sigh. "Good."

"You thought I would turn you down?"

"I hoped not. I didn't want to think too much about that."

She grabbed him and hugged him, and they kissed. She

broke it and leaned back. "Anyways, it was about time you got around to asking me," she said.

"Yeah? You could have asked *me,* you know?"

"Nope, I'm an old-fashioned girl. That's the man's job."

" 'Old-fashioned'? You?" He laughed. "You're a butt-kicking, hardheaded woman who looks over my shoulder at work."

"Oh, well, you won't have to worry about that much longer."

He looked at her. "How come?"

"I'm going to quit work."

"What?!"

"I intended to keep the job when I took it, but something better has come up."

"A better job? It's not too far away, is it? I was just getting used to having you around."

"Oh, don't worry, I'll be around." She put her hands over his shoulders, then slid them up to behind his neck. "The job is going to be something completely different."

"Yeah? What?"

"I'm going to become a full-time mommy."

He stared at her, stunned. "You . . . you're . . . ?"

"Yep," she said, grinning like a fool. "I'm pregnant."

Then they were both grinning like fools.

The Bestselling Novels of
TOM CLANCY

RAINBOW SIX
John Clark is used to doing the CIA's dirty work. Now he's taking on the world...

"ACTION-PACKED."

—*The New York Times Book Review*

EXECUTIVE ORDERS
The most devastating terrorist act in history leaves Jack Ryan as President of the United States...

"UNDOUBTEDLY CLANCY'S BEST YET."

—*The Atlanta Journal-Constitution*

DEBT OF HONOR
It begins with the murder of an American woman in the backstreets of Tokyo. It ends in war...

"A SHOCKER CLIMAX SO PLAUSIBLE YOU'LL WONDER WHY IT HASN'T YET HAPPENED."

—*Entertainment Weekly*

THE HUNT FOR RED OCTOBER
The smash bestseller that launched Clancy's career—the incredible search for a Soviet defector and the nuclear submarine he commands...

"BREATHLESSLY EXCITING."

—*The Washington Post*

continued...

RED STORM RISING

The ultimate scenario for World War III—the final battle for global control . . .

"THE ULTIMATE WAR GAME . . . BRILLIANT."

—Newsweek

PATRIOT GAMES

CIA analyst Jack Ryan stops an assassination—and incurs the wrath of Irish terrorists . . .

"A HIGH PITCH OF EXCITEMENT."

—The Wall Street Journal

THE CARDINAL OF THE KREMLIN

The superpowers race for the ultimate Star Wars missile defense system . . .

"*CARDINAL* EXCITES, ILLUMINATES . . . A REAL PAGE-TURNER."

—Los Angeles Daily News